The Outcast and The Rite

Also published by Handheld Press

The Outcast and The Rite

Stories of Landscape and Fear, 1925–1938

by Helen de Guerry Simpson

edited by Melissa Edmundson

Handheld Classic 26

This edition published in 2022 by Handheld Press
72 Warminster Road, Bath BA2 6RU, United Kingdom.
www.handheldpress.co.uk

ISBN 978-1-912766-60-4

1 2 3 4 5 6 7 8 9 0

Series design by Nadja Guggi and typeset in Adobe Caslon Pro
and Open Sans.

Printed and bound in Great Britain by Short Run Press, Exeter.

FSC
www.fsc.org
MIX
Paper from
responsible sources
FSC® C014540

Contents

Acknowledgments

My thanks to Kate Macdonald of Handheld Press, for commissioning me to curate the stories in this book.

I would also like to express my sincere gratitude to the family of Helen Simpson. Her daughter Mrs Clemence Hamilton and her granddaughter Kate Hamilton have supported this project from the beginning and have graciously provided documents from Simpson's private papers and manuscripts.

My appreciation goes as well to the National Library of Australia for making so many primary sources freely available through Trove. The introduction to this edition could not have been written without this invaluable resource.

I also wish to thank Jeff Makala for his feedback on the introduction and for his editorial assistance.

And my gratitude, as always, goes to Murray, Maggie, Kitsey, and Remy for their furry support.

This book is dedicated to Mrs Clemence Hamilton,
daughter of Helen Simpson

Melissa Edmundson is Senior Lecturer in British Literature and Women's Writing at Clemson University, South Carolina, and specializes in nineteenth and early twentieth-century British women writers, with a particular interest in women's supernatural fiction. She is the editor of a critical edition of Alice Perrin's *East of Suez* (1901), published in 2011, and author of *Women's Ghost Literature in Nineteenth-Century Britain* (2013) and *Women's Colonial Gothic Writing, 1850–1930: Haunted Empire* (2018). Her other work includes essays on the First World War ghost stories of H D Everett and haunted objects in the supernatural fiction of Margery Lawrence, as well as a chapter on women writers and ghost stories for *The Routledge Handbook to the Ghost Story*. She has also edited *Avenging Angels: Ghost Stories by Victorian Women Writers* (2018). Her Handheld Press titles include *Women's Weird: Strange Stories by Women, 1890–1940* (2019), *Women's Weird 2: More Strange Stories by Women, 1891–1937* (2020), and Elinor Mordaunt's *The Villa and The Vortex: Supernatural Stories, 1916–1924* (2021).

Introduction

BY MELISSA EDMUNDSON

In a newspaper feature on Helen Simpson, written during Simpson's visit in 1937 to her native Australia, the author Coralie Clarke Rees recorded her appraisal of Simpson:

> Not content with being a first-rate novelist—one of the few Australian writers who have a wide oversea public— she is a biographer, an expert on cookery and homecraft, a prominent lecturer and radio talker, an authority on witchcraft, and a talented amateur musician. Such is her interest in world affairs that she reads daily papers in four different languages—French, German, Italian, and Spanish—besides her native English. During the recent troublous times she has displayed an active interest in the struggles of the workers of the world against Fascism. Her physical and mental vitality can only be described as super-normal. (Rees 1937)

Rees's description encapsulates many of the attributes and talents that made Helen Simpson unique. Her writing career spanned roughly two decades, and her time as a novelist was even shorter. In just fifteen years, from 1925 until her untimely death in 1940 at age 42, she distinguished herself as a gifted historical novelist, publishing bestselling books set in her birthplace of Australia and in her adopted home of England. She had a long-standing business partnership with William Heinemann, who published most of her books. This includes one which remains unique in her oeuvre: *The Baseless Fabric*. This was Simpson's only collection of short fiction and contains most of her supernatural writing. For almost a century, this collection has been forgotten. Yet its stories represent some of the best—and most chilling—supernatural and macabre fiction written during the interwar years, a period which saw a resurgence in such literature. These stories range from tales of obsession and vengeance to haunted houses, ominous landscapes, and possession. Along with these collected stories, the present edition adds two supernatural narratives which Simpson published later in her life. These once again showcase her lifelong interest in the occult and the paranormal. *The Outcast and The Rite* is the first modern reprinting of Simpson's short fiction and reclaims an important and distinctive voice within the supernatural tradition.

※

Helen de Guerry Simpson was born on 1 December 1897 in Sydney, Australia. She was the daughter of Edward Percy Simpson, a solicitor, and Anna Maria Alexandra Guerry de Lauret, daughter of Auguste Pierre Clement, Marquis de Guerry de Lauret. Simpson's maternal grandfather was a political refugee who had left France for Australia in the 1840s and acquired land near Goulburn, a town in New South Wales that lies between Sydney and Canberra. She was educated at her family home in the Sydney suburb of Point Piper under the direction of her governess, Winifred West. Her parents later separated, and her mother moved to London. Simpson remained with her father and was sent to the Convent of the Sacred Heart in nearby Rose Bay, Sydney, from 1910–1911, and later to Abbotsleigh, a private girls' school in Sydney, from 1911–1912.

When she was sixteen, Simpson left Australia in order to study music in Paris (with the hope of becoming a composer) but because of the outbreak of World War I, decided to go to Oxford to study languages in the hopes of helping with the war effort. There, she joined the Society of Oxford Home Students (which would later become St Anne's College). She published her first book while still a student at Oxford and founded the Oxford Women's Dramatic Society.

During the war, Simpson joined the Women's Royal Naval Service (WRNS) and worked as a cable decoder with the Admiralty in London. She then volunteered to work as an interpreter in France and Tunisia. She spoke fluent French and spent mornings at the Berlitz School learning Italian and Spanish while working nights at the Admiralty (Ussher 1931, 22). In a 1937 interview, she recalled that this time 'was really most thrilling, doing interpretations and working on codes' (Simpson 1937a, 13).

After the war, she returned to Oxford, intending to complete her Bachelor of Music degree. There are different reasons given as to why she left Oxford without a degree. In interviews, Simpson said she failed her exams, but another possible cause is that she staged a play in which both male and female students acted (against the regulations) and was subsequently sent down.

Her first books were published in Sydney by Angus & Robertson. These included a collection of poems, *Philosophies in Little* (1921), and the play, *A Man of His Time* (1923). William Heinemann published her collection of stories, *The Baseless Fabric*, and her first novel, *Acquittal*, both in 1925. Simpson's arrival as a novelist actually came about because of a bet. She recalled:

> I was deriding the modern novel, and stating that anyone could write one in three weeks: a novel good enough for publication. The girl to whom I made this somewhat boastful statement ridiculed the idea and bet me £25 that I couldn't write a novel in three weeks and then get it published. I accepted the challenge—set to work with a will—finished the book on the 21st day—sold it to the first publishers I approached ... and won my £25! [...] And so, after this extremely surprising literary achievement, and realising that I was evidently not cut out to be a composer, I turned to writing as a career. (Simpson 1937a, 13)

Her relationship with Heinemann continued throughout the 1920s and 1930s. Her novel *Cups, Wands and Swords* (1927), as the

Tarot-inspired title suggests, includes mystical and supernatural elements. *Mumbudget* (1928) is a collection of Irish fairy tales for children. The semi-autobiographical *Boomerang* (1932), a historical novel that moves between eighteenth-century Paris, New South Wales, and France during the First World War, won the James Tait Black Memorial Prize for fiction that same year. *Boomerang* also represented a substantial increase in Simpson's earnings as an author. She told Coralie Clarke Rees in a 1933 article, 'I got £30 for my first novel, £40 for my second, and £600 for "Boomerang"' (Rees 1933).

In 1933, Heinemann published *The Woman on the Beast*, a fantasy consisting of three linked novellas across different eras but with common themes. The book begins with a Prologue set in medieval times, then moves to sixteenth-century India, revolutionary France, and finally to Australia in 1999. Her historical romance *Saraband for Dead Lovers* (1935) was adapted into a film in 1948. *Under Capricorn* (1937), set in colonial New South Wales in the 1830s, was adapted as a film in 1949. Her final novel was *Maid No More* (1940), published the year of her death. By all accounts, Simpson was a highly disciplined writer. Her work was a constant source of pride for Australia and throughout her career she was known as an Australian novelist. Most of what we know about her attitudes toward authorship and publishing comes from the many personal interviews and reviews of her work published in newspapers throughout the country. In July 1937, the Melbourne *Argus* went as far as to say, 'No other Australian authoress has had such success abroad as Miss Helen Simpson' (Anon 1937). In a September 1937 article for the *Newcastle Morning Herald*, Simpson discussed the importance of maintaining a daily routine for her writing and keeping to a schedule. She first wrote everything in longhand using a pencil, then her secretary typed the manuscript. There was a round of editing, then the manuscript was typed again (Simpson 1937c).

Simpson knew many fellow authors in the interwar London literary world. Beginning in the late 1920s, she collaborated with the playwright and novelist Clemence Dane for a popular series of detective novels published by Hodder & Stoughton. These included *Enter Sir John* (1929), adapted as a film by Alfred Hitchcock in 1930, *Printer's Devil* (1930), and *Re-Enter Sir John* (1932). The two writers formed a lasting friendship, and Helen named her only daughter after Clemence. Simpson was also close to the novelist Margaret Kennedy, who, during Simpson's illness and hospitalization in wartime London in 1940, took the young Clemence to live with her in greater safety in Surrey along with Kennedy's own children, and later moved Clemence with her children to Cornwall (Powell 1983, 171–72). Clemence is called 'Claire' in *Where Stands A Wingèd Sentry* (1941), Margaret Kennedy's memoir of the war.

Simpson and Dane were invited to join the Detection Club in 1929, after the publication of *Enter Sir John* (McDonald 2021, 209). The Detection Club's other members included Agatha Christie, Gladys Mitchell, and Dorothy L Sayers. Through the club, Simpson and Sayers developed a close friendship and after Simpson's death, Sayers wrote a posthumous tribute to her in *The Fortnightly*, praising her ability to relate to people and her intense interest in the world around her (Sayers 1941). In a letter to Sir Walter Wilson Greg some months earlier, Sayers had written: 'We shall feel the loss of Helen Simpson very much; she had one of the finest minds I know and an extraordinarily vivid personality. I don't think I ever met anybody who was so intensely interested in every kind of person and thing she encountered on her passage through life, and I feel that her death at this moment is a blow not only to her friends but also to the country; she would have taken a vigorous part in the post-war re-building' (Reynolds 1996, 184).

On 21 April 1927, Simpson married fellow Australian Denis Browne, a prominent paediatric surgeon at The Hospital for Sick Children in London. The couple first lived in Holborn near the

Law Courts and then eventually settled in a 200-year-old house in Queen Anne Street, further west. Their only daughter, Clemence, was born in November 1928. In addition to collecting books on witchcraft, Simpson's hobbies included horse riding and fencing, as well as collecting silver, old musical instruments, snuff boxes, medieval recipes, and Elizabethan cookbooks. She credited her French mother for instilling within her a love of cooking; along with homemade jams and jellies, Simpson made her own wine. In addition to her involvement with the Detection Club, she was a member of the PEN Club and served as a committee member for the Stock-Heinemann Prize.

Simpson wrote biographies of Henry VIII and the explorer and folklorist Mary Kingsley. She also wrote about domestic subjects, in *The Happy Housewife: A Book for the House That Is or Is to Be* (1934) and the cookbook *The Cold Table: A Book of Recipes for the Preparation of Cold Food and Drink* (1935). Her cookery talks on the BBC were some of the most popular programs broadcast, often resulting in thousands of fan letters. When it came to women and domestic economy, Simpson held progressive views. She told Coralie Clarke Rees: 'Women should know all about where the money comes from and where it goes to [...] and how the domestic economy of each household is linked to the larger economy of the whole country and that in turn to the whole world. [...] Girls should have at an early age experience of handling money and of making it go as far as possible' (Rees 1937). These feminist ideals extended beyond the domestic realm as well. Simpson contributed a chapter titled 'Man the Magpie,' to *Man, Proud Man*, a collection of feminist essays published in 1932. She felt that the literary work of women should stand on its own merit and disagreed with the practice of singling out the achievements of women based purely on their gender: 'The work of women [...] should be judged precisely in the same light as that of men—without the label of sex being attached' (Simpson 1937b). Though she admitted that men's literary output was historically greater than that of women, she said that women's writing was unique: 'But they have something delicate, delightful, and very real to say for themselves, something no man ever has or can imitate' (ibid).

Simpson was a frequent contributor to popular magazines throughout the 1930s, including *Cosmopolitan, The Illustrated London News, The New Yorker, Nash's, Pall Mall, The Passing Show, The Strand, The Tatler,* and *Lovat Dickson's Magazine.* Many of these stories showcase her sharp wit and sense of humor, such as 'A Posteriori,' which was published in *Lovat Dickson's Magazine* in July 1934 and presents a comical take on the traditional spy story. This humorous side was showcased again when she contributed an updated version of 'Puss in Boots' for *The Fairies Return* (1934), a collection of modern fairy tales contributed by famous authors of the day. In addition to her published writing, Simpson gave lectures and frequent radio talks on a variety of subjects for the BBC. In 1937, she returned to Australia to visit family, as well as to promote her recently published novel *Under Capricorn* and to do research for a forthcoming novel (left unfinished due to her illness and death). During the trip, she also gave a series of talks for the Australian Broadcasting Commission. She then completed a lecture tour in the United States before returning to England in 1938. The following year, Simpson turned her attention to politics, becoming the prospective Liberal candidate for the Isle of Wight's seat in the House of Commons. Her political career was cut short, however, when she was diagnosed with cancer.

In a letter to Lady Ethel Mary Boileau, Dorothy L Sayers wrote, 'I don't really quite know just what was the matter, but immediately after [Simpson's] operation, I gathered that things had not gone well and that they had found something more extensive than they expected, so that from the beginning I rather feared the worst' (Reynolds 1996, 199–200). In *Where Stands A Wingèd Sentry*, Margaret Kennedy also gives further information about Simpson's ongoing illness. In an entry from July, she says:

Claire's father is down for the week-end. He looks ghastly, but he has more than the war to worry him, for Claire's mother is very ill again. She has had one major operation, and now she has to have another. He, being a doctor, knows too much. He won't talk about it, but I can see he is tortured with anxiety. (Kennedy 1941, 122)

In an entry from September, Kennedy describes how the bombings in London directly affected Simpson's recovery: 'The hospital where Claire's parents are has been hit. Neither was injured. Claire's mother is terribly ill still, and they are moving her to the country. I fear the shock and fatigue will be very bad for her' (152).

After leaving a London hospital, Simpson stayed in the village of Overbury, Worcestershire, and died on 14 October 1940.

※

Helen Simpson had a longstanding interest in the occult. Her library of books on witchcraft and demonology included many rare titles from the sixteenth century and earlier. In a 1932 interview for Sydney's *World's News*, she discussed her collection, saying, 'It is a costly hobby, for these books are very rare and have to be diligently sought. There are many more I would like to have, but, alas! they are too dear' (Anon 1932a). She enjoyed the challenge of finding such books, saying in another interview: 'Books on demonology are exceedingly rare and it is the collector's instinct within me which always sends me hot on the trail of rare things that prompts me to collect them' (Simpson 1937a, 15). Among her books was one 500-year-old volume that contained a facsimile of one man's agreement to sell his soul to the devil, written in blood. Other books in the collection contained various spells and incantations for summoning demonic forces. Although she was often skeptical about the ceremonies she observed and read about, Simpson kept an open mind about such practices, claiming: 'Not all occult manifestations are sinister. I firmly believe our actions have an influence in the spirit world. If we live right the powers of darkness cannot harm us' (Anon 1932a). She later stated, 'As for witchcraft, black magic and other psychic phenomena, [...] I attribute them solely to tricks of the mind and examples of mental power, over which some people appear to have remarkable control' (Simpson 1937a, 15).

She gave talks about witchcraft for BBC radio as well as on lecture tours. In an undated draft of a speech on 'English Witches,' held in Simpson's personal papers in the possession of her family, she focuses on the lives and confessions of three seventeenth-century witches (including the infamous Elizabeth Styles) and draws from contemporary written accounts of these women. The speech covers a wide variety of topics related to witchcraft (including pacts with the devil, spells, shapeshifting, and familiars) and showcases Simpson's vast knowledge of the subject. She ends the speech with a summation of her particular views on witchcraft:

> You do not dispose of a belief by saying that it concerns itself with something untrue. The power lies in the belief itself, and not in the peg—religion, witchcraft—that it is hung to. [...] You can't move mountains by faith; you can't, that is, interfere with the physical world that runs by large laws of its own. You can, however, once you have got into the microcosm the little world of which a man's mind is the governor, lay about you and change things there. (Simpson nd)

Simpson also traveled to Austria and Hungary to study local customs and gather stories relating to witchcraft, vampires, and other occult practices in the region. In 1932, she visited Brocken, Austria, a site famous for its connection to black magic and the infamous he-goat ceremony in which a goat is supposed to transform into a young boy (Anon 1932b). These personal interests eventually found their way into her novels and short stories, with most of her supernatural fiction being collected in *The Baseless Fabric*.

Yet *The Baseless Fabric* almost never saw its way to publication. According to Simpson, Heinemann's reader was unsure what to make of the book. By chance, Clemence Dane came into the office and the publisher gave her the manuscript to read. Shortly after, Simpson received a postcard from Dane inviting her to the latter's house to discuss the stories (Anon 1927, 10). Simpson credited Dane with helping her to finalize the collection for publication and after this meeting the two became friends and collaborators. Dane favorably mentioned *The Baseless Fabric* in an April 1926 essay as one of the best contemporary collections of supernatural stories along with May Sinclair's *Uncanny Stories* (Dane 1926).

Reviews for *The Baseless Fabric* were positive, and the collection gained the notice of newspapers in both Simpson's native Australia and in Britain. The *Spectator* noted the nuanced treatment of the supernatural that eschewed the typical generic formula in favor of atmosphere and landscape: 'They are not ghost stories, but often they are much more frightening. The intangible atmosphere of dank woods, old houses and the downs can sometimes affect us more than visible ghosts' (Anon 1926a). London's *Weekly Dispatch* called it 'a book of short stories hovering on the line that separates the real from the supernatural' (Anon 1926c). The *Australasian* likewise praised the liminal nature of the stories, saying that the collection was 'an excursion into that shadowy borderland between the conscious and the unconscious' (Anon 1925b). The reviewer appreciated the distinctiveness of the stories and how they differed from other supernatural fiction popular at the time, saying, 'The uncanny story with its atmosphere of horror, and its terrifying suggestions of occultism, has been with us a good deal recently. But these stories are different again, their rather vague mysterious endings suggesting that the writer avoids the usual tragic climax. And more than a sense of the uncanny and fearful, they convey a sense of the beautiful' (ibid). Indeed, the subtle yet ominous nature of the stories represented a uniqueness that appealed to reviewers and readers alike. The *Montrose Standard* praised the 'evasive' and 'elusive' qualities of the collection:

It is difficult to correctly classify this volume of short stories, for they are very evasive. This is not to be wondered at for the authoress deals with a mystical evasive side of life lying as she puts it 'just beyond the reach of the five senses.' [...] There is originality and freshness and a sense of depth in all these stories. The authoress has tried to capture very elusive emotions and has succeeded to a remarkable degree. (Anon 1925a)

The Sydney *Sun* remarked, 'About the technique of Helen Simpson there can be little complaint. It is clever work, displaying a high capacity for fine writing and no little measure of dramatic power' (Anon 1926d).

One of the most insightful reviews of *The Baseless Fabric* appeared in New Zealand's *Saturday Review* on 20 February 1926:

There is a broad, fertile, infrequently visited territory—it lies midway between the fantastic short story and the impressionistic sketch—which holds limitless opportunities for the writer adequately equipped to enter it. Miss Simpson has worked in that abundant land and returned with tokens of a sombre and unique beauty. These are embodied in the eleven profoundly imagined creations here contained, each one, perfect in the exact balance and unfailing accuracy of its veiled suggestion, concerned with the potencies for good or evil latent in the invisible realm which separates the conscious senses from the surrounding world. Only in part, however, does the author rely upon the intangible for her medium, joining it, as she does, skilfully to an atmosphere of reality and invading the beings of living people with the uncanny powers of agencies beyond their comprehension.

A prodigal diversity of effects is enlisted to evolve the individual form of the illusion which dominates each character. Here and there a very slight hint of the supernatural or the mildly deranged creeps in, but these exceptions are unobjectionable breaks in a firmly held continuity of design whose burdens are the mute forces of nature in close concentration upon deep hidden frailties of the human soul. One protagonist may suffer from the company of a 'haunt' perceptible only to himself, another from the acute spiritual torment of his conscience for the desecration of a venerable inanimate thing, a third from the fatal blight of a fixed idea at last materializing in a tragic actuality. (Anon 1926b)

As the reviewer notes, these stories combine Simpson's interests in both human beings and the 'invisible realms' that lie just beyond the living senses. Her imaginative fiction allows readers to discover unexplored supernatural worlds while also confronting the very real imperfections that exist within the living world and the interior consciousness of the individual person.

After Simpson's untimely death, however, her work disappeared from the literary landscape and most of her books went out of print. This certainly applies to *The Baseless Fabric*, as Simpson's only collection of short stories fell even deeper into obscurity and was, until now, almost all but forgotten for its contribution to imaginative and macabre interwar fiction. It is perhaps not surprising that attempts to reclaim her place in such fiction have been most sustained in Australia, where Simpson's work was consistently praised during her lifetime in numerous contemporary reviews, interviews, and retrospectives. Of particular note is the work of James Doig, who included 'The Pythoness' in his anthology *Australian Hauntings* (2013). Doig is also responsible for one of the few critical appraisals of Simpson's writing. In his 2013 article 'A Sombre and Unique Beauty: The Stories of Helen Simpson,' he gives an overview of Simpson's life and work before focusing on the stories from *The Baseless Fabric*, which he calls 'quiet, elusive psychological studies' (Doig 2013, 51).

These stories, in addition to the supernatural stories Simpson published in popular magazines during the 1930s, represent a wide array of weird subject matter. As several reviewers noted, she often places readers in the grey areas between the natural and the supernatural, a quality which lends an even greater degree of uncanniness and uneasiness to the narratives. Other stories may have more overt supernatural content, but this content is always linked to very real psychological struggles experienced by the characters. The opening story, 'Grey Sand and White Sand,' concerns a mentally unstable artist who becomes increasingly suspicious of his partner's attitude towards his paintings. The coastal landscape begins to have a weird hold over the artist as he becomes obsessed with translating its elusive inner life onto the canvas. Simpson's taut style reveals the increasing tension that builds inside the artist as he becomes more and more desperate to depict something that is unreachable and ultimately unseeable. His solution to this dilemma results in a final break that leaves both the artist and the reader in an overwhelming (and literal) darkness.

The uncanny hold of the land over a person is also a central concern in 'The Outcast,' in which the unburied body of a fallen soldier who cannot fully rest is directly connected to the inability of a memorial tree to grow in a rural town in the British countryside. Simpson engages with the aftermath of the First World War and how the town's ostracism of the soldier ties into the abandonment of his body on the battlefield.

'The Rite' and 'Young Magic' concern restless adolescence and how such restlessness experienced by the young women in both stories leads them into dangerous mental and physical territory. They seek an escape from their lives, but each must pay a price for such an escape. In 'The Rite,' the dark, otherworldly landscape of Parvus Holt, a wooded area which remains unchanged since Roman times, encompasses an uncontrolled wildness in the plants and flowers that grow there:

> [The creeping flowers] grew low, obscenely shaped, and
> when they were plucked wilted at once and turned brown
> before they died; the villagers would never touch them,
> for they hated the wood and all the things that grew there.
> Parvus Holt, they called it, and there was a saying, black as
> Parvus at noonday. Certainly it was always very dark there,
> and not cool. (22)

For those who dare to enter, the forest landscape simultaneously encloses and exposes desire, or, as the narrator describes it, 'the darkness that could so reveal hidden things' (28).

There is an intimacy between the characters and otherworldly beings in several of the stories as their interior lives are invaded by these supernatural presences. In 'Good Company,' a young woman on a walking holiday is suddenly possessed by the spirit of a Catholic saint. She struggles to regain control of her body and mind, now inhabited by two people. Once again, Simpson's writing beautifully describes such a frightening invasion:

> The terror withdrew, or rather she twisted away from it as
> a diver turns his hands to the surface and comes slowly
> up through the yielding pressure of water. She lay face
> downwards on the bed, her mouth writhed open, feeling
> her heart thud against the mattress. After a time she
> had breath to think of other matters, and to remember
> moments of fear, of insistence, of acquiescence, of
> possession. (105)

Likewise, in 'A Curious Story,' a famous stage actor feels the presence of a long-dead actress. He asks a friend to communicate with the spirit but when this attempt fails, it becomes clear that the actress appears only to those who are attached to the theatre. Like the saint in 'Good Company,' the ghostly woman uses the living to express something that has been loved and lost, yet these women's associations with the living world remain tenuous. The spiritual world on the borders of the everyday 'gets lost in words' and 'slips past us' (132). Throughout *The Baseless Fabric*, Simpson reminds us that the connection between the natural and the supernatural will always remain elusive, and will always resist our attempts to discover the source of the mystery. As the actor's friend concludes, 'We don't know so much of life, after all' (132).

The power of the imagination returns in 'The Man Who Had Great Possessions,' which concerns a writer and how one of his fictional creations gradually moves beyond his control and develops a life of her own. The woman created in the author's mind, who has 'lived' with him since he was sixteen, threatens to overwhelm him and destroy his career as a writer. To reclaim himself, he must exorcize her by putting her into written words, moving her spirit from his mind onto the page. Like the imaginary friend Binns in 'Young Magic,' this adolescent creation is easily summoned but not so easily abandoned. The imaginative impulse of youth becomes an emotional weight in later years, one that threatens the very life and well-being of the characters in these two stories. 'The Man Who Had Great Possessions' is an effective study in how writing can bring ideas into the world, but also how it can allow us to free ourselves from personal demons. In 'Young Magic,' the protagonist Viola is not so lucky. In the final paragraphs of the story, Simpson shocks both her main character and her readers by making it clear that such supernatural forces may have a greater hold over us than we realize. In so doing, the story subtly moves from one of innocent make-believe and precociousness to something very ominous as the imaginary friend of Viola's youth is revealed to be a foreboding uninvited companion in adulthood.

'As Much More Land' is an extended study in fear and in many ways encapsulates the mood of the entire collection. During a visit to a relative's supposedly haunted house, the skeptical protagonist insists on discovering the secret of a locked room. Yet what he finds there goes beyond the room itself and into something more primal. As he sits in the room one night, trying to convince himself that the claims about the room are false, he begins to lose control of rational thought. The more he tries to control those thoughts the more fearful he becomes:

> It would be frightful if a room were suddenly to come alive. (Let those ideas alone, can't you?) Well, of course it can't, so it doesn't matter thinking about it. [...] But if it were to come alive, and be somehow malignant, hating me. Walls of white membrane, stretched tightly. And they would begin to pulse, moving in and out ever so slightly, like a creature breathing. [...] One would watch them and think at first that it was only the shifting light. One would think so until one couldn't fool oneself any longer, and that would be fear. (51)

The man's description of the inability to escape the room becomes the perfect description of the inability of the human to escape from their own mind, their own thoughts and fears. The physical room with its membranous walls becomes a symbol for the brain, that other living mental 'room' in our body in which we are forced to reside:

> You might run at the soft walls, and they would give a little, but you could never tear the stuff apart. It would feel clammy and sweatily warm, like living guts, so that you would rather go through hell than touch it again. You would wait in the very centre of the room, and watch it closing in. (51)

In the story, Simpson allows readers to experience the suffocating feeling of helplessness as the character tries to rationalize and put order to the irrational. This is the psychological ghost story at its best.

'Disturbing Experience of an Elderly Lady' and 'Teigne' likewise focus on the malign influence of houses. The terrible prophecy of the latter house comes true, and in both stories, the houses ultimately exact their revenge. Simpson described *The Baseless Fabric* as a book about 'houses which are alive' (Anon 1927), and she had the remarkable ability to craft stories that centre these houses as central characters who look, think, and feel. In 'Teigne', the house waits patiently for its prey: 'From the woods to which Anne had fled in her terror he spied upon the malignant house, watching it as though it were an enemy; it stood, triumphant, secure, and the great artificial keep mocked him with its strength' (159). While in 'Disturbing Experience,' the house silently enacts its revenge before uttering its final, chilling statement of triumphant possession. Indeed, in these haunted house stories, possessing and possession take on new and terrible forms as the dwellers first voluntarily possess these domestic spaces in the physical sense only to be involuntarily possessed psychically by these ominous properties.

The interior world of the characters—and how that world is disrupted by exterior forces—is a central focus of 'The Pledge'. It features another coastal landscape and a woman who mourns the loss of a lover at sea. The sea looms large in the story and represents a wider world that the protagonist Miss Alquist once knew. This world is juxtaposed with the smaller, lonelier world of her lodging room, which contains treasures brought to her from distant regions by the sailor. The sea represents a form of escape as well by the end of the story. It assumes a supernatural quality as it comes onto land to carry away the woman who is seemingly reunited with her love.

The last two stories in this volume were published a decade and more after the stories collected in *The Baseless Fabric*, and they represent Simpson's writing for the popular magazine market. These stories show Simpson moving even more firmly into the supernatural mode with her short fiction and offer an intriguing possibility about whether such stories would have continued if not for her death a few years later. 'An Experiment of the Dead,' originally published in the 19 October 1938 issue of *The Tatler*, concerns the aftermath of an aristocratic woman's murder trial as she waits to be hanged. A dubious clergyman uses her impending death as an opportunity to carry out an occult experiment which ultimately backfires on him.

'The Pythoness' originally appeared in the short-lived *Lovat Dickson's Magazine* in January 1934. Dorothy L Sayers referred to Simpson as 'the Pythoness,' remembering how she would read Tarot cards for friends and acquaintances, even going so far as to removing the Death, Tower, and the Ace and Ten of Swords cards so as not to upset anyone. On other occasions, Sayers recalled that Simpson would put her library of black magic books to use for those in need: 'forlorn ladies whose neighbours were undermining their constitutions with black magic wrote imploring her aid, and were comforted—not with advice to consult the physician, call in the parson, or pull themselves together—but with "a good strong charm" suited to their condition and extracted from an authoritative manual of sorcery' (Sayers 1941, 55).

'The Pythoness' involves a Spiritualist medium, Ruby Bain, who falls in love with a man whose wife has recently died. In order to become a respectable wife, Ruby tries to free herself from her life as a medium but as an acquaintance says, 'You can't suddenly padlock a gate that people have got used to using' (195). Towards the climax, something (or someone) does indeed come through that gate, as the victim of a crime appears in order to reveal a terrible secret using the body of the medium. The ambiguous ending—and the fact that Ruby may or may not be faking her ability to communicate with those of the other side—provides a nice twist on the longstanding tradition of short fiction inspired by Spiritualism and séances.

✳

The title of Simpson's 1925 collection is fittingly taken from Prospero's speech in Act IV of William Shakespeare's *The Tempest*:

Our revels now are ended. These our actors
(As I foretold you) were all spirits, and
Are melted into air, into thin air,
And like the baseless fabric of this vision,
The cloud-capp'd tow'rs, the gorgeous palaces,
The solemn temples, the great globe itself,
Yea, all which it inherit, shall dissolve,
And like this insubstantial pageant faded
Leave not a rack behind. We are such stuff
As dreams are made on; and our little life
Is rounded with a sleep. (Act 4, scene 1, lines 148–158)

Helen Simpson's stories give us that dreamlike quality, where we must question what is real and what is imagined, what is natural and what is supernatural. But along with dreams come nightmares, and Simpson gives us plenty of those, too. Dark forests, marshlands, and barren hills confront us with an ominous presence that we cannot quite fathom. Likewise, her haunted houses force us to confront the unexplainable and the irrational. Fear is an active force in these stories, and it leads the characters to question their motives, their insecurities, and their darkest desires. Reading these narratives, we are struck by their originality, by their inventiveness, and by a style of writing that elegantly describes almost indescribable terrors. It is tragic that Helen Simpson's life was cut short. Perhaps she would have entered a political career that would have benefitted those she served. Perhaps she would have published that epic novel of Australia that remained unfinished at her death. But what we do have of her published work remains a treasure. Her supernatural writing gives us another voice to add among the 'greats' of genre fiction during the interwar period. Like her contemporaries, Helen Simpson gives us a glimpse into worlds we could scarcely otherwise imagine. The fabric of her vision can still excite us, can still chill us, and can still allow us to appreciate the terrible beauty of a fine-crafted supernatural tale.

Works cited

Anon, Review of *The Baseless Fabric*, *Montrose Standard* (Scotland), (20 November 1925a), 6.

—, Review of *The Baseless Fabric*, *Australasian* (Melbourne), (19 December 1925b), 52.

—, Review of *The Baseless Fabric*, *The Spectator* (16 January 1926a), 100.

—, Review of *The Baseless Fabric*, *The Saturday Review of Literature* (New Zealand), (20 February 1926b), 580.

—, Review of *The Baseless Fabric*, *Weekly Dispatch* (London), (18 April 1926c), 19.

—, Review of *The Baseless Fabric*, *Sun* (Sydney), (23 May 1926d), 20.

—, 'Difficult Publishers,' *Daily News* (Perth), (19 March 1927), 10.

—, 'Incantations: Helen Simpson's Queer Hobby,' *World's News* (Sydney), (4 May 1932a), 9.

—, 'Toured "Vampire Country"', *Herald* (Melbourne), (7 June 1932b), 7.

—, 'Talented Australian Authoress in Melbourne,' *Argus* (Melbourne), (26 July 1937), 3.

Dane, Clemence, 'New Lamps or Old,' *The Bookman* (New York), 63.2 (April 1926), 166–171.

Doig, James, 'A Sombre and Unique Beauty: The Stories of Helen Simpson,' *Wormwood* 20 (Spring 2013), 45–53.

Kennedy, Margaret. *Where Stands A Wingèd Sentry* (Bath, 1941, 2021).

McDonald, Louise. *Clemence Dane: Forgotten Feminist Writer of the Inter-War Years* (New York and London: Routledge, 2021).

Powell, Violet, *The Constant Novelist: A Study of Margaret Kennedy, 1896–1967* (London: Heinemann, 1983).

Rees, Coralie Clarke, 'An Australian Novelist of Many Talents,' *Sydney Morning Herald* (1 June 1937), 21.

—, 'Helen Simpson: Talented Australian Novelist,' *West Australian* (Perth), (1 April 1933), 4.

Reynolds, Barbara (ed.), *The Letters of Dorothy L Sayers*, Vol 2, (New York: St. Martin's Press, 1996).

Sayers, Dorothy L, 'Helen Simpson,' *The Fortnightly* (January 1941), 54–59.

Simpson, Helen, 'My Recipe for Happy Living,' *Table Talk* (Melbourne), (5 August 1937a), 13, 15.

—, 'Women and Books: Miss Helen Simpson's Views,' *Sydney Morning Herald* (10 August 1937b), 16.

—, 'Women's Realm: A Writer on Writing.' *Newcastle Morning Herald* (New South Wales), (10 September 1937c), 16.

—, 'English Witches,' nd. Personal Papers of Helen Simpson, held privately.

Ussher, Kathleen, 'Helen de Guerry Simpson: The Australian Authoress,' *Sydney Mail* (4 March 1931), 22.

Bibliographical details

The following stories were originally collected in *The Baseless Fabric*, published in London by William Heinemann in 1925. This present volume uses the 1925 American edition, published in New York by Alfred A. Knopf.

'Grey Sand and White Sand'
'The Rite'
'The Outcast'
'As Much More Land'
'Young Magic'
'Disturbing Experience of an Elderly Lady'
'Good Company'
'A Curious Story'
'The Man Who Had Great Possessions'
'Teigne'
'The Pledge'

'The Pythoness' originally appeared in *Lovat Dickson's Magazine* in January 1934. The present text is based on this publication.

'An Experiment of the Dead' originally appeared in *The Tatler* on 19 October 1938. The present text is based on this publication.

Obvious typographical errors and inconsistencies have been silently corrected.

1 Grey Sand and White Sand

When he had put his canvas safely inside the door Hilary Monk went out again to watch the storm coming up from the south-west over the marsh, wondering as he always did at the swift darkening of so immense a sky. He had finished his picture while the sun lasted, and now saw without resentment or impatience the transformation effected by the changed light. The marsh had no outlines. There were no trees save the three thorns a mile away, slanting northwards as though they yielded to a perpetual wind; no hedges, but only a darker, richer line among the grasses where reeds bordered the dykes. The land was a monotone, a flat screen on which the light played.

He leaned his folded arms on the top bar of the gate, looking southwards. The storm was miles away yet, advancing steadily across the yellow fields, and he could see the foremost clouds fringed with falling rain. An hour ago these same fields had been almost gay with light; now they were sullen as a dirty sea, and the wind drove the grass in waves which made a little sound like the hiss of breaking spray. It was, he thought, an unnatural country, more like water than land, taking its colour and moods from the sky as water does; changing as water. Below this inconstancy lay some quality which he could not discover, disguised by the passing shows of sun and wind, an unpaintable quality which disturbed him, and which he was constantly trying to fix and place in his mind.

The wind came more strongly towards him, bending the dark plumes of the rushes. It pressed against him, and set a lock of hair threshing across his eyes. He hated this wind. It was the spy sent out to watch and drive away intruders that the parties to an intrigue might meet in safety. He thrust the lock of hair upwards, pulled his hat tightly down on to his head, and folded his arms again upon the top of the gate, almost smiling at the childish tactics of the wind. It plucked suddenly at his coat, stood off for a moment, and advanced roughly from a different quarter to worry the brim of his hat; howled against the southern chimney; finally it came at him full strength like a squadron of cavalry, charging, retreating, wheeling, charging again. It did not intend that he should ever approach the secret which the patient and sinister land was hiding.

A week ago he had begun to know that such a truth existed, and had almost surprised it; that was on a grey day when land and sea were one substance, and on the horizon hung low white clouds curling forward like surf. Then he had seemed to be present at a colloquy between the elements; but while he listened down came the wind to break the strange single-coloured whole into its parts; the sea was itself again, the sky was patterned with cloud. When he tried to make his eyes understand it the wind harassed him, blowing straight into his eyes, and when he could see again it was too late, and the marsh was back again, not a field out of place.

Since that day he had watched, though the wind would not let him alone and the marsh offered a dozen new aspects to enchant him from his purpose. He was not deceived. He painted the moods, got them safely on canvas, but he knew well enough that they were only tricks of light and shadow; a series of masks.

Wind was pulling the clouds forward at a great pace. Suddenly, as he watched, the grey pyramid of the town five miles away was obscured by a curtain of rain, whose soft sound he could almost hear beating into the ground like the sound of many distant hoofs on grass. Already the sheep had turned their backs to the force of the storm; the wool on their backs was blown apart, so that they had an absurd appearance of having been carefully trimmed with a comb. Hilary Monk lowered his head, but faced it, and would face it while the light lasted. Light was important. Vaguely he felt that it was connected in some way with the secret, which ceased to be powerful when darkness came; for this he was thankful, since otherwise he must have watched by night as well as by day. As it was, he did not sleep very well, nor for long at a stretch. He was afraid of missing the dawn, and it was necessary that he should watch from the very earliest coming of the light. He did not quite see why this should be so, but some personage deep down in him insisted, and he obeyed, though once or twice he had caught himself thinking: If anyone else got to know of this they might think it was funny. For this reason he said nothing to the woman who lived with him, to whom he referred for convenience as his wife. Often, going out into the expectant darkness to wait for the sun, or while he felt the rain soaking his coat at the end of a wet day, he wondered if it could be what doctors called an obsession, and was a little frightened. The personage would have none of this and there were discussions. Even now, standing by the gate, the adversaries argued in his mind, so that he frowned, and his mouth took on an obstinate look below the alert and unwavering eyes. He knew how the debate would shape itself, even to the turn of a sentence. Wearily he listened as it went forward.

How much longer is this to go on? Till something happens. Till what happens? Till I find out. It was an illusion. Perhaps; in that case it may come again. If it does? I'll paint it, and you'll see a miracle. Are you going to spend your life waiting on a chance? Why not? That's what most of us do. Poor fool. Here comes the rain.

He stood passively while it lashed his face with little strands of water. The light was almost gone, but until the last green was withdrawn from the grass he did not dare to shift his ground. There could not be long to wait, for already his eyes were puzzled by the approaching night. He thought with satisfaction of the fire whose smoke streamed in the wind horizontally from the southern chimney, and was conscious that he lacked food, needed it, yet did not want to eat. In spite of the comfort of fire he knew the evening would seem long. His vigil ended, life had no meaning until it could be renewed. He knew how his wife would look at him when she thought his eyes were closed. She had learned not to comment, but there was no way to stop her wonder except by getting rid of her altogether. She did a great many things for him. She was useful, fond of him, and not as a rule very shrewd. Besides, she had nowhere to go. He dismissed the thought.

Rain was muttering on the wide darkened brim of his hat, falling straight now, for the wind had ceased to drive it. The town five miles away was quite lost, and when he looked down at the grass by the hinge of the gate it was grey. He gave a little sigh for the twelve hours without opportunity that lay before him, lifted his arms slowly, stretched, and turned towards shelter.

The door of the cottage opened into the room where they lived. He opened it and stood for a moment with the latch in his hand looking into the warm disappointing stillness of the room. Outside there was movement, water slanting to the ground, making channels there, grass beaten down and lifting again, the whole sky marching. Here the lamp glowed steadily, and the walls stood firm. Flames had gone from the fire, so that it stared red between the bars of the grate, not blinking. She sat by it with her hands in her lap. The whole scene was stripped of motion as a body lately dead.

He let the latch fall, and went towards the woman in the chair, treading heavily, his boots stiff with wet. She did not turn her head. He stood by the chair, balancing while he unlaced the boots and threw them down before the fire; then she leaned forward and arranged the clumsy things with their soles towards the warmth. His feet left wet impressions on the brick floor. When she saw this she rose, and went towards the stairs, but he stopped her.

'It doesn't matter.'

'But you can't sit about all wet like that.'

'I'll take them off. Is any wood left?'

'In the kitchen.'

She went, and returned with two small reddish logs. He said almost apologetically as she put them on the fire.

'They're more fun.'

He was a little touched by her immediate submission, and decided that the evening might seem less long if he talked to her. It was not easy, for he had no longer any curiosities about her, nor any need to display himself for her approval, and except when one of these necessities roused him he was a silent man. He thought that it might be as well to begin by showing her his picture.

He had to call her attention to it; she was looking into the fire, now crisp with burning wood.

'Here's what I did to-day. Do you see what I'm trying for?'

She gave it her attention, turning her head on her hand. He was intent on the canvas, and would have waited for the non-committal answer he expected, if the flaming wood had not sent a spark towards her that seemed to fall on her hand. It did not touch her, and she did not move, but he was startled and looked involuntarily at her face. The hand shadowed it; she was silent. He saw with incredulity that her eyes were laughing, and the mouth, too, stirred derisively for a second.

While he looked it was gone. She had hidden it as quickly and as securely as the marsh hid its secret, and he heard her saying the expected thing.

'First-rate, old man. Just the way it looks.'

The voice at any rate was not mocking. He might have thought that the light had tricked him. He tried to think so. He knew her so well. But all the time he was sure, and his conviction was betrayed in his answer.

'The way it looks; not the way it is.'

'Well, of course, it's always changing about, every time there's a breath of wind.'

'That's not the real change.'

He broke off, looking at her; she looked innocently, blankly, in return. He went on, putting into words the thing he had not told her for fear she might think it was funny.

'The real change comes when everything is quite still.'

She asked politely, humouring his desire to talk, 'Does it? What happens?'

'I believe you know.'

She gave one quick glance upwards that did not quite reach his eyes, and laughed openly.

'I believe this old marsh is getting on your nerves.'

'Why did you look at my picture like that?'

'Like what?'

'As if you knew.'

'Knew what?'

He gave it up, lifting one shoulder in a kind of despair, and put the picture away. She went into the kitchen to cook their supper, leaving him by the fire; but he was restless. He came padding after her, and stood in the doorway of the kitchen, watching. She made movements which he had seen repeated for two years, carelessly breaking eggs into a bowl, handling a frying pan with assurance. Her short hair was familiar, no more and no less untidy than when she had first come to live with him. Last winter he had seen her knitting the fawn-coloured woollen dress she wore to-night. She stood firmly, not shifting her feet, moving as she worked her body sideways and forwards on the axis of her big hips. Her face, bent down with only the curve of the cheek showing, her left hand with the crooked third finger, the slight shaking of her breast when she moved suddenly, the square back of her head, all were familiar and entirely disconcerting. These aspects of her made up something new, the queerly shaped prison that concealed a stranger, a woman who had laughed at his picture just as a person who knows the answer to some riddle will laugh at a random guess. He was excited by that knowledge of hers. Perhaps she followed his thought, for she looked at him once or twice, and put a hand to her hair. Outwardly they were both calm, silently eating, without one glance towards the picture leaning in a corner of the room with its back to them.

When supper was over and she had washed the dishes he went forward to meet her as she came back from the kitchen, and caught her left hand, that still was damp and smelled warm, turning with her across the room. She was surprised, and stood still. He let her hand go free.

'Don't you like me to touch you?'

'Of course I do.'

'Why do you look like that? Is it so strange that I should want to?'

He knew very well that she might consider it strange, and perhaps discover the reason; but he took comfort in the thought that she was a woman of experience and knew desire to be a rhythmic thing, recurring at fixed periods like a strong beat in music.

That night he said nothing more about his trouble. When he woke, from habit, just before dawn, he could feel her body pressing against him and sinking away as she breathed, and told himself that he must have patience. Discoverers were always patient. He moved his hand to feel the warmth of her, surprised that she could so easily baffle him just by sleeping, or being silent, or talking over the surface of the immense question. His watchfulness had now a double object; one held the answer to the other and at times they were distinct, and at times were one. It was dark yet, but he looked down at the woman's face, seeing it clearly, smooth, and placidly smiling, as the fields did. Speech could stir it and change it as sun stirred the fields, laughter could wrinkle it as wind wrinkled the grasses on the marsh. He moved away from her, carefully, so that she should not wake, for while she slept the secret was safely locked away and he was not tempted by it. He got out of bed and furtively dressed to be ready for the dawn when it came.

It came with admirable slow dignity into a sky swept clear by the night wind. The misted fields revealed themselves. They lay open to the sun, blandly, without guile, while the sheep which had crowded together during the night began to wander apart from the flock one by one to find new patches where they might feed; for here the tough sea-grasses lay on the green like drifts of grey sand. At such a moment Hilary Monk distrusted his vision, and would have been glad to abandon the search. This first hour of light was so sane. It laughed at him, not as she had laughed, but rather tenderly, mocking, inviting him to be happy. In the beginning he had almost been taken in by this pleading, and only remembered just in time the innumerable masks, the sly thrusts and whisperings of the wind. After ten days, he could remain unmoved by the gentle promise of the morning.

There were gulls hovering above the grass, looking surprisingly big as they wheeled and settled. He noticed that when they came to rest on the ground they did not stride about as crows do, not hurry like thrushes; they stood in one place shifting their feet as though they were used to feel a yielding surface under them. They trod the ground for a moment as though it had been water, and were off again, dipping, soaring, turning sideways to feel the grass tickling the tips of their wings; sweeping above the sheep, who disregarded them, or when they came too near stood nervously with heads erect to face them. The birds were indignant to find the sheep tranquilly pasturing in their chosen spaces, and could be heard screaming in protest, making a harsh noise that would not have mattered among the tremendous sounds of the sea. Above their assaults and advances the sky was darkening to an unthreatening and uniform grey. Hilary thought that there would be no more sun that day, and he went out by the lane which led from the cottage into the main road, meaning to follow its zig-zags as far as the village called Martinchurch which lay in the centre of the marsh, hidden behind a hedge of dwarfish trees. As he walked, the hope which the clouded sky had roused in him sank away; the wind paid him no attention and did not try to lure him out of his path by fluttering from him like a bird guarding its nest, nor to drive him indoors by squalling and spitting at his face. It blew steadily, without purpose, in a manner that showed it was off duty. He went on, a conviction increasing in his mind that the enigma might be pursued at home with more chance of success.

It was odd, he thought, that she should have made the discovery. He knew, however, that the most foolish and improbable people may sometimes by chance become possessed of power which they have not the imagination to use. He saw that he had made a mistake last night. It was always, with women, a mistake to beg instead of bullying. Even the least wise of them must understand that when a man wanted a thing which she could give, his desire became her weapon so long as she chose to withhold. Fortunately they, women, always wanted to be giving; it was at once their luxury, and the weakness by which they could be vanquished. A man must constantly demand of them, or else pretend to be indifferent to gifts in order to get the most out of them. Here lay his difficulty, for in the two years of their liaison he had not accustomed her to be generous, and pretence, in this matter at least, was out of the question. He wondered if a frank appeal would have any effect, but when he thought of his question translated into words it became grotesque, and towered up in his mind like a genie with a foul and ludicrous expression. Has this flat earth a life? Are these moods that I trace and set down the changing attitudes of some living and possibly sinister thing? Have I seen one of the moments in which that thing shows as it is? Whichever way he turned it, the question was unaskable.

At the sullen end of day when he went back to the cottage he was still undecided. There was a feeling behind his eyes as though they needed a different kind of sleep, as though the ordinary darkness and forgetfulness could not satisfy. The light was not quite gone, but he went indoors, to see her sitting in that same posture, looking down at the timid new fire. She spoke at once.

'You haven't been painting?'

'No.'

'Just as well.'

'Why?'

She did not answer immediately, and he repeated, 'Why?'

'I only thought you'd been doing a bit too much lately.'

She went on hurriedly, seeing him look quickly at her.

'I don't mean you haven't done some lovely things. I think these last ones are the best you've ever done. Only you're looking a bit tired, that's all I meant.'

'As if that mattered.'

'Well—I was thinking perhaps it would do you good to get away.'

He was really startled.

'Away from here? I can't do that.'

'I don't see why not. We haven't been spending much. You could go up to town for a week.'

'What about you?'

'I'll be all right here. I don't mind. I think you ought to go.'

'Yes, I daresay you do.'

She began to talk of other things. He responded. They had supper, and she went early to bed. Hilary Monk remained by the fire, smiling. He was amused that she could suppose him capable of being taken in by such simplicity, and he was content to have this proof of her share in the conspiracy of silence. She permitted him to go to London and disperse his energy in follies, while here on the marsh something was about to happen of which she was aware; the secret unfolding. It was childish of her; as silly as the everyday antics of the wind, trying to push him here and there about the roads. He stayed for a long time with his feet stretched towards the fire, lazily blinking, not sleepy. The dissatisfied feeling behind his eyes grew stronger. At last there was no more warmth in the ashes, and he went upstairs.

He did not sleep at all that night, but he was calmer, and time passed easily in thoughts of the miracle. It would explain, he thought, a great many things; and though the actual happening might be too swift or too subtle for a brush to define it, something might remain, a kind of light showing the reason why the land looked as it did, why it took on these aspects and rejected those. For, he thought, what is the use of going on painting surfaces for ever? Every man in his full five senses knows all about surfaces. Painters must try to get at the reason, otherwise there is no excuse for them. Most of them are far too easily satisfied; they go to a country, and put down on canvas its more superficial aspects, together with a few of their own more or less random convictions and prejudices; then they run about crying that they have caught beauty and caged it, whereas in their haste and their little knowledge they have done no more than put salt on beauty's tail.

This matter seemed to him very important. He reflected that he would be the first man to understand the truth of landscape, and he felt an honest disdain for the work he had accomplished so far. It lacked, not sincerity, but vision, as indeed all such painting had lacked till now. Those pictures of his that were to come would be hated perhaps, or patronised, which would be worse; but the little critics pass, and their opinions make the first quick prey of fire. After them would come the men who were not concerned to be considered almighty, at whose nod none trembled. These would give the final verdict, which he might never hear. He would be to them the man who had seen. A good epitaph.

The woman who lay beside him twitched in her sleep; he put out a hand to her and she lay still. He felt for her that regard of the fighter for the honourable enemy. She had tried to keep the tremendous knowledge from him. No doubt she had her reasons, jealousy, caution, fear; none of them mattered. He was too strong, too amply determined; and if he wondered that she should have known of the search, it was only a momentary astonishment, such as comes to all reticent creatures surprised by intuition in their innermost strongholds.

Night passed, splendid with proud imaginings and dreams of conquest. He made twenty different futures and tried them on one after the other. There was the future in which he walked about the marsh as now, solitary, while poets and great names waited, and came forward bareheaded to greet him as he unlatched the gate, with his old wide hat riding aslant on his head; or the future which saw pilgrims standing at his grave; or that best future of all when trees and the grassy hills knew him and let him come near, like shy animals tamed.

When he knew, by some indescribable change in the darkness that filled the window square, that it was time to become real again, he sighed, and at once began to dress. The routine of breakfast, the usual cocoa heated on the oil stove, was soon over. It was no more than the necessary delay between one gladness and another. This joy of another day was balanced by an increase of the curious feeling of unrest and desire that brooded behind his eyes; he was not impatient, however, knowing that the feeling, which was not pain but a kind of uneasiness, would go when the delicious moment came.

Mist lay thick and white above the morning fields, an October mist that passively awaited the sun. October, he thought, was the best of the months, with its calm days and savage nights that assailed the trees and stripped them; October night winds were ravishers. But when they had done their work, what a clean and marvellous world remained! Trees like lace, white sheets of water in the hollows of the fields, and all the westerly windows flaming together at five o'clock in the evening. A naked month. A month in which things happened.

All day there was no wind. He could look without hindrance at the faint horizon, where above the sea lay a line of white clouds, which did not move all day. He could look inland, and carry his glance along the line of hills that made the boundary of the marsh, like the line of a coast viewed from the sea. Wherever he walked he could hear the frequent sound of water. A cart filled with roots swayed across the ridgy field beyond him with the labouring motion of a ship caught in a tide. He was not nervously alert, as he had been during the past week. The hours slipped by him, round and yellow as amber beads. He sat on the arched coping of a culvert, motionless, while his shadow, that had been only a dark inch or two, swung round, lengthening, towards the east; not needing to seek occupation, entirely ready for that which was coming.

When the afternoon drew to sunset he was not disturbed. He had passed from suspicion to an absolute trust in the marsh, and did not suppose that it would cheat him. If it chose to withhold itself a little longer he could submit. He remembered how he had despised women who yielded too soon. A man coming from the lane behind him heard him talking, and laughing gently at the capricious marsh.

'That's a woman,' he was saying, 'it's the same with you. Once she's said the first yes, none of the no's that come afterwards count for very much. You know, at first I was inclined to be frightened; I thought that what lay underneath could be nothing very good. But I only had a moment's glimpse; I couldn't see; and there was the wind. This is the first day's peace we've had together. It's been good, but it isn't knowing you. Not as I want to know you. She tried to send me away; she suspected. We must be gentle with her. She understands partly. Well, to-day's over, and I've had nothing from you. She needn't have worried.'

She was standing at the gate when he reached it, standing as she always did with her arms folded on the top bar, looking across the fields to the apex of the distant town. As he came up to her she said, 'What a day.'

Looking at her very seriously he answered, 'Yes.'

She went on.

'Doesn't seem to have done you much good.'

'It isn't over yet,' he said, smiling in a tolerant sort of way, and went past her into the house. She came after him slowly, puzzled by his appearance and that smile, wondering what she could do. Something suggested itself.

'Would you like some tea now, instead of waiting?'

'I don't mind. Yes. All right.'

While she moved about in the kitchen he stood by the window; when the tea was ready he took his cup to the window and drank it standing there, incredulously becoming conscious that the light was going, was almost gone. At last he could not pretend to hope any longer. The day was over. She heard him sigh as he pulled the red curtains together.

In bed that night he was restless. His thoughts no longer moved in splendour to the tune of immortal homages. They twisted away from him when he tried to face them at the future and ran murmuring into dark corners of his mind where he could not hear what they were saying. He tried to lay the whole position before them in a reasonable way, but they howled him down, beating and surging behind his eyes just where he most needed rest, and nothing articulate emerged from their clamour but the single phrase, No use waiting. Why not? he asked, what other way is there? The thoughts hesitated as though they could have answered, but would not yet, and when he pressed them they began to howl again so that he was afraid to ask any more questions and afraid to sleep lest he might miss something. The night seemed long. He was glad when morning came and his senses had something to do.

For some reason he chose that day to walk towards the sea. As a rule he hated the shingle, which yielded and sank at each step with small grinding noises, and the dunes of white sand continually being shifted and built into other shapes by the sea wind. To-day he came to it as to a refuge. He climbed one of the dunes with sand streaming into his shoes, and sat down to be free for a while from the interrogation of the fields. He offered the sand and shingle to his thoughts.

The sand was very white, bleached, he supposed, by salt water and the sun. It lay in smooth drifts, dimpled here and there, and behind it the shingle was gathered, a flat invariable stretch of rounded pebbles over which the sea had once had power. The pebbles were three or four feet deep. They smothered the earth so that no grass could thrive to bind the sand. Each year after the big tides these stones received reinforcements from the sea, which swept away the barriers of sand and deposited more stones; then it built up the sand again, and the beach was rough with occasional pebbles which had proved too heavy to be carried beyond it by the force of the water.

Idly Hilary worked his stick between the stones, and levered up others from the layer beneath. They were dry, coloured dull grey and brown, not to be distinguished from that had been above them. It occurred to him that there could be no better hiding place than this very shingle for something which need never be found again. There would be no way of marking the spot, except perhaps by a pattern of stones. A cairn would soon be blown down or otherwise levelled. The vague outlines of the dunes altered from day to day. The hidden thing would be more securely forgotten with each new tide. He had the idea of burying immediately a shilling with which his left hand had been playing; a gift to the sea or land, whichever chose to claim it; a recognition of their long patience with men; a kind of sacrifice.

At that word all the thoughts began to leap and yell in his head, just behind his eyes. He sat stunned, unwillingly listening. At last, when they became too insistent, he laughed and spoke aloud, landwards.

'Old as all that, are you?'

He began to understand what they meant when they said that waiting was useless. The patience of one man could not match the huge patience of the land, though he gave his life to it. But this other idea was more tolerable. Old memories revived, fragments of books he had put aside since his schooldays. Rams and bulls and cocks were acceptable, he supposed, and there must be formulas, which he could not recall. A bull was beyond his means; besides, with so large a beast and a celebrant so inexperienced the ceremony might not proceed according to plan. He was unwilling to search with a knife the throat of one of those rams, who, with the flocks they governed, made the whole riches of the ungenerous marsh. A cock, however, was not out of the question. There was one in particular, a black creature which he had often seen parading in the early sun, gripping the earth with strong talons while he acknowledged the new day. Hilary looked carefully and long at the idea, and was not displeased by it. It possessed and soothed his mind so that he lay back full length with his hat pulled down at the back to meet his collar and protect his neck from the sand, in a kind of abandonment of the senses that had nothing to do with sleep. The sea birds soared over him, crying; he could just hear the wash of waves retreating. A calm sky was set with grey and yellow clouds shaped like fields, almost rectangular, with thin lines of blue that might have been water running between them. He regarded them curiously as they passed above him in unvarying formation, and thought of fields seen from a slowly moving train. But on the whole he was tired of this eternal masquerading. It was unsatisfying. Real things might be hateful or terrible, but they satisfied. They were bedrock, the final statement. He was tired of questions.

It was hardly four o'clock when he stood up, stretched, and decided to go back to the cottage, not so very far away across the zone of sand and shingle. Occupation awaited him there, something different. He felt no wish to use the skill of his hands in the accustomed way, for it meant thinking and that in turn meant the noise of thought too near his eyes. It would be good to smoke. He was surprised to find that he, who all his life had been unaware of the hours, should now be intolerant of the mere dead weight of time that hangs between decision and action, and he imagined that his life must until now have been running along the surface of things. He could recollect no previous emotion or desire which had been strong enough to make him impatient. He had loved women, but they had never kept him waiting. His was not the temperament that longs for happiness, grasps it, and longs again for some new satisfaction. Things came to him, and he possessed them, discovering in the moment of possession that they were the things he wanted. Until he had achieved he was indifferent.

The cottage, when he reached it, was empty. She had gone off on her bicycle to visit some neighbours a mile away along the road; not long ago, for the fire was piled with coal through which rose thick yellowish smoke. Her absence brought things nearer, halved the weight of time. He had made up his mind to wait till she was asleep; that would have meant midnight, or after. But his luck, that thing in him which could compel opportunity, was with him still. He began at once to make preparation.

First he looked for a knife, and found in the middle drawer of the dresser the very instrument, a black-handled thing with a pointed triangular blade that she used in the kitchen. It was not very sharp. While he hunted for the steel he remembered that it might be as well to secure the black cockerel at once. He could see it stalking in the yard, holding its head high, and looked about with a questing haughty stare. Going out, he cornered and caught it without difficulty, and came back to the kitchen carrying it tucked in his left arm with his hand round its throat. It struggled and fluttered noisily to the floor, where it strode to and fro, suspiciously turning its head to watch as he continued his vain hunt for the steel. He would not waste more time. He shut the window to keep the bird safe, and took his knife to the living room, to the smooth hearthstone, and crouched there, stroking the blade backwards and forwards across it with a twisting movement of his wrist. A sound came to his ears, the light deliberate steps of the cockerel; it had followed, and stood inquisitively surveying him. There must have been another sound besides, but he had begun again to scrape at the stone. When her voice sounded close behind him, he leapt up, sideways, holding the knife back as though to strike with it. She had said,

'What are you doing with my knife?'

As he turned and she could see his face she ceased to smile. She stood rigidly, looking at him with eyes wide open. He wondered at her expression and answered.

'It's for something I've got to do.'

She stared at him still, and he began to feel oddly helpless, as though her eyes were weaving strong ropes to hold him. He wanted to escape. He wanted just to walk past her in the most ordinary way, and could not. She did not speak. He implored her.

'Why don't you let me alone? It's getting late.'

She watched him steadily, as he stood awkwardly before her, his head hanging, looking up from under his lock of hair. His hand held the knife pressed backwards, so that he could feel the blade flat and hard along his forearm. Time was passing, the light was slipping away. He began to sweat and to whine, in an agony lest he might, after all, have to wait more endless hours.

'Let me go. There's only just time. They want me to do it. Honest. Truly. It's to please them. If I have to wait, something may have happened. It's behind my eyes, something. If I do this, they'll tell me. I only just want to know. I tell you it's getting late—'

The black cockerel, with a sudden gasp and rustling of feathers, scrambled to the windowsill and out into the darkening yard. The unexpected sound made her start, and for a second her eyes were not steady. Hilary saw his chance; in a desperate rage of fear, knowing that she would not let him go, he gathered all his strength into one blow and ran past her with his head down, blindly pushing her from him as she fell. He wrenched at the door, and when the latch did not yield immediately he beat with his hands against it, in a panic lest even now she should prevent him. It opened, and he stumbled through into the air; as it rushed cold into his lungs, he apprehended something. He looked enquiringly at the rounded horizon and laughed with understanding, shaking his head reproachfully at the immense waiting sky. Then he noticed the fields.

The fields had been colourless, and very smooth. Now, though no wind troubled them, they began to toss and sway in tiny patches which seemed always to move nearer, never to attain. These patches were continually being broken and reformed. They advanced angrily; beneath them were depths. The strange fields were cold. They hated to feel life moving above them; they hated the colour of warm things; they stirred passionately, the rebellious, lashing fields, against the men and cattle that walked on them in safety, the opaque green of grass, the square houses that should have been narrowed to a keel. They came piling and smashing forward in a fury, and the sky had curled itself down so that it lay flat, withdrawn as if to spring. Hilary Monk waited, seeing it happen from the tail of his eye. At last, when the furthest sky had darkened and contracted unbearably and the sound of the fields grew thunderous, he jerked the door open and went in.

She was lying on the floor with her head drawn down to her shoulder, sideways, as though she had tried by that natural pressure to hold together the edges of the wound. She did not move, and Hilary had no time for her. He groped in one corner for a canvas, found his brushes near, and the tubes of colour, and sat down to paint. The room was completely dark. He fumbled a good deal at first and had to find his way about the canvas by touching with his fingers, but evidently it had to be done soon before he could forget, and it was not the kind of picture that could very well be painted by daylight. He sat working at it all night, unaware of noises in the quiet house.

2 The Rite

Save for the sighing of the trees it was a silent little wood. No birds nested there; the thumping of the rabbits could not have made itself heard on the moss which was spread underfoot like a soft couch for lovers; no stream ran by it. It rose from the valley, a thin shaft of darker green against the slope of the grass, and spread out at last to compass the top of the round hill. The shape and secret look of it had not changed since Roman days. Thick undergrowth tangled the space between the trees, such as must have stifled all smaller growths, all flowers, with shadow; yet flowers grew there. They were curious flowers, spotted with purple and green, fleshy, and they seemed to creep upon the ground, giving forth a warm and sleepy smell. They were not like the honest flowers of the hedgerows that cling close to the earth or send a spire of blossom towering into the air. They grew low, obscenely shaped, and when they were plucked wilted at once and turned brown before they died; the villagers would never touch them, for they hated the wood and all the things that grew there. Parvus Holt, they called it, and there was a saying, black as Parvus at noonday. Certainly it was always very dark there, and not cool.

On this spring day, impregnated with the warmth of the later year, Len was drawn to it. She had gone out of the house in a sullen temper, leaving her work, angry at being obliged to choose and at having the choice forced upon her always by her mother's hints and insistent comparisons. Since her mother was so willing to have her gone, Let her see what it's like, Len thought, when I'm married and there's no one to help. So she walked out into the street as though she were going for water; but there was no bucket in her hand, and she went on past the pump, the shop, and along the road that skirted the hill on whose farther side Parvus Holt lay. There was no plan in her mind, but rather a blank fury which would permit no thought.

The morning was far advanced. Already it was almost twelve, and as she walked, hatless, the high sun struck down upon the crown of her head like a powerful hand. It forced itself upon her consciousness. Through her anger she became aware of it, unwillingly, but it suited her fierce mood and she walked defiantly on. The dust clouded about her feet as she trudged; the air was busy with insects; unheeding, a bee droned past her. She longed for a stick with which to cut down the drowsy nodding heads of the flowers by the way. Her hands grew red and heavy, swinging by her side, the road was pitiless, and she knew that it ran bare along the hill for nearly two miles more before it came to shelter; but she was obstinate. She thought, I don't care if I drop. Serve her right if they were to come out here and find me lying dead. She was not afraid of death, which had its picturesque aspects, but this penetrating awful discomfort was unbearable. For a while she soothed herself and employed her thoughts by imagining how she would look lying pale on the roadside, to be discovered by a horseman riding past. He would dismount, and kneel beside her. He would take her hand or lift her up with an arm about her shoulders, but she would be silent, with closed eyes, and he would know that she had died because nobody cared. Her eyes were blurred with the pathos of this scene before an unsuspected stone striking her toe revealed to her the world of facts again; and the facts were that she would not be pale but red if she died of the sun, that there were no horsemen now, and that her whole quarrel with life was being wanted too much.

The sun was malignant. It held her neck and shoulders in a strong grip, from which she could not escape though she writhed the muscles and put a hand to the back of her neck.

The dust, swirling higher as her feet moved more listlessly, had a sharp and acrid smell. She hated it, and trod heavily, as though by doing so she could prevent it from rising to vex her nostrils. The insects became more persistent, more infuriating. A cohort of flies wheeled and circled about her head, brushing her skin, settling upon her hair; and she was defenceless. Every moment her resentment changed its quality. It ceased to be dull and general, and became actively directed against the causes of her present discomfort, the sun, the dust, and the flies. She even thought longingly of the house she had left an hour ago, and the cool front room that faced away from the sun. She turned the corner of the hill, and lifted her eyes to find the dark trees of Parvus before her.

As a rule, Len, like the other villagers, feared Parvus, and would not set foot within its shadowed and dangerous borders; now it seemed to welcome and invite her. The motionless trees would make a constant shade where she might soon forget the white furnace of the road. She halted, wondering. Then the sun smote her on the cheek she had turned to it, and with a hand lifted against treacherous branches she broke through the hedge and into the mystery of the wood.

There was no path; but, looking about, she discovered a way between the trees where the growth was less dense, and followed it, stepping high over the bracken and the unnamed flowers; even in this relief of coolness she was afraid to tread those hateful things underfoot. She went forward and upward, seeking a clear space where she might lie and perhaps sleep; the trees closed in behind her, a silent regiment. She went forward still, putting aside the branches whose thorns held her, towards a point where it seemed that the trees grew more sparsely at the top of the hill. Her hands and forehead were sweating; the climb had been a steep one. She paused, and took the pins from her loosened hair, meaning to coil it afresh, but it clung about her hot hands and would not be settled comfortably. She let it lie upon her shoulders, the roots darkened with sweat, the ends gleaming gold even here where there was no sun, and breathing deeply went on. The trees began to shoulder each other less closely. The undergrowth, with its speckled, creeping flowers, ceased altogether, and she trod now upon moss in which her footsteps were lost, springy to the tread. Panting, she stopped at last, and with a quick animal movement lay down, her body supported by the forked roots of a tree, feet pressed against a rounded stone which stuck up out of the moss smooth and grey; on the side turned away from her were little marks and slashes as though it had once been carved to some semblance of life.

Now that the more immediate annoyance of heat had ceased, her mind returned again to its problem. She considered it without passion, lazily, as though it were a matter with which she need not concern herself; but for all that it was urgent enough. Her mother had said that very morning that Arthur would not wait forever; there were lots of girls after him, with his medals, and his farm, and both parents dead. If only her mother could have let her alone, she would have given him her answer long ago; but she did not care to seem as though she had no mind of her own. She knew it was a good thing for her, without all this telling. But there was Steve.

She wanted Steve badly; she admitted it. The very thought of him tempted her; he was strong and fair, the sort of man she liked, the sort of a man a girl would be proud of for a husband. He was only a labourer, and he lived with his mother in a dirty cottage by the river from which sometimes they were flooded out in winter. There was no furniture there like Arthur had in his house. There would be only an old iron bed with a thin lumpy mattress, and the old woman groaning and tossing in her sleep so that you could hear her in the next room. And she was pious, always God this and God that. Not like Steve. He was a real man, strong; he didn't go whining, pretending to be grateful and all the time afraid of hell. He wasn't afraid of anything or anybody. But Arthur had the money. There was the problem, nakedly set out. Arthur had the money, and Steve had something, not looks exactly, but something she wanted. Well, there it was. She couldn't have both.

Len's resentment began once more to gather. She was angry with a world where such alternatives must be faced. The thought of her mother's triumphant eyes if she took Arthur was odious to her; but the thought of the solid shining furniture going to another was odious too. She kicked the bedded stone, and shifted uneasily, rubbing her shoulders against the rough bark of the tree. The current of her thought changed as the movement recalled her surroundings. What would they all think, if they knew she had been alone in Parvus, walked right up into it? Why did they make such a song about Parvus? It felt all right, though the flowers were funny. People used to say they died as soon as they were picked. She wondered, idly at first, but later was stirred by curiosity to rise and go through the trees a little way to where a cluster of pale leaves grew, with greyish petals showing above them. They felt warm to her hands, like flesh, and the stems did not snap but yielded softly, in a sickening way. She gathered a handful, however, with some of the leaves, and going back to the tree by the stone lay down again with the flowers in her lap. They were not shaped much like flowers, she thought; more like animals; and there were ugly purple spots on the grey surface. She began to twist them together, the long soft stalks and the pale leaves, into a round shape like a crown; they hadn't begun to die yet. Perhaps it was all a lot of lies. The wood was all right. It hadn't done anything to her.

She thought again of Steve. But what was the use? He must get some other girl. If he worked all his life he could never be as rich as Arthur. Money was the only thing that mattered, in the long run. Other things, perhaps, for a time; but they didn't last. Youth went so soon. And soon, when a man had got what he wanted, he didn't care. Oh, God!

But what was the use of that? God was forever talking of houses, the beauty of his houses, his many mansions; God would be on Arthur's side. If there could be a god of gardens and woods it might be worthwhile to pray, here in this chapel of trees whose branches gathered to a vault above her, nobly ordered as though they sprang, not from the mutable flesh of growing things, but from the obedient stone. Such a god would listen and be kind.

She looked down at the circle of flowers, and it seemed in the green twilight that already the edges showed a brownish tinge; but they stood firmly, and the leaves had not yet begun to droop, those strange leaves that felt warm as her fingers closed upon them. The moss, too, was warm. In the dim loneliness of the wood she would have liked to feel that softness against her bare skin. She could lie there with her hair about her shoulders all the afternoon till the heat was gone, unseen, unknown; in this light her body would look green, like a dead thing. For an instant the thought startled her, but she stretched upwards with her hands into the shadowed air and felt life pulse in the fingers, and was reassured. It would take a lot to put out that life, running so strongly. But what was the use of it?

She knew how she wanted to give herself, but her heart rebelled at the thought of the one-sided bargain. It would be fine to flare up like a great flame; but in a while that would be done with, and he might change or be false, and the power, the great force of her body, be withered away. Youth gone. Love gone. So soon, and for so little.

The flowers were dying. They seemed to droop and fail like animals, and the petals were discoloured with a darkening stain that spread as she watched, like blood. With a sudden spurt of impulse, unaccountable, she threw them from her, and the crown fell upon the stone and hung there. She laughed aloud, defiantly. Let the Old Face have them, the ugly things; dead already.

The words beat their way into her mind. That was what she would be if she married Arthur, dead, and buried in a bed with a man beside her who didn't even know that she was not alive any more. She would go walking about, and talking; but something would be dead. It wasn't right. It was against something. Life ought to come first. But with Steve, would that be life, any more than the other? Ah yes, even there in that dirty house, in poverty, even though it didn't last, it would be life. There would be something to show for the years, not happiness, but a longing satisfied, a purpose fulfilled. Life ran deep, its meaning and end were dark as this wood—dark as Parvus at noon.

A sudden horror came upon her, a dreadful fear of the darkness that could so reveal hidden things. She scrambled to her feet and stood, holding her fear in check, madly seeking with her eyes the way she had come. She found a broken branch and another, and followed slowly down the almost invisible track of her own passage, slowly, her heart stilled with terror, not daring to run lest she should lose her reason and be caught for ever by the menacing trees, the vile flowers. Slowly, stepping high as though in some solitary measure, she made her way down the hill, and her staring, shifting eyes found at last the glow of warm light from the road.

Now it was almost evening, and the leaves began to waver in a faint breeze. They whispered, and once there was a sound almost of laughter. The crown of flowers that had fallen upon the stone hung there still, and sent out upon the air that warm and sleepy odour as of beasts lying close; but the flowers were not dead. They hung there, living; and they were still alive when a great wind came up from the south two days later and scattered them.

3 The Outcast

It was after seven when I came, tired, to Chantry St Owen, walking sharply through the closing October night. It was a small village, and the street lamps were infrequent, but the red blinds of a tap-room guided me, and I knocked at the door beside them. A woman opened it. I asked for a bed, and she stood aside to let me pass into the light before she answered. In those parts they were accustomed to see strangers with packs coming in for shelter at nightfall, and they can tell at a glance the mock tramp from the real. My hostess did her reckoning more quickly than most. She marshalled me into a room on the right of the door and stood over me while I shouldered off my pack. It was a forbidding room, a parlour. The vast table seemed hardly to allow space for the chairs to stand ranged about it in a hollow square; no breath of wind had ever tumbled the woollen balls that edged its cloth. There was an oval mirror framed in red plush and painted with water-lilies, and above the flimsy sideboard with its gothic niches occupied by china pigs and yellowing photographs, a picture hung, vaguely religious in significance. There was no fire. Through the open door, from the bar across the passage, I saw a warm light leaping and glowing on the walls, and turned towards it, but was quelled by the woman's eye. 'This is the parlour,' the eye seemed to say, 'and you, by your shoes and other signs, are accustomed to parlours. You will therefore stay here and give no further trouble. *Noblesse oblige.*'

So I sat meekly on one of the unyielding chairs, and was even grateful to it, for my feet had borne my weight for the last three hours and they now confessed to weariness. The hostess took up my pack and bore it away, probably to inspect its contents at her leisure. She said nothing about a fire. I was still warm, with the inner heat of my body coming tingling through to the skin, but from pure laziness I should have liked a fire, to stare at the tireless flames, the wild thing tamed to a hearth. Hunger, which fatigue had deadened, began to stir in me. I pictured to myself, and could almost savour, the meal which would appear in a few minutes' time. There would be a cottage loaf with the top torn off, and the crumb showing flaky and white; butter; cheese in a flowered dish with a wedge-shaped cover and gilded handle; best of all, there would be beer, ladylike in a jug. I waited, stretching out my legs, contemplating in a pleasant lassitude the new shoes which now were ripening to a brown and satisfying glow. So much for a week, and a week's weathers. I was too tired to summon memories or anticipation, and drowsed, staring down at my toes, feeling the blood course and throb in my body. The blessed weariness was on me that makes of sleep a pleasure more luxurious than the loves of a caliph. Silence impelled me. Slowly my head drooped forward.

Five minutes later I woke, cold. The inhospitable inn was silent, save for the creaking and whining of its sign, whereon, as I knew, a stately sheep was painted; in that country all inns bear the sign of the plough or the fleece. The parlour seemed no longer a refuge; it had grown larger and stuffier and less warm. It was absurd, I thought, watching the firelight dancing still upon the passage wall, that I should be compelled by the memory of that decorous eye to remain sitting here while a chill advanced perceptibly upon me. A gust swung the sign, protesting, and the shrill sound made my parlour more intolerable. I got up, stuffed my feet again into the shoes I had loosened, and advanced into the room across the passage.

It was cheerful, with red blinds, and a red flagged floor, and a fire. The landlord leant sideways on his bar, reading a closely folded sheet of newspaper. By the window sat an old man, nursing a pint pot, who stared at me as I entered, and suddenly drank from it with an air of having got the better of me, just as a dog will hurry over a bone he thinks is in danger. There was nobody else in the room.

The landlord turned when he heard me, and cut short my explanations with sufficient civility.

'The missus is gone to get a bit o' meat for supper. She'll be back in no time. Sit ye by the fire. This is the last of the weather, I'll lay.'

He came from his bar and indicated a chair, wooden but adequate to human curves, kicked the innocent fire, and returned to his paper after serving me with a half-pint. I sat, gladly thawing. The old man, after watching me for a time, abruptly finished his ale, and with a short sigh set down the pint pot, finally void of its treasure. He did not speak, nor did I. The landlord's paper was too compactly folded to sound as he turned it; no footsteps came down the passage. It was a comfortable silence, broken at last by the opening of the tap-room door; a tall man, his boots muddy, came clumping in. The landlord did not look at the intruder, but taking a small glass, went immediately to a pink china barrel labelled Rum; the man waited while the clear spirit trickled down. When the glass was full, he received it carefully, and holding it in both hands, addressed us in general terms.

'Comin' on for wet,' said he.

'Clear to Beacon, weather'll thicken,' said the old man, speaking for the first time, in a strong voice that creaked like the stanchion of the sign outside.

'You got her in just in time,' said the landlord, abandoning his paper and ringing the coin into the till.

'She'll do,' said the thin man, 'but where's the use? Come June it'll be to do again.'

'Not if it rains like it ought,' said the old man, 'That's what yews want. A dry summer'll kill any yew.'

'If it rains till Christmas this one won't take hold,' the thin man responded.

He put the glass to his mouth and seemed to throw the contents down his throat. I could not see that he swallowed.

'You got no right to say that,' said the landlord.

'I tell you, I know,' the other answered, rather angrily.

'Perhaps you do,' the landlord said slowly, with a significant nod at the old man, 'You never did like Jim Hewish.'

'Nor I did,' the thin man agreed, 'but I wouldn't go for to cheat a dead man. I planted his tree good and deep like I did the others. It's good soil, all of it; churchyard soil. A tree's nought to do but grow.'

'And you say it won't?' the landlord asked, sarcastically.

'I know it won't,' said the thin man more calmly, but with decision, 'they'll go on dying till Vicar's tired o' plantin'.'

'Is it a special tree?' I asked.

'It's what they put here for our memorial,' the landlord answered. 'There's always been a hundred yews in Chantry churchyard. So Vicar says, and I think myself it was a good idea, we'd plant seventeen more, one for each man that was killed, like they was lying in their own earth, same as if they'd died here. Godsell planted 'em. Now he's got this notion into 'is head that one of 'em won't never do well.'

'It'll die, I tell you,' said the thin man, 'wherever they sets it.'

'That's him,' said the old man, 'restless and wandering. That was Jim Hewish. He can't lie quiet.'

'What's that?' said the landlord scornfully.

'I don't say it, but maybe it's truth,' the thin man answered. 'He had Gippo blood, they do say. When we was in Palestine you could see it plain. He had the beaky nose and the high look same as those men you see on the hills above Jordan. He'd 'a took to their ways, too, but for discipline.'

'Army's no place for a man like that,' the landlord said, his underlip pushed out.

'Earth's no place for a man like that,' the thin man corrected him, 'not to stay in. But he was great on a march. He loved the road. Never seemed to feel his feet under him. But he'd go silent when the rest of us was singing.'

'That's gipsy blood,' said the old man, 'they'll go walking till they drop, so I've heard, same as he did.'

'Ah,' said the thin man, looking into the fire, and added, after a little silence, 'He'd 'a been alive now but for that.'

'Well,' the landlord broke in roughly, 'He's dead now, right enough.'

'Name on the monument, and all,' the old man confirmed him.

'I wouldn't be too sure,' said the thin man, 'yew won't grow for him.'

'He's dead all right,' the landlord repeated, 'you saw him yourself.'

'So I did,' said the thin man.

He went on, talking to me.

'We never buried him. Left him there where the road tops the hill when the column retreated. Two days after, when we'd got our water and come back, he was there and picked clean. I brought his cap-badge home for his missus. It was all the birds had left, about. That wasn't burying ground. Too hard even for picks. And t'would a' been sweat wasted for such as Jim.'

'You've sweated more for him since,' the landlord chuckled.

'I have that. When the first tree died, nobody thought anything of it. Plant another, they says, and it'll come right. I planted another. What happened? Dies. Vicar says to me, when he sees it turning brown, "Dig deeper, Godsell, or try another place. Maybe there's stones or roots down there to hinder it." So I dug another place for this one. You saw the pit.'

'I did,' said the landlord.

'Clean, sweet earth,' said the thin man, 'like he could never hold to. The others, they clung on as if the roots was hands. But Jim was always different.'

'I'm not defending Jim,' said the landlord, 'He was no good. I know that.'

'He was a stranger,' the old man murmured.

'When they said War was declared,' the landlord went on, leaning impressively above the bar, 'that very night Jim Hewish come in here. "Heard the news?" I ask him. "I have," he says, "and thank God for it. Now's a chance to get out of this bloody hole for good, and I don't care if I never come back." He'd had nothing to drink. It was just his way of talking. Used to remind me sometimes of Vicar when he was feeling strong about hell; that same desperate way of talking that don't mean much. Well, then, that very night after he went out of here, he walked into Borthwick to enlist, but the office was shut. They took him next day though, and glad to get him. Fusiliers, wasn't 'e, Godsell?'

'That was Jim all over,' said the thin man sourly, 'too high and mighty to go to the regiment where he belonged.'

'You was a Fusilier yourself,' the landlord reminded him.

'I was,' retorted the thin man. 'And why? Because some old madam of a colonel couldn't read.'

'Well, it's a good regiment, too,' said the landlord.

'I know that,' said the thin man, 'though the officers was half of 'em ladies' pets, and the men was half of 'em scum like Jim Hewish. The regiment was all right. I reckon there wasn't much fighting we wasn't in, some of us. It was as good as a medal, that grenade I sent her off his cap.'

'She's well rid of him,' the landlord said.

'And on with another, they say,' said the old man, brightening at the prospect of gossip. 'Inglesham's looking her way. Well, it's no surprise to me. She's a neat-looking woman, and Jim treated her wrong.'

'Well, it's a funny thing,' said the landlord, 'you and me don't get our names on a monument and trees planted, only the men that died. Seems a waste, when they can't see it.'

'Jim'll see it, I bet,' the thin man said, 'he was like a cat in the dark. Funny to think of them great birds getting at his eyes. It's the first thing they go for.'

He spoke slowly and thoughtfully, without apparent disgust. The old man rose, and carried his pint pot to the bar. The landlord took it with a non-committal expression, and cast it into some limbo of pots beneath the counter. The thin man stretched himself, and the flames threw a grotesque gigantic shadow of him towering up the wall and halfway across the ceiling. I heard movements, clinkings and rustlings, in the parlour, and I could not wait to hear the end of the discussion: indeed, I had the impression that it was already ended. Too hungry to remember dignity, I almost ran across to the forbidding parlour which now held promise of repletion. There was the meal as I had pictured it, save that the beer-jug was empty. The woman took it, and went across into the bar, where already the voices had ceased; perhaps they only talked for an audience. When she came back I said to her, 'They were talking about a man called Jim Hewish.'

But she was not to be drawn. She set down the jug, wiping it carefully first on her apron, and answered, 'Oh, indeed, m'm? Yes.'

She moved towards the door. With a final spirt of curiosity I insisted, 'And how his tree won't grow.'

She answered, indifferently, it seemed.

'The tree? Yes.'

I gave it up, and begun to help myself from the slices of meat set out on a plate with tomatoes. I no longer expected anything, or desired anything, other than what lay before me. But to my surprise, as I took the first mouthful she paused in the doorway, and said in a sombre, almost angry voice, 'Why do they go talking of him? He was a low sort of man.'

I said nothing, having found occupation. She added, as though to herself, 'An ugly sort of a man; more like a foreigner.'

She closed the door, and I heard her steps going across to the tap-room. The sign creaked and cried, like an animal in prison, and the same wind that swung it bent the stem of the tree that would die, that stood for his body, a little heap of bones on a bare hill; the vultures would have left it long ago. I thought that a tree would take root if they planted it there, in the close yellow earth where he lay, to which he belonged, the earth that was too hard even for picks. Then the wind, that had been no more than one sudden gust, dropped, and the sign was quiet. I went on eating.

4 As Much More Land

'It must be marvellous for you, having this,' said the young man, looking about him.

Certainly the room was delightful, long, and not too high, with shallow bow windows looking west; the walls were panelled, and painted an odd lush green, the colour of grass after a wet summer. Against the panels stood two or three bookcases filled with brown volumes. There was a mantelpiece with cherubs drawing some deity in a chariot, and the door had above it a broken pediment whose angles rose like horns. It was the kind of room the young man could appreciate, and since his hostess had not long been its owner she did not disparage it in the usual way, but answered, beaming, 'Marvellous!'

And stared as he had done, with almost equal rapture.

'He must have been a charming uncle,' the young man went on, 'and a person of discernment besides. Otherwise he would have left it to your cousin James just because he is a man; and James would have had quantities of children as soon as possible, who could be trusted to ruin every inch of the house. The uncle suspected this, and left it to you instead, because he knew you'd adore it, as of course you do.'

'Oh,' said the hostess happily, 'it's such fun to have somebody to gloat with. You do like things; not as much as I do—no, no, not as much really. I've had twenty-three years longer than you, all of them spent with other people's things, in other people's houses. Now I think I'm absolutely happy.'

'Poor Anne!'

'I did so want it. And now I've got it, I want it just as much as I did before I had it. That's funny, isn't it?'

'Not a bit. Come and show me the garden while we can see the colours.'

They went out, and there at once was the garden, not mellow yet, for the spring was late, but full of anticipation under a pale gold sun. Anne knew very little about gardens, and was content to listen while her guest lectured on borders, and condemned the star-and-crescent-shaped beds that defiled the southern end of the lawn. He approved the sun-dial, faintly engraved with the maker's name, a date two hundred years old, and a motto; *laedunt omnes, ultima necat.* It was depressing, he admitted, but not immediately so, for the hours kill slowly, and it was not undignified to be able to say at the end, I yielded only to Time.

She listened gravely, and thought that undergraduates nowadays were certainly more civilised. They read poetry in public places, and made themselves appear a little wilfully precious, but they could talk knowledgeably of flowers, and to an older person without condescension or boredom. They were not ashamed to be sensitive. Altogether, she thought, in spite of newspaper outbursts, they had improved a good deal. She wondered if the Universities were trying at last to help people to discover themselves, and their place in social relationships.

'Are you doing anything at Oxford, now?' she asked, and added, when he looked surprised, 'anything that interests you, I mean.'

He was off at once. There was a monthly starting next term to which he should contribute; it was to be called the *Patrician*, and its policy was to voice the reaction of intelligent persons against what he called the present-day tousling of a language that once was chaste. One might say anything one pleased, he explained, but it must be said in form; the phrases must be smooth, yet have a rake to them like the tilt of a three-cornered hat. He had an essay in the manner of Addison ready for the first number. It was concerned with

Extravagance, and proved that balance was the first essential of any work of art.

'Do you know why you like your house so much?'

'Yes. Because it's the first thing of my own I've ever had.'

'That's sentiment merely. You like it because it's in proportion. The rooms, the books, the whole decor; it's of its period, homogeneous. It's serene. It's right. Only the neatest and most orderly emotions have governed it. Gentlemen have taken wine together at your round table, after a chase; and gentlewomen, submissive to the will of God, have yearly been confined in your bed with the green curtains.'

He paused, and she thought that he was memorising this as being something rather good, but quite suddenly he began to laugh.

'How absurd, when I've only seen two rooms. But it's like that, isn't it?'

'Most of it.'

'Do you mean to say you're not entirely at peace here?'

'I am, yes; personally. But it seems there's somebody who isn't.'

'Not a ghost?'

'Not quite a ghost.'

They moved towards the house as they talked, and its red brick seemed, in the failing sun, to take on a purple bloom like that of a grape. It looked spacious and friendly, not sinister at all, or ghostly, or anything but the sort of house most people would like to live in; although the rounded windows had caught the last light, which set them flaming, pane by pane.

'Tell me about it,' said the young man.

She told him what she knew. It seemed to be the usual thing, a room with an unaccountable feeling, servants frightened, and frightening others.

'But how did it start? What's the story?'

'It started in the fifties of last century. There was a wild young man, my uncle's cousin, who used the room a good deal. He used to shut himself up there and nobody knew what he did. Then he went away to London, and the room was disused for a time. One night the keeper was passing outside and saw a candle burning. He went round to the kitchen—it was about half-past nine—and told the maids. One of them had been in there with a candle some three hours before, but she remembered, she thought, bringing the candle away. She went up with another girl to look, and came down in a fright to say that nothing was there; no light, and no candlestick on the table. They didn't believe her, but others went, and could find nothing. Next day came the news that the wild young man had died in London.'

'Naturally? Not murdered?'

'No, he just died of pneumonia; congestion of the lungs, they called it then. But he left something very restless in his room.'

'What form does it take?'

'No form, that's the worst of it. It just makes people dreadfully afraid. So they say; I haven't felt anything, and I don't think I believe in it. But it seems to be a cherished tradition of the house.'

'I see. Queer,' said the young man, quite seriously.

'Don't people laugh at such stories nowadays?' she asked, astonished.

'They're not such fools,' he replied, in the voice of one who had forgotten for the moment to react as a patrician.

At dinner that night he talked of it again when the service was finished and they were left alone. Anne laughed, and offered to tell him twenty stories more authentic and alarming; his interest persisted.

'I won't have you spoiling my house for me. It's a friendly house. I don't want this idea encouraged. It's too ridiculous.'

'But you don't put people in the room.'

'How do you know?'

'I asked. And I asked which one it was. The maid said it was always kept locked.'

'I don't want to lose my servants.'

'What a liar you are.'

'Hugh!'

'A prodigious, adorable liar. You're proud of that room, and frightened to your marrow. Only with your Victorian upbringing you think it's enlightened and creditable of you to pretend about it. You're only being sceptical and haughty because that was the pose twenty years ago. You're not being real at all.'

Anne sat meekly, looking down at her table in which the candles shone.

'You won't confess to being a coward. I do, quite frankly. Things I can't explain terrify me, and I can't put them out of my mind. I hover about them. It's too incredibly silly.'

'Perhaps you're not really afraid. People will say anything nowadays to be different.'

'Oh no, I'm really a coward. I should have had an appalling time at the war, if I'd been old enough. Afraid of being hurt, and yet not wanting to miss it. I should have lost my balance, as the others did, and pretended that I didn't mind it, and was brave and hearty. Curious, that. As soon as poise is lost, a pose of some kind seems inevitable.'

Again that fixed expression, as of memory at work. Anne got up, and said rather maliciously, 'So you've discovered that.'

'Long ago,' he assured her. Then, his voice dropping to the cadence of an epigram, he added, 'One should distinguish between the discovery of a principle and its application.'

And she saw him grin. Really, she thought, they are very disconcerting. In the old days they were pompous, and could be laughed at without their knowledge. Now, though they were pompous still, they stood outside themselves, and perceived their own absurdities sooner than their elders could. It was unnatural, Anne felt, to find them being amused at their own antics. Of what use were twenty additional years if youth could share the Olympian perspective and see itself as the older generation saw it? But later in the evening when she watched him disgustedly reading Elizabethan dramatists, and heard him complain of their extravagant verse and lunatic plots, she felt that there still were joints in the shining armour of youth.

He read and made notes till half-past ten, while she sat, not occupied, but comfortably aware of companionship. When a tray with drinks and candles appeared, he looked up with relief, and made as though to throw down the text-book; but a speech caught his eye, and he declaimed:

> Think'st thou that Faustus is so fond, to imagine
> That after this life there is any paine?
> Tush, these are trifles and mere old wives tales—

'That's your opinion, isn't it? But he went to hell in spite of it. When are you going to show me that room?'

'I'm not going to show it to you.'

'Why not, if there's nothing? You're inconsistent.'

'Why do you want to see it?'

'I explained that at dinner; because I rather like being frightened.'

'Nonsense.'

'My dear Anne, you don't know anything about it. Fear is an experience like any other experience; up to a point it may be enjoyable. But you have to learn how far you can go; when you know that, it becomes amusing.'

'That sounds very decadent.'

'Better than taking the immensities seriously. There's some fun in playing catch-you-last with death and hell. That's what your Elizabethan did.'

'Not in this self-conscious way.'

'You're a barbarian. Of what else may we be conscious, if not of ourselves? We can know ourselves, and only ourselves? The rest is guesswork. You, for example; there is a certain amount of circumstantial evidence to show that you exist, but such evidence is notoriously unreliable. I can't be completely aware of you, as I am of myself; I haven't the data. You may be a delusion for all I know, the merest projection of somebody else's thought; and you have the impertinence to deny me an experience which will extend my consciousness.'

'Doesn't that almost seem equal to proof that I do exist?'

'Perhaps; curse you.'

The candlesticks were unusual, made of wood, and shaped like shallow bowls with iron sockets for the candles. They were old and smooth and dark. Anne said, as she held one out to him, 'It was a candlestick like this that was seen in your famous room, with a living candle in it.'

'Yes. Interesting,' he answered abstractedly, taking it; then looked at her. 'Seriously, Anne.'

But she shook her head.

'Your mother said that you were to be looked after and fed and kept quiet, because you had some kind of examination quite soon. Be good, please.'

He seemed to give in.

'Oh, well,' he said, and went up the stairs obediently enough.

But in his room he knew that he was excited, and not likely to sleep. Leaning against the sill of the window with arms stretched wide and hands pressed flat against the folded shutters, he began deliberately to consider the geography of the house. His room was at the end of a wing with windows to the east and south, Anne's at the other end of the main building. Servants, he supposed, were above. It would be easy enough if he waited an hour or two; there was no hurry.

He pulled a chair towards the window and settled down to wait. Pity I've let myself in for this, he thought. Anne obviously doesn't want me to interfere; but it would be too absurd to have her going about like Bluebeard with the one key that's not to be used jingling under my nose all day. I don't want to see the room; but for that passage of arms at dinner I shouldn't have insisted. Anne ought to have known better than to talk like that, as if I were two. If she hadn't been so tactless it would be all right. And I'm not sure that I'm capable of deriving any pleasurable emotion from fear. In fact, the whole theory was rather impromptu; but I shall go through with it. The penalty of not being real at the time is that one has to be so heavily real afterwards.

I wonder about the room; whether the story as it stands is true. If it is, there's nothing so very alarming. A careless maid leaves a candle alight in a room which has been used by one particular person. By a coincidence the candle goes out and the person dies at the same hour. Nothing much in that. The candlestick and candle cannot be found five minutes later. Then they must have been moved. By whom? A dozen people, possibly. Another maid coming in who had not cared to make her presence known; stealing, perhaps. All very reasonable. But the fear? It may not exist; Anne hasn't felt it. At least, so she says, but with these courageous eighteen-ninety liars one can never tell. The whole thing seems to rest on the evidence and persistent cowardice of servants. And yet it doesn't sound like a servant's invention; not definite enough, no tall white figure, no unaccountable noises, just a fear. Why should any person go out of his or her way to set up and support so uncomfortable a legend?

But the whole thing is so slight. So irrational. So capable of being explained. Then why is there no explanation? Why does a normal middle-aged woman like Anne—rather a dear,

Anne—keep the door constantly locked? Lest her servants should become frightened? But she's not the woman to encourage that. It would be more like her to go and sleep in there deliberately, to shame them out of being cowards. So there must be something. It's possible that I don't know the whole story; she may have left out some detail, kept something back. That's it, I should think; because as it stands it's rather silly. Well, if there is something I'll soon know. Why go into the thing at all? Why not let it alone? I couldn't now. 'Your mother said you were to be kept quiet.' Really! Besides, I want to find out. Besides, what fun to come down in the morning and tell Anne.

'Do you know, I think your ghost has been rather over-rated. I think it must be a secondhand one that you got cheap. I took a lot of wear out of him last night.'

'Hugh! You didn't get in—but it's impossible.'

'My dear, on the contrary it's ludicrously simple, with that little row of bricks projecting all the way along. You'd better latch the window in future. Burglars mightn't know the story.'

By the way, how if the window should be latched? Oh, well, in that case obviously nothing can be done. One can't break glass to prove a theory, unless it's more vital than this one. And the servants might hear. How important servants are! One comes up against them at every turn.

Another cigarette; when that's done it will be almost time; or I'll give them another half-hour, and then slip out. That delicious brickwork is about three feet below my window, on the south wall; the room I want is four windows away, to the right of the front door. The spaces between the windows are equal, I should think, about five foot six, which I can easily span. I must take a light of some kind, so that I can see the place when I get there. Matches, and a candle. Why not the candlestick too? It's flat, it would go in my pocket. 'In my school days when I had lost a shaft, I shot another in the self-same place,' or something like it; that cad Bassanio. But there may be something in it; this candlestick may find the ghostly one. Well, if it does, it will be an experience, a discovery. That's always worthwhile, if one can make it for oneself.

> And from th' Antartique Pole, Eastward behold
> As much more land, which never was described,
> Wherein are rockes of Pearle—

If only all this will stay in my head till schools are over! Hysterical stuff, enough to poison one's style for ever. Similes as barbarous as arrows; disproportion, horseplay, flaring inconsistencies! And Racine was giving out that exquisite verse sixty years later! Hardly credible, that such a gap should so soon be bridged. Half-past twelve; no sound. Time!

He took off his shoes and got up; lit the candles on his dressing table, extinguished the other between his finger and thumb, and put it, stick, matches and all, into the pocket of his dinner jacket; straddled the sill, found the brickwork with his feet, and leaned sideways till he felt the stone sill of the next window under his fingers. He stood for a moment stretched like a man that is to be flogged, and moved again, silently, along the face of the wall. The fourth window gave him pause, for the top of the sash was just out of his reach, and he could get no leverage with his hand spread on the glass. Then he remembered the gold knife that lived uselessly on a ring with his keys, opened it with one hand and his teeth, and slipped the blade under the frame of the window, pressing gently lest it should break. The window yielded an inch, so that he could thrust his fingers into the opening. It went up. He crawled into the room, lit a match, and surveyed it.

It was disappointing, rather; a square white room like a bandbox, with a plain marble fireplace, the top slab supported by scrolls, and an egg-and-spoon decoration bordering the ceiling. A dark solid cupboard stood in one corner, and against the wall were two chairs. There was no smell of any kind. It was quite clean, quite ordinary. He surveyed it without enthusiasm, and allowed his thoughts free rein.

Well, now what's to be done? I suppose one has to give it time; one sits down and takes no notice and things happen. I'll give it an hour; that's about all that's left of the candle. This chair isn't bad, and I can put my feet on the other. The candlestick goes on the floor. Now:

> Let no deluding dreames, nor dreadfull sights,
> Nor sudden sad affrights—
> Ne let hob-goblins, names whose sense we see not
> Fray us with things that be not.
> Let none of these theyr drery accents sing—

I forget the rest, and I don't believe that's right. Rather a good exorcism, all the same. Apt. Neat. But this room is the wrong period.

White; curious how we make continual use of it. It isn't a good background. It doesn't suit people who wear it; makes brides look coffee-coloured as a rule. If snow be white, why then her breasts are dun. Quite so. I don't know the Sonnets so well as I ought. Not that it matters. Nobody seems to know what he was driving at, or they think they know, and shy away from it. Pity one should always think so colloquially. White. It's distressing to consider how we are obsessed by it, and how it persists in decoration. Because really it is a negation, a denial. This room, for instance, is a creed turned upside-down. I disbelieve in the almighty sun, the quickener, by whom all colour was created; in fire, in blood, in trees, in deep water; in all things living and changing, I disbelieve. Nonsense, of course, but not badly put. Odd that so many of us go through life and never realise the sinister significance of our bathrooms.

Nothing, as yet. I shall tease Anne beautifully in the morning.

An uninteresting fireplace, compared with those downstairs. If one thinks about it, fireplaces of this type are absurd. Two upright slabs with a third slab laid on top; like Stonehenge, only white. All the better; the blood would show. Is that the meaning of white? But it's no use as a background. Think how ineffective it always is on the stage. In life, though? Green clefts in snow; leprosy; a shark's belly slowly turning to the surface.

He shifted in his chair, and sent orders to his mind, which had set off, galloping, into some cloudy distance, to return to duty.

Think of something else; not the Elizabethans, they're full of horrors. 'My soul, like to a ship in a black storm is driven, I know not whither—' 'Hell is murky, light thickens.' My God, the candle's going!

The flame dwindled, seemed almost to die. Then it spat, and flared, and steadied itself in the form of a long triangle as before. He was angry to discover in himself such appalling readiness, such power to fear, and his exhortation did not lack vigour.

You bloody fool, it's all right; something wrong with the wick. It's always happening with candles. Think of something, can't you? (Pity I didn't bring a book.) There's a noise. Yes, rats. It must be rats, the scurry, and the soft thud like a dead hand dropping. (Oh, shut up.) There goes one of them. I won't look at him; animals hate it.

This ceiling is quite badly cracked. The long one in the corner that twists back on itself is rather like a noose. A vile death, to be hanged. They say it's painless and instantaneous and all that; I wonder how they imagine they know. I don't suppose anybody has ever given the hangman a testimonial. One would stand there on the drop, bound and blinded, and thinking, 'This is my last conscious moment; no, this; no, this.' What a waste of time! And then it really would be the last. I wonder if they think as they fall, and waste more time wondering how far they are from the end of the rope. Then the jerk. What sort of pain would it be? Nothing tremendous; just a thin pain like a long needle running from the snapped spine into the back of the head. Arms and legs flung about, jerking upwards; no, not the arms, they'd be tied. It must be very nearly funny to watch; dreadfully funny, like the faces people make when they're in agony. What a filthy thing to think!

He came back to normal a little unwillingly, for there were a dozen fascinating guesses still to be made, and looked at his watch.

Half an hour gone, anyhow. I haven't been frightened yet. Not properly. I've been making my own terrors. If only this room were not so bare; there's no starting point for thought. One ought not, of course, to need anything of the kind. It's this habit they have at Universities of not being able to start thinking unless someone comes and gives them a push from behind.

This floor slopes a little. The candlestick isn't set absolutely straight, the flame rises from the wax at a very slight angle, like a spear point that has been bent. And yet the house is not very old, not old enough to have the floor warped like that, and the atmosphere. Warped. Twisted altogether away from the normal by something. I can't think of anything that doesn't lead to some beastliness. But why? Suggestion, probably. If Anne hadn't told me, I should have felt nothing; and that's so absurd, because there is nothing. Nothing at all.

This room is quite square; a cube. The length and breadth

and height are the same. Odd to think of us all calmly living in cubes, in a set of cubes arranged in rows, one on top of the other. It would be frightful if a room were suddenly to come alive. (Let those ideas alone, can't you?) Well, of course it can't, so it doesn't matter thinking about it. It's neutral, or whatever the word is. It has never lived, it's only a shell. But if it were to come alive, and be somehow malignant, hating me. Walls of white membrane, stretched tightly. And they would begin to pulse, moving in and out ever so slightly, like a creature breathing. (The candle makes it look like that. Why can't it keep its flame still? There's no draught.) The walls would begin to contract very gradually. One would watch them and think at first that it was only the shifting light. One would think so until one couldn't fool oneself any longer, and that would be fear. Because there would be no escape, no doors in that sort of substance. You might run at the soft walls, and they would give a little, but you could never tear the stuff apart. It would feel clammy and sweatily warm, like living guts, so that you would rather go through hell than touch it again. You would wait in the very centre of the room, and watch it closing in. But perhaps you would die before it could come utterly round you.

A room lighted from the floor looks different and rather horrible. My chair and I cover nearly the whole of one wall with our shadow. If I spread my hand above the flame I can obscure the ceiling, except for the little fiords of light that run between the fingers. If I lift it the shadow grows smaller, but still it is menacing; the shape—'a thing armed with a rake that seems to strike at me.' Close up the fingers quickly.

It's moving. Not possible; steady, steady. I tell you it's moving, the shadow. I'm looking quite steadily at the ceiling. I'm holding my hand quite steady, and yet the shadow is slewing round so that it shows in the corner and on the edge of the wall. Further. Don't look down. Is this fear?

Imagination, all movement seemed to cease. In his mind a stillness remained which had all the agonised quality of flight. He wanted and dreaded to know. Curiosity overcame fear; he looked down. A rat was dragging the candlestick along the floor towards the dark cupboard.

He drew in a long breath and his foot moved involuntarily as though to kick. The rat at the same instant let the candlestick go and ran noisily out of sight behind the cupboard. He lifted his hand to his face, and the light traced twenty little rivers on the palm. His thoughts, after the momentary stoppage, hurried on.

So that's it! This is what happened to the first candle. Evidently. Good old Bassanio! End of the soul-stirring drama entitled 'The Bloodstains on the Wall, or A Dead Man's Hand.'

He hung across the sill, found the brickwork with his toes, drew down the window without noise and climbed back to his room. He had earned another cigarette, he considered, and he kept it in his mouth while he took off his waistcoat and tie. Standing in front of the mirror he surveyed his face, with the smoke curling up one side of it and the eyes, in which the candle flames were reflected, looking romantically intense. He spoke silently to that careless insolent face in the glass, the face of a person incapable and disdainful of fear.

I wonder if I'll tell Anne. It's her tradition, after all. The mysterious room. There's a curious story about one of the rooms here. If I tell her, she may begin to use the place again, and that wouldn't do yet. There's something there; nothing definite; just fear.

But why? Why fear where there's no cause for it? God knows; people are like that. They don't think. They just let themselves be afraid, and that's fatal. It leaves something. Fear is so strong. It must be, to have preserved the race. Say what you like about courage, but a brave race dies out sooner than a cowardly one. With honour, no doubt, but what's that? Who hath it? He that died o' Wednesday. Look at the Jews.

Yes, that's all right, but what about this feeling? The story may be a lie, but the feeling's authentic. I was most dreadfully afraid. Something was there, twisting my whole mind out of shape. But what? All those other people, perhaps; all the fools that have let themselves be afraid in that room; piling up a kind of dreadful treasure for the next comer. Fear is so strong. I can feel the tension still, even now that I know the whole thing. Seventy years. People, one by one, invoking fear until it came. Lord, what fools—!

He heard a clock strike two somewhere in the house, but it was difficult for him to quit the seductive face looking out from the mirror with the eyes of some very interesting person, a cavalier, or one of those gentle Elizabethan poets whose verses were scanned to the clink of swords. He lingered, reflecting.

Resume and conclusion. Fear, up to a point, as I told Anne at dinner, and as I have just proved rather convincingly, may be considered an admirable thing. (Bravo, our old friend poise—or pose? Return of the prodigal.) Tradition too is admirable. Combined—how doubly excellent! They create atmosphere and promote talk, two essentials of civilization; therefore I shall not tell Anne. On the other hand, it would be amusing to tell her; not quite all, but enough to make a good story. (Only one good story, as against the many that will grow if the tradition remains undisturbed. I hope I'm artist enough not to hesitate.)

The candles are nearly down. I hope no one noticed that light. I ought to sleep after this.

Darkness hid the face in the glass as he blew out the candles; his last vision of it was with lips pursed and cheeks flattened, blowing like one of the four winds, with an eye slanting to watch him. He left it, and climbed into bed.

Breakfast was at nine. He was punctual and hungry, so he told Anne, who sat reading her letters, a big silver tray with coffee in front of her.

'I'm glad,' she said, 'there's food on the side table. Take plenty, and give me an egg. Did you have a good night?'

'Marvellous. I think your ghost is rather over-rated.'

'You didn't see it too?' she said quickly.

'See what?'

'A light. But of course you didn't. Servants are a strange race, aren't they?'

'The room again?'

'Nonsense again.'

She added, unwillingly, in response to his look, 'The traditional candle, but rather later than usual.'

'Oh? What time?'

'About half past two.'

'Half past which?'

'Two. What's the matter?'

'Nothing. I was wondering how your visionaries fixed the hour.'

'Alice had been sitting up with the gardener's wife to let the husband get some sleep. He walked back with her just at the half hour and they both saw it. Now I suppose everyone will leave.'

He gave her the egg and went back to the side table for a spoon.

'Why did you say that about the ghost?' she asked.

'I was being funny,' he answered, laying the spoon neatly by her right hand. She looked at him, but the curious expression was gone whose twist she had seemed to catch as he turned. His eyes were wide and innocently young.

'Ha, ha,' she said, obligingly.

And they both laughed.

5 Young Magic

When Viola was very little she used to play by herself exactly as a cat does. She would fix her eyes upon an invisible adversary, stalk him, and fly from him when her manoeuvres could not take him unawares. It was a very good game to play in a garden, especially in autumn when the taller flowers came out, delphiniums, and a strong kind of white daisy; but curiously enough in the garden it was never a success. Viola used always to hope that one day it would be. She used to run out of the house pretending not to care, not looking behind, and would hide, allowing some part of her dress to show in a most alluring way. It was no use, though sometimes she caught a grown-up, with whom it was no fun to play, for such persons showed a long way off, and trod heavily, and were awkward at dodging. The grown-ups considered her a good child, always amusing herself and not noisy. They thought it was perhaps a little odd, the way in which she talked and nodded to flowers or patches of shadow, and they used to question her.

'Is that a fairy you're playing with? Oh, how nice! What is her name?'

Viola would stare at them, realising that some answer was required if she were not to be rebuked for sulkiness; and when the enquirer asked again, wheedling, for the fairy's name she would contemptuously answer, 'Binns,' and go on with whatever she was doing. This always caused laughter, and as a rule put the grown-ups to silence. Persistent ones, however, would keep at it.

'And what is Binns like?'

'Thin.'

'Oh! And what does she do?'

At first Viola used to ignore this question, but when she found that it meant being told not to be silly she invented an occupation for Binns. She hated more completely than anything in her experience to be told she was silly. So she would answer, 'Washing.'

And sometimes when people were looking she would pretend to be washing, so that they would believe her when the inevitable question and answer came along. But it was all the purest invention. She did not like the way other people came trampling into her mind, just as they often walked unheeding and made dull marks on a nice-shaped patch of dewy grass she had been treasuring since morning. And they would have said she was silly if she told them truthfully that there was no Binns, only a feeling, and this feeling was not a she, and that he did no washing and was not thin; he was rather soft and big. She did not know what he looked like. He played with her only in the house. Perhaps for that reason Viola lost touch with him in summer. She liked to be a prince in summer, and her throne was a tree that had split in two low down, and was easily to be climbed. In the rounded fork she would sit with a sword tucked into her leather belt, and sometimes other trappings, a piece of gold braid round her head or a few bits of ribbon pinned on for medals. She was not often a prince in the house, and never wore decorations there, because if she did somebody was sure to comment. She was sure to be asked where she had got the braid from, and if she were playing soldiers. She knew when they asked in that voice and smiled in that way that they thought she was being silly, even when they said quite kindly, 'Having a lovely game, darling? Don't get in Annie's way, dear.'

So she was only royal in the garden; in that special part of the garden where nobody ever bothered to come, and where she was not watched. She would make tremendous speeches there, standing up in the fork with her left hand on the cross hilt of the sword to make it stick out; her subjects all adored her, because she was so very noble. Once or twice she allowed herself to die in battle, and lay with her arms stretched out on the daisies, that felt damp but were only cool, listening to the sad things her people said as they passed. They all thought that there could never have been a prince so brave or so good. They said, 'What we'll do now I don't know, I'm sure.'

And Viola listened, every moment inventing new and more splendid things for them to say about her. When she had to go in to her dinner—and she knew, when the shadow of the big branch got as far as the fence, that it was about time to go in—the contrast was too great. It was too big a distance to be bridged in a moment. There had to be a period of readjustment, of coming back, and during this period she was silent and aloof, paying no attention to the small talk of the table; this habit, when she neglected to answer questions immediately addressed to her, sometimes led to trouble, accusations of sulkiness; or nurse would say, from sheer caprice, when she had finished and wanted to go out again, 'Now you don't want to go off by yourself in the garden. Stay about here where I can see you. Don't go running off.'

It made Viola angry to be told she didn't want to go off by herself when she did. Often she wondered if it would count as a lie against nurse when she died, for it was as untrue as possible on the face of it. In her more savage moods she hoped that it would count, and that Jesus would say to nurse when she wanted to get into Heaven, 'What about all those lies you told Viola?' For it was one of nurse's favourite expressions. It cropped up in relation to almost every impulse of Viola's life.

'You don't want to look like those little dirty children. You don't want to be always running wild in the garden. You don't want that old tin soldier in bed with you.'

If nurse had had her way, or what she liked to pretend was her way, Viola would have been very nearly always in the house; but in fact nurse, though she scolded and bullied a little for form's sake, was glad enough not to have Viola underfoot and always permitted the garden in the end, so that during the long days, of which only the sunny hours remained afterwards in her memory, Viola was happy by herself.

But towards the end of October things would begin to happen which she could recognise, and which meant that there was to be no more summer. One day as she sat in her throne a yellow leaf would fall on to her knee, half-a-dozen others following; she would look round her and see that all the trees were losing their green. Then the branches would begin to lash about and sweep the air, making a wind that sent the poor leaves running on the grass, lost and homeless. When they were quiet again the thick shade that had lain like an island under her tree would be pierced with holes when there was sun to show them; looking up, the sky showed clearly in a hundred places. At last no leaves would be left at all, but only the branches, ugly against the sky, like lace without any proper pattern, or cat's-cradle when it came very tight and muddled towards the end. The prince game ended with the green year, and the warm free days gave place to an infinite time without colours, or any outdoor play except the official walk before tea. The house was big, but there was nothing much to do in it except watch cook now and then. Viola could not read, for her mother always thought it so unwise to force children. In the winter which held her ninth birthday she began seriously to play with Binns.

These games were something quite different; not in themselves, for there were still fairy tales to be acted in which she was the prince; but this indoors winter prince was a more romantic figure, dressed like one of the photographs in the drawing-room, with a shining breastplate and a long-tailed helmet. People did not weep over him; he had no people, and no need of them with all his magic things, the table that was covered with food each time he rapped on it, and the sword that could kill twenty enemies at a blow. He was less real than the other prince, but he went better with an audience she could not see or touch, and which did not interfere. She knew Binns was there by the sounds he made, and by the feeling he brought with him, which nurse always said was a draught. At first he could only make very little noises, like the cracks that furniture makes in the night. Viola knew that it was not the furniture because the sounds came from the air, quite near her; as they increased in strength she began to understand what he said; and at the end of a month of rain, when she had had to stay in the house nearly all the time, she knew all his meanings. His noises did not make sense if you thought of them as words; he could not give a plain answer to a question, yes or no, so many cracks for each. One sort of crack meant that he was pleased, another sort meant that he wanted her to go on playing, and after a time he learnt to make four or five cracks close together, like a laugh.

The first time he did this she was frightened. Nurse was quite near, just at the door, and the cracks were so deliberate, not like anything that furniture could do. Nurse heard, for she turned her head suddenly, and said that it was time they had somebody to see to those loose boards. Then she went out, and Viola told Binns not to do it again, but he was proud of his achievement and would not keep quiet. Fortunately nurse had gone. Viola tried all sorts of ways of making that sound, so that she could pretend, if anyone else heard, that it was her own. She tried bending a nice round stick that she had found and peeled, but it had gone dry and soon it broke. She tried with a cotton-reel against the leg of a chair, but that made a dull, woolly sound. The problem was not solved until the afternoon of her birthday party, when she found in a cracker a black piece of tin shaped like a beetle, which, if its wings were pressed down towards its stomach, gave out a sound exactly like Binns' laugh. The grown-up who had pulled the cracker with her said, 'Oh! It's only a nasty old locust. Never mind, I'll find you one with something pretty in it.'

While she was away Viola dropped the locust right inside her clothes, where it felt cold for a moment before her skin warmed it. She was afraid that Binns might come to the party and crack at the grown-ups. However, he stayed away, and she went to sleep with it under her pillow, relieved from the fear that they might be discovered and somehow not allowed to play anymore.

The locust answered its purpose well for a day or two, until the morning when nurse kept her in the sewing-room trying on dresses and underclothes. There was no need for her to stay. Most of the time nurse was occupied with the sewing-machine, a reluctant thing that always clucked angrily before it began to make its regular thudding buzz. Viola was interested in the almost human unwillingness of the machine; it had one or two tricks, such as refusing to swallow the stuff, and holding it fast in one place while it stabbed the needle down a dozen times, savagely, that pleased her for a few repetitions. But soon nurse got what she called the knack and the machine obeyed her, and roamed over Viola's clothes-to-be just as nurse wanted it to go. Still Viola was not allowed to put on her dress and go away. She stood by the fire, trying to see how the flames grew, hoping that soon they would turn the coal into bright pinky hills; but the fire was new, the lumps of coal were hardly red even underneath, the thin yellow flames did not look as if they would burn if she were to put her finger into them. She thought that it would be fun if flames could be picked like flowers. They would be alive, snaky, all twisting about in the hand that held them; much nicer than flowers, that stayed still, and never cared for being in a house, but died soon. Fire didn't mind houses, it was used to them; it wouldn't need water in its vases; it would always be twisting and straining and doubling back; nice bunches of flames; and her mother would say, as she often did about flowers, 'Wonderful how a vase or two will brighten a room.'

Viola watched the hot flame-flowers growing, and would have liked to put her hand into their funny black garden, but nurse saw and said, 'Come away from that fire at once. You'll be getting chilblains.'

Viola would have liked to say that nurse was wrong, and that only servants got chilblains; but she knew that such answers annoyed nurse, who called them arguing. 'Don't you argue with me,' was one of nurse's speeches that Viola feared. There was temper behind it. So she moved away from the fire and went slowly over to the window, to breathe on it, and make patterns in the breath that got caught on the panes. Nurse said at once that she was in the light and told her to move out of it. She obeyed, feeling sulky and impotent, and wishing with all her strength that something would happen to nurse, that she would get very ill, or go away to some other child as she had often threatened to do. She wished the scissors would stand up on their round ends where the holes were for fingers, and snap at nurse's hands as they flattened the stuff under the quick needle. Viola looked very hard at the scissors, wanting them to get up and walk on those round feet towards nurse's hands. She put herself on her honour not to blink, which would break the strength of the wish, and she stared at the scissors, lying with their blades a little open on a pile of stuff. She stared so long that her eyes began to draw towards each other and to feel watery; to drive away the feeling she moved them up and down, following the white line that shone on one of the blades; the other was dull, shadowed by the stuff on which it lay. She thought that she would make her eyes like magnets; she could almost think that they were becoming that shape, like a thin round horseshoe. She had to keep herself from winking by bits at a time. 'Not until I've counted twenty very slowly; another twenty; ten.' Just as she finished the last second of the ten she forgot why she was counting. She could see the scissors beginning to move, twitching themselves up in little jerks, and she thought with triumph, 'I can do magic.' She could see the dent the weight of them was making in the stuff, the little movements in the stuff as they twitched themselves upright on it. Nurse did not see, busily making the machine slave for her, but she was warned of something by the child's silence. She stopped the wheel with her right hand and turned round to see what Viola was doing. When she found her standing quite still, very white, with eyes, as nurse said afterwards, that put her in mind of a maniac, she turned back again to find out what the trouble was, and saw the scissors standing upright, but unsteadily, like a man walking a rope, and moving with timorous jerky steps towards the hand that still held the wheel. Nurse gave a scream that made Viola start and cover her face, a scream so loud that she could not have heard the double crack that sounded close beside her. The scissors dropped, and lay innocently on the stuff again; but now the line of the light showed along a different blade.

Nurse looked then as Viola had never thought any grown-up could ever look. She was ugly with terror, more frightening than the happening that had surprised her. She made a scrambling movement towards the door, but halted, and came back to catch Viola by the arm and push her first out of the room. The key was on the outside, and nurse turned it before she let Viola go; then she seemed to forget her, and ran down the back stairs to the shelter of the kitchen.

Viola waited while the stairs hid nurse bit by bit, until even her head was gone, and went back into the room which, now that nurse with her ugly fear was out of it, was calm. The fire still climbed, the scissors had not moved. Viola went to the window, feeling happy. She blew on the glass and started to draw in the grey vapour that began to shrink at the edges almost as soon as it was there. She drew a face, and her own name, and nurse's name, and then another face in a big piece of breath that was the size of a whole pane. This last face was not very like anyone. It was more like an animal, a slug or a fish. It was different from anything Viola had ever seen, and she was proud of it. She watched it for a long time with her face close to it so that she could breath it back again as soon as it began to fade. Then she could hear voices in the passage, Annie's scornful voice, and nurse protesting. She heard Annie say, 'I thought it must be a fire or something. You want to be ashamed, yelling like that.'

'I take my God to witness—' said nurse.

But Annie interrupted, 'You ought to take something for your nerves; not what you do take, neither.'

'I never—' said nurse.

'Oh, get on with you,' Annie interrupted again. 'Well, let's see into the room. Whatever it is can't have got out.'

Viola could hear the dry refusing sound a key makes when it is turned back as far as it can go. Annie shook the door.

'Oh, don't,' said nurse, 'No. What's the good?'

'Whatever have you done to this lock?' Annie asked, paying no attention.

Viola turned away from the window, unable to attend to her drawing while they disputed. At the sound her feet made nurse screamed again, and the horrible noise angered Viola. She ran to the door and opened it, but before she could say a word nurse caught her by the arm and roughly shook her, so that everything she had meant to say went out of her head.

'What do you mean by going back in there, you naughty girl?' said nurse.

Viola did not answer because she was still being shaken. She had felt proud, contemptuous of nurse and able to shame her; now she was silly again only because nurse, though a coward, was strong. She began to cry. The shaking continued, and nurse's voice went scolding on in the full vengeful flood of her relief from fear. Then she saw Annie put her fingers and thumb on nurse's arm and give it a good wringing pinch. The noise and the shaking stopped. Viola could hear her own sobs, which were bigger and more uncontrollable than any she could remember. Annie said, 'Let that child alone. She's got more sense than what you have. Let her go, now, or someone'll know about it.'

Annie waited for a moment, looking very hard at nurse, and went on in a different voice, to Viola, 'It's all right, lovey. Don't cry. Where's your dress?'

She advanced into the sewing-room, picked up the dress and called, 'Come while I put it on for you.'

'You bring that dress here,' said nurse, holding Viola.

Annie laughed and brought it. Nurse snatched it from her and hurried it over Viola's head, not caring how it caught one of her ears and almost pulled it away.

'You be off,' said nurse. 'And you're not to say anything to Mummy; mind what I tell you, now. Go along to the nursery, and don't you move till I come.'

Viola went along to the nursery, where she sat doubled up on the floor near the fire. After a moment she went to sleep, quite unexpectedly, and when she woke it was dinner-time. The morning seemed almost not to have happened. Nurse said nothing. She did not repeat her warning. In any case Viola would not have told, lest her mother might find some way of putting a stop to the magic, but the knowledge lay in her, golden as a treasure, with all her senses on guard about it.

After this the games became great fun, when they could be played; they needed secrecy because of the cracking, whip-lash noises which grew louder the more they played together. She tried to put him through all the fairy tricks, one after another, but he was as obstinate and as unteachable as a cat. There was no magically spread table for Viola, no walnut shells with dresses inside, not even a leaf of the cabbage that could turn people into donkeys. In the mornings, at the forlorn hour when nurse brought her two uninteresting biscuits and a cup of milk covered with wrinkled white skin, she used to wish that he had never come. Before, it had been fun to pretend; the things she imagined she was eating used to taste as distinct as the food at dinner, so that she had once asked her mother if thinking you were eating would do instead of really eating. Now, somehow, the fun had gone out of pretending. She could not build those steep fairy castles in her head, nor ride through those forests. She had made her inside world as a place to slip into when the green ordinary world was dull; now it could never be dull, because she never knew when it might suddenly flare up into magic, and flames might begin to lift and curl instead of flowers in the vases. And a great sword swinging in a castle gateway was less marvellous than a pair of ordinary scissors walking across the sewing-room table on their round heels.

It was disappointing to realise how little Binns could actually do. He could move things and he could make noises, and that was all. And the only improvement Viola could notice after a month's training was that he could lift heavier weights and the noises were louder. He spoilt things for her. He had taken the keen edge off the old games, and would not help with the new ones. She could not think of anything that she really wanted to do, and used to stand by the nursery window watching the sky go past, wondering how the trees could make, with their bare winter arms, enough wind to drive the heavy clouds at such a rate. At the end of such stormy vacant days there was nothing to go to bed for.

Six weeks after her birthday her godfather came, a little man in spectacles so large that she thought he must be a diver. She was taken down to the drawing-room after tea to see him, and her mother said, 'Here's Uncle Godfrey, darling, who gave you that nice fork and spoon. You've never seen him before, have you? At least, you don't remember.'

'Don't be so sure of that,' the little man answered, shaking hands politely with Viola.

'Oh, my dear,' said her mother, 'at the font!'

'Well, why not?' asked the little man. 'You have no right to assume that people forget certain events merely because they happen at a time when the mind has no pigeon-holes ready for them.'

'But you haven't seen Uncle Godfrey before, have you, Viola?' said her mother.

Viola stared at him.

'Of course the child can't in one moment bring to the surface of her mind a thing which happened before the crust of consciousness formed. But I dare say she has the appropriate dreams.'

'She doesn't have dreams, do you? Not at night, anyhow.'

'No,' said Viola, very shortly. She knew the question about Binns was coming.

'Very wise,' said Uncle Godfrey, 'they're a great waste of good sleeping-time.'

'I'm afraid they waste a lot of play-time too,' Viola's mother said; and rather wistfully added, 'It's difficult down here. They're all octogenarians; no children at all on this side of the county. It's difficult with only one.'

'Parents always suppose that children must be lonely by themselves. It's the sentimental instinct of creatures that live in a herd, but it's quite false. How is a child to develop an imagination if you crowd it up with half-a-dozen others and give it elaborate toys, and illustrate its books to the last scale on the dragon's tail?'

'I'm not listening to you,' said Viola's mother, pulling Viola's sash straight.

'I know you're not. But sense is sense even if nobody hears it, as a table left solitary on the top of Everest at the end of the world continues to be a table after all consciousness has perished; though there are people who dispute that.'

'People with a great deal of time on their hands.'

'Possibly, though that's not relevant. A wise man knows that time on the hands is worth eternity on the clock. But the point at issue is this. You suppose that your daughter must be lonely and dull if she is left alone with her imagination, because, similarly left, you would yourself be lonely and dull. And why? Because you, in common with most fully developed persons, physically, are in the habit of restraining your imagination.'

'I'm sure I don't.'

'You're not listening. I say you do. You permit it to depict for you only such happenings as are strictly possible.'

'I often imagine quite impossible things; you behaving like an ordinary person, for instance.'

'I repeat, the most you allow your imagination, which is your power of creation, to do for you is to provide ropes of real pearls or an admirer like a young Greek god. Both lie conceivably within your power of attainment; utterly dull, utterly remote from the fantastic. Sky-scrapers limit your empyrean. Now the child—'

'You're too absurd. Do you talk this nonsense to your undergraduates?'

'I can't understand how women who are not good listeners ever get married. No, of course I don't. What is the use of talking nonsense to undergraduates or fairies to children? They both know more about it than I do.'

'Oh, you have some limitations?'

'Certainly. My only claim to distinction is that I recognise them.'

'Viola knows all about fairies,' said her mother, bringing her into the conversation.

'I've no doubt she does,' said Uncle Godfrey.

'She has a fairy who comes and plays with her, and helps with the doll's washing.'

'Not she,' said Uncle Godfrey, 'that's not the sort of thing a fairy worth its salt would do.'

'But Viola sees her, don't you? She really plays in the most uncanny way sometimes, just as if somebody was with her. Tell Uncle Godfrey what Binns does.'

Viola did not answer. She felt that Uncle Godfrey would see through the usual answer. Her mother went on.

'Binns comes and helps her to be a queen when they're not busy with the washing. She's very thin, isn't she, Viola? And they have a lovely kingdom down in the far corner of the garden where we burn the rubbish.'

Viola wanted to explain that her mother had got it all wrong, every single word of it; but that would have meant giving up her secret. She stood very square on her feet and kept quiet.

'It can't be much of a fairy,' said Uncle Godfrey. 'What's the use of setting an elemental power to do menial jobs like washing, or running a kingdom? I reject Viola's domestic fairy as I reject your Greek gods. You fail, both of you. You bind fire with chains; for two pins you'd set Pegasus to pull the municipal dustcart.'

'What is the matter with you? You scold me first because I'd rather she had other children than these funny plays of her own; and then you scold her and say her fairies are no good. Of course they're good. Why shouldn't her Binns be a nice friendly person?'

'Because in that case she might as well have been given an undersized body and sent out into the world, with a reference from Lady Stick-in-the-Mud, to replace your kitchen-maid.'

'He's very unkind, isn't he, Viola? Well, we're quite happy about Binns. We know she's real.'

Viola's mind was in a tangle. She could see that it was Uncle Godfrey who really understood, and that her mother, who defended her on the surface, inwardly, deep down, thought the invention of Binns rather silly. She wanted to do something to show them both the meaning of the unseen companion, and it was her mother's attitude which made her want to come out into the open, abandoning her secret place; the tone, not exactly condescending, but affectionately tolerant and kind. While the decision hung in the balance her mother added something which snapped, like a spider's thread, Viola's resolution to hold back. She said to Uncle Godfrey, 'We won't let you play with us. You can't pretend.'

Viola had no words with which to answer this. It was too wrong, more wrong even than her mother's account of the fairy games that were Viola's own property, and of which her mother, unasked, ignorant, assumed control and patronage. Viola smiled, and a hot misty feeling mounted from her stomach to where her throat began. There was a loud crack just by her right hand, a crack more arresting than any she had yet heard.

'What's that?' asked her mother, startled.

'My locust,' Viola answered, keeping her hand shut tight.

'What a hateful noise! Don't do it again.'

'I'll try not,' Viola answered, with unusual meekness.

But she knew very well that she had no control over Binns in these proud fits; almost immediately he cracked again.

'Viola!' said her mother, 'I asked you not to do that.'

'I know,' Viola answered; a third crack sounded in the middle of her words. Her mother got up from her chair.

'Give me that thing at once,' her mother commanded.

Viola withdrew the hand and held it behind her back. She could not afford to have it examined, for it was empty. Uncle Godfrey stood looking on with interest, as though they were acting a play for him. Her mother repeated, 'Give it to me, Viola.'

Viola took a step backwards, not answering. Her mother made a sudden movement, intending to become possessed by force of the clenched hand which her strength would be able to open. To Viola, frightened already, it seemed the most important thing of all that nobody should open that hand. She had somehow to distract her mother, and make her abandon her intention. She stretched out her left arm with a jerk, pointing at a jar of heavy painted poppy-heads that served for flowers in winter; the jar was a foot distant from the longest of her pointing fingers, and much higher. The odd, stiff gesture surprised her mother, who stopped, looking at the outstretched hand, expecting to see in it the scrap of black tin; instead, she saw one of the poppy-heads begin to lean towards it. It leant out at an impossible angle, and when it was free of the jar it seemed to fall very slowly towards Viola, as though it were sliding down a solid invisible slope, and it hung in the air just short of her fingers for a definite moment before they closed on it.

Viola could not remember what happened after that. She had an illness almost at once that lasted for weeks and obliged her to forget; then, as soon as she got well her mother took her away to a village in the south-west of France. They stayed there for two years in a whitish villa roofed with curved red tiles; at the end of those years Viola could speak French with a savage facility which she had acquired in self-defence. She was never, for more than ten minutes at a time, left by herself; not even to sleep. At first she was inclined to shut herself up in her silent castles, but they were no longer the same. They would not build themselves easily in France, within a bee's flight of a real castle, to which she could climb. And the village people were different, more vivid, and they were always singing; the songs were queer, like pictures drawn in sound. Viola could not learn them; there were no words on which to hang the slow, balancing phrases; but she loved to listen, and during the second year, because in French it was something of an adventure, she learned to read. Overtaken by that immense new interest as by an enveloping sea the castles disappeared, and the princedoms, and the memory faded of solitary games played in an empty room.

When she could read pretty well, and after a serious French doctor had examined her, she was sent to school at an establishment on the south coast of England where her mother had been assured that a healthy tone prevailed. At first she was not homesick, but after a year or two a longing grew up in her, not for the villa backed by mountains and the dark cheerful people with their unhappy songs; some unreasonable fraction of her wanted, and saw clearly in dreams, the house where she had played alone. She crowded the stupid longing out of her waking thoughts, and did not speak of it to anyone. When she was seventeen they went back to the house.

She had looked forward so long and so eagerly to being there that the actual arrival felt a little flat, as though the house, which for years had been busy with strangers and their affairs, had forgotten her. She came as an acquaintance into the brown hall, looking about her, unrecognised. She remembered everything, the positions of the furniture, the way the light came in from the autumn afternoon outside. Forlorn and restless, with the vacant feeling of a person newly arrived in a new place, cheated of habits and at a loss for occupation, she wandered about, while her mother dealt with the servants and the unpacking. She went into the nursery, where she was no longer to sleep; the patterned birds on its walls had scarcely faded at all. Going down the passage from the nursery she came to the sewing-room, and thought with a pang of wonder, 'Could I have been that child?' She could see the child as though she had been someone else, one of the children who used to come to tea; sulky and secret, and very sure of the worlds she had created. The child had been safe, her strong imaginings had protected her; the invisible thing had been no more and no less real than they. Now it was as though one of those imagined creatures had escaped, taking body and power apart from her; huge, towering above the dwarfish company her grown mind could picture for her. It would be dangerous now. And she had a feeling of courage and elation, like a moment before battle.

She had been given a different bedroom. Grown Viola could not make for herself a golden hall in an attic, nor conjure a pattern of parrots and cherries into a tropical forest at night. She had been robbed by the years of these splendours, and instead was given the room which before had been kept for the most important guest. It was on the first floor, very light, and there were flowers on a small table in the window. The nursery had never been given flowers, except the frail things that Viola used to pick from the hedges and put in a doll's teacup with the water forgotten. There were writing things, as for a guest, and cupboards for clothes. But when she had unpacked and put her own belongings about it still felt empty; and she thought, 'Hiding.'

At dinner her mother said that it was delightful to be home again, not to be nomads any more. She said the house gave one such a friendly feeling, as though it were making one welcome. She said she had almost forgotten what it looked like, and supposed that Viola had, too. She was civil about the departed tenants, except that they had let the garden get into a dreadful state. Viola agreed with it all.

Next day she announced that she would like to have the sewing-room as her own room, to sit in.

'But there are plenty of places for you to sit,' said her mother, astonished, 'and your own room is quite nice. There's a comfy chair. What are we to do if a woman comes in to sew?'

'She can have the old nursery.'

'But that little room is so inconvenient, right at the top of the house. Dark—'

'Oh, please. Really I'd like it.'

'Well, of course—But I can't give you any more furniture. I really can't have anything taken out of the other rooms.'

'I didn't ask for anything. I don't want anything.'

'But you can't leave it like that, without any proper things. I don't see why you want it; you've got all the rest of the house—'

In the end Viola was allowed to keep the sewing-room just as it had been. A fire was lighted there each morning, and this was the only sign that the room expected anyone. It had always been a room that lived by fits and starts. Its guests were the shadows cast by some passing emergency, sewing women, monthly nurses, housemaids in quarantine. It was unaccustomed to people, and during the first weeks of Viola's tenancy it continued to have an air of awkwardness, like a person who is willing to be friendly but has not the habit of civility. Then it began to respond to her continued presence; and although its furniture remained austere, although there were no flowers on its table, it began to look, as her mother said, quite habitable; quite human.

Viola used to sit there for hours, doing nothing, trying to

make her mind empty, a long bare attic such as children love to play in. She was sure that if she could succeed in doing this he would be tempted out of hiding, but she could not banish altogether the furnishings that the years had collected and stored there. And there were people, too. There had been a great many of them in the nine years of absence, and they kept coming in, without warning, to the bare room of her mind; people she thought she had forgotten, or had hardly known, shop-assistants, schoolgirls, gardeners. While they were there he did not come. At night she would sit in the dark, staring at some glowing promontory of coal; the red ashes moved as though they breathed light, and the running white glow sketched for her hills and cities she had known; real places always, not the steep, thin towers of her childhood with bridges curved like scimitars leading to their gates. He was obstinate, but she was more patient than Viola the child had been. She tried other ways. Once or twice she spoke aloud, on windy evenings when nobody could have heard.

'You're afraid. You won't come because you know I'm stronger than you. Can you hear me? You're afraid.'

'Do come. I can't remember you, it was so long ago. We used to have such good games. I want to find you again. Oh, do come on. I know you're there—aren't you?—listening. You needn't be frightened of me. I won't ask you to do anything.'

Silence; then, in a burst of temper.

'All right, you silly beast; you coward; you ugly dirty beast. I'm sick of you. Good riddance.'

Between the sudden thrusts of the wind she could hear silence waiting in the room, full of tiny prickling sounds, unguessed movements, and knew that he was there. She wondered if there could be anything in herself that shut him out; sought, but could find nothing, except that she no longer had entry to her invisible, obedient world.

Then James happened. He was an ordinary young man but for one or two engaging tricks which made him more adorable to Viola than the Greek god of her uncle's taunt. His hair grew very close to his head in the shape of a wig; he had large feet and large limbs that contrived to arrange themselves in soft puppy-attitudes. He had a mark like a little arrow-head near each corner of his mouth from smiling so often. Viola sat in the sewing-room more than ever, thinking; but now every part of her thought was concerned with James. She even brought him up once to see it, and gave him tea. He thought it an odd room for her to have chosen, and said so; he was not to know how she felt about him, nor why she was allowing him to see the place where her very self lived. At first he temporised.

'I suppose you feel more on your own up here, out of everybody's way?'

'No, I just like it.'

'Well, you're high enough up. Is there a view?'

But the sewing-room looked on to a couple of nondescript trees and the shed where the servants kept their bicycles.

'No. I hate views. I've had to live with too many of them.'

'What do you do up here, then?'

'Nothing. I don't read or sew or play the violin or cat's-cradle or learn anything or make anything.'

'Just one of the idle rich.'

She laughed because he did; and when he tried to lean back in the unyielding chair and fold his legs comfortably together in their usual way she laughed again because it was so obvious that he would have been happier on the sofa downstairs. She did not mind when he said that women could not understand comfort, for she knew it was true, and when he said that she was a Spartan and he must give her a little fox she was delighted with him for being so funny and so dear as to talk, even in joke, of giving her anything. She fussed over his tea, wanting it to be just right, and made one or two of the little faces she had noticed in her glass and hoped that he would like. While he coaxed a pipe she looked hard at him so as to be able to remember the shape of his head as it bent forward, and his face, serious for once, the arrow-heads quite smoothed out with the pursing of his lips. She thought he would look like that kissing someone; kissing her; serious and intent, thinking only of one thing at a time. She was friendly and natural, not herself exactly, but the sort of self he probably liked, and which she played for love of him so that it almost became the real Viola. She let him laugh at her chairs, and her unattractive view, and the complete absence of what he called the woman's touch.

'I know just the sort of house you'll have when you're married. You'll go to the firm that does station waiting-rooms and give them a free hand. And you'll say to your husband, "There's a sale at the Office of Works to-morrow, dear; they're selling off a lovely lot of iron seats from the parks".'

'I'll marry someone who won't notice. Or someone that's never at home.'

'A commercial traveller.'

'Or a policeman. Or one of those men that sit all night with a street when it's up, with buckets full of charcoal.'

'Good idea. He might let you have the bucket to put an aspidistra in by day. I'll give you one for a wedding present.'

'Thanks, but it's to be a very quiet wedding. The bride and bridegroom will leave by Tube for the Edgware Road, which will be their address for the season.'

'It's funny about you. You've really got a sense of humour.'

'I had the three permanent jokes in *Punch* carefully explained to me when I was little. Since then I have used no others.'

'You are an ass. But nice.'

'Thanks. Your old-world courtesy is charming.'

When they came downstairs and were under observation once more she was casual and normal, and there was not a word to be got from her that was amusing. She interested and stimulated him, so that he found himself that night writing a marvellously good letter to the lady in Ebury Street who had taken charge of his sentimental education. While he wrote and admired Viola sat in her room, or walked irrepressibly about it, with her arms lifted above her head. The room of her mind was to be bare no longer; it should be hung with tapestries and have a thousand candles in gold sconces alive on the walls. She stared into the fire, smiling, trying to see it there as the red and white heats shifted. She thought, 'I wish I had lots of things that I could give him. I wish I was rich and most frightfully beautiful, and that he was poor. I'd ask him to marry me and he'd be surprised and would hate not having anything of his own. But I'd make him and we'd be together. Happy.'

She could see herself, dressed in silver and much taller than at present, standing with him on some balcony, some terrace which looked out on to water. There was no moon, and no light except that which came from a long window open behind them. He would be looking at her, dreadfully in love; and then she would put her hand on his and say, 'We love each other. What does it matter who says it first?'

She did this scene over several times, improving it here and there, changing the décor. At the end it went beautifully, with several admiring people looking on, unseen, of course; but she heard their comments afterwards.

After this her own bedroom, with white lights everywhere and incorruptible mirrors, was an anticlimax, and she went to sleep at once, in a prosaic attitude.

She saw him often, for a time. He had a car and would call for her at odd hours, just after breakfast, just before luncheon. They would race through sixty or eighty miles of country while he tried to draw her out and make her say the things which tempted him to wit. She knew what he expected and gave it, thinking that even to make him laugh was something; but compared with the other gifts she wanted to put into his hands it was rather pitiful.

Upstairs in her room she tried to send messages to him, patiently imagining him as he might be at any given moment, sitting with his legs crossed and one foot twisted under the other ankle; reading a newspaper; bending over the shining body of the car. She made herself see these pictures of him so clearly; even the grain of his skin and the way his eyebrows grew were visible to her as though she were in the room with him. And holding him like this in her company she would talk to him, and give him those other things. Now and then his head would lift as if he listened, and tilt on one side as though he could not hear all her nonsense, or her passionate boasting.

'You don't know all the things I can do. I can make ordinary things not be the same. You feel that when I'm with you. I'm a kind of witch. I could do all the magic, godmother things for you. Can you feel me now, standing beside you? I've gone out of myself, I've left myself quite empty, to visit you and talk to you. I'm strong, aren't I? That's why I can come to you like this. When I go back I shall be weak, because I'll have left part of my strength with you. We'll share. I love you when you laugh at me.'

At the end of three weeks he said that he was going back to London. It was dreadful. She was shocked by the thought of not having him near her, and by another thought, that perhaps it would not take him long to forget her. Only one thing could have made it bearable, if she could have been sure that the night messages reached him. She was almost sure—the pictures were very real—but she was afraid to ask him, lest, to tease her, or because he would not admit he was sensitive, he might deny it. The day before his departure she begged him to come. He refused, lightly, offering some very reasonable and acceptable excuse. She insisted, with a curious force that surprised him.

'I want you to come, please.'

'But I've got ten thousand things to do.'

'One more won't matter, then.'

'No, seriously—'

'Seriously, I want you to come.'

'Any particular reason?'

'One.'

'Tell me now.'

She lifted her left shoulder, and the hand that held the receiver, in a shrug.

'It's far too indelicate.'

'What's that?'

'Nothing. Will you come?'

'Only for a minute, then, and probably cross. About six-thirty.'

'Right.'

She spent the day waiting, and wondering if the whole thing were madness, or a kind of primal sanity. She had not the energy even to smoke. She was utterly listless, surprised at the outgoing of her strength. It could not, she thought, disappear like a blown candle-flame; it must go somewhere, touch something. It was satisfying to imagine those waves of strength beating continuously against the strong wall of his mind. It was worth being tired to have that going on, but she had to keep away from mirrors in order to believe it. Her square child's face and body made an incredible shrine. If she could hardly believe, seeing herself, how should he?

When he came he found her sitting by a fire that was red and low, with only a candle beside her to light the room.

'Well, Cinderella,' said he.

'The light's fused. Can you put up with a candle?'

'I'll fix it.'

'No, don't. Let it alone. You're going back to marble halls to-morrow.'

'So I am, and not a thing packed. What's this indelicate secret?'

'It's not, really.'

'You said it was. Why do you tell such appalling lies?'

'I thought you probably wouldn't come if I didn't.'

'Perfectly correct, I wouldn't have.'

'I thought not.'

'Well, what? Are you going to make an offer for my hand?'

'Not quite. It's something that's been worrying me. I want to ask you something.'

'Don't make it too difficult.'

'I—you see, when I was little I could do all sorts of funny things. Make things move just by willing, and so on.'

'Things? What?'

'Oh, well; a pair of scissors, once. Flowers.'

'Move?'

'Yes. I know it sounds silly, but other people saw them too. This hasn't anything to do with it really, only it sort of leads up. I used to do it for spite, chiefly, then. It was something in the house—oh, I don't know. At least, I do, but it's no use my explaining that part of it. Anyhow, these last few weeks I've been trying something else.'

She leant forward. The light, placed a little behind her, showed her round head and thick shoulders; her voice was that of a child, and all the candle did was to make her outline correspond to the voice. But already she had forgotten why she had arranged the candle. He felt that he must say something.

'All sounds pretty necromantic.'

'Yes, that was; the first part. This is different, what I'm trying to do now. I'm thinking how to put it. Well, I've been trying to communicate with people. I get out of myself somehow and go to them.'

'Good lord, who?'

'You, for one. And I'm sure I've got you once or twice.'

'Viola, look here—'

'No, let me tell you. Two nights ago did you go out at ten minutes to six to look at the car? Pat was with you. He put his paws on the mudguard and you knocked him off because he scratched the paint. Did you?'

'I don't know what I was doing at ten minutes to six on Tuesday. I think all this is a trifle far-fetched.'

'Well, last night, then. Did you go to bed about eleven and take two books up with you, and drop one on the stairs?'

'No.'

'Don't just say that. I mean, don't tell lies just to snub me. I'm frightfully serious about this. Did you?'

'No.'

'But you must have felt something. Did you hear me saying I was strong?'

'No.'

'Have you ever thought you could hear me talking to you? You mightn't have known what I was saying. Did you ever think I was sort of there?'

'No.'

'Honour?'

'Yes.'

'But where's it gone, then?'

He was alarmed by the change in her voice; it cut through his indifference and his impatience. He tried to cover it up, talking loudly, even advancing to pat her shoulder.

'Of course I often think about you. Look here, don't you

think this sort of thing is rather unhealthy? You're only a kid. Eighteen is only a kid, after all. I don't like to think of you taking it out of yourself over a silly thing like this.'

She was not listening to him. She was leaning sideways and back, behind the candle, watching a shadow that was beginning to take shape on the forget-me-not patterned wall of the sewing-room. It was a shadow without definite edges, almost formless, but certainly there. It was a sleek shadow, not angular; like a fish, perhaps, or a slug. She began to laugh when she saw how it was growing, and James, who had his back to it but was frightened, ran to the switch by the door and pressed it down. Instantly light flooded into the room, overwhelming the candle and its shadows, and he was brave again, so that he could even bear to kneel by her and hold his arms round her while she fought with her laughter.

6 Disturbing Experience
of an Elderly Lady

'Ostcott Manor was granted by King John to Stephen de Percys in the year 1210, and was held by his descendants until the reign of Queen Elizabeth, when, in 1579, it passed to Roger Furnivall on his marriage with Anne Percys, the heiress. It remained in the possession of the Furnivall family until quite recently, and during that time has welcomed more than one of the sovereigns of England beneath its hospitable roof, notably the ill-fated James II, who left a chased gold snuff-box, which is still preserved, in memory of his visit. Ostcott Manor is now the seat of Mrs Jones.'

That was the version in the guide-book; and by the mere iteration of those splendid names the guide-book contrived subtly to put Mrs Jones in the wrong. She was the usurper. She had tempted the improvident Furnivalls with an incredible sum of money, which they, with hardly a moment's hesitation beyond what decency demanded, had accepted, and immediately confided their poor loyal old house to the invader. They were a stupid lot, the Furnivalls and Percys; but then seven hundred years is a long time. They had been fighting men during the first two centuries, then couriers, then statesmen; in the eighteenth century they were poets and gamblers; in the nineteenth century, by an inevitable reaction, they were dull; in the twentieth they had lost all imagination, virility, loyalty and enterprise, and had become smart. Now they wanted, above all things, money, and the house meant money, if it could be properly advertised.

But Mrs Jones was unexpected. Nobody could think why she should be willing to pay that enormous sum, which brought before the dazzled eyes of the Furnivalls a glittering vision of smart years; as all their friends said, she would have been much happier in a villa at Surbiton, expensive and up-to-date, with a garden. Odd Mrs Jones, to wish to exile herself from all that her previous experience demanded, to shut herself off from her kind in a patchwork house with a Norman Keep, a Tudor gallery, and an eighteenth-century music-room where in the corner still stood a tall shrouded harp, and the marble mantelpiece was carved with shepherd's pipes, garlanded.

She had been nobody, came from nowhere. Her husband had acquired a fortune, apparently without effort, during the last years of the war; then the strain of money told upon him and he died and was buried at Brookwood, beneath the weighty presence of a lamenting angel whose upturned eyes— was it only a chance?—displayed, when viewed from the side, an archness of expression more feminine than becoming. The angel represented a type that Mr Jones during his lifetime would never have dared to address, and it was, perhaps, a sudden flash of perception which induced his wife to set such a guardian above the body which had so lately been forsaken by its desires. She had often watched Mr Jones when they walked towards their Tube coming home from a theatre, and had seen his eyes as the women brushed by him, scented a little rankly for the night air, walking languidly westwards; but Mr Jones never knew. Mrs Jones was too clever for that. Even to the monumental mason she had only said that it was sweetly pretty, and had realised that it would cost a lot and that the costliness would have pleased her husband.

But Ostcott, though it too was expensive, so that its price had set the Furnivalls whirling afresh like wavering tops slashed by a whip, Ostcott would not have pleased him. He would have grudged the thousands of pounds that were represented by the panelling, and the wide shallow staircase;

even the fifty pounds which had secured the James II snuff-box and allowed it to gleam still in its setting of faded plush, he would have grudged. He liked to see value for money; but Mrs Jones was content.

She had passed by this place years ago, in August, when the trees about it were at their most mellow green. She had been in the company of some twenty-five other persons in a charabanc; but they had been too much occupied with sandwiches, and the unostentatious holding of elbows, to take much notice of it, beyond a casual word as its roofs appeared above the elms. They had all enjoyed themselves a good deal, and noisily. Someone had offered to hold Mrs Jones' hand, and as she squealed with laughter, glancing towards her husband who rose in a mock-heroic attitude, she saw Ostcott, silent, immutable in its dignity, watching her. She blushed, as though for a moment she saw herself with other eyes; she felt cheap. For the moment she hated the house, bitterly, as though it had been another woman; then there were other things to think of, and much talk, much laughter, so that she could truthfully agree with Mr Jones when he reckoned that the outing had been cheap at eight and six a head.

When, after his death, she found that all the money was hers, to do as she liked with, hers without question, she could not at first so extend her ambition as to contemplate a yearly expenditure of more than a tenth of the income. She had no children, and disliked her relations. For years she had ordered her life within the limits of a few hundred pounds, and found it difficult to understand that she might, from the security of her thousands, make raids upon those other worlds which she had come to look upon as being altogether outside her own. Liberty stupefied her. She was afraid of it, and unused to it, for the late Mr Jones had been secretive and close in the matters of money. It takes time to acquire the habit of spending. It had taken the Furnivall centuries, and this now was their only legacy from their chequered history, a mysterious exquisite elegance and carelessness in spending.

Mrs Jones remained motionless for over a year, incredulous of her freedom; then, one day, she saw on the back page of the *Times* a photograph of remembered grey roofs, which had lifted themselves above the elms to shame her, long ago, before the war. She read the particulars, noted the acres of garden, the various royal bedrooms, with a certain wonder that it should be possible to possess so much of the living stuff of romance, and a hint of spiteful joy that the proud house should have been brought low. It then occurred to her, with a serene splendour as of revelation, that if she wished she could buy it, merely by writing a cheque for an unreal sum on a piece of pink paper.

The whole business was so surprisingly simple; that was what at first amazed Mrs Jones. That so many hundred acres, so much carved timber and stone could belong to one person, and an hour later, by reason of one or two illegible scribbles at the foot of an incomprehensible document be ceded utterly to another person, a stranger, was astonishing to her, who had always looked on 'business' as compact of intricacies and delays. And she hesitated long before she accepted the invitation of the Furnivalls to come to Ostcott as their guest before she came as their successor. They were civil, the Furnivalls, and far from resenting her, they felt that she had paid them a good deal of money, and was entitled to have the worth of it. Therefore, they were willing to be polite, to ingratiate themselves with the mammon of unrighteousness, and even to introduce her to the less important neighbours.

So that Mrs Jones, when at last she came with rather too much brand-new luggage, was made welcome. Mrs Furnivall showed her a gentle courtesy, tempered with a faint annoyance when she remembered that in a month's time packing would begin, an operation which she hated even to supervise;

Stephen took her for long, tangled walks, maliciously aware of her heavy breathing as she plodded by his side; and Edith, tall and cool in her summer clothes, showed her the gallery and the sliding panel, and gave her tea under a big coloured umbrella on the terrace above the lawn. They quite liked her, they found. She was common, of course, but she did not talk loudly, nor wear a red blouse, nor cringe to the servants. They were pleased with themselves for enduring her so politely, and never knew that as she walked down the oak stairs, her too-heavy footsteps echoing, she was thinking only of the house, protected still by their mere presence, soon to be left undefended. Her obstinate will still found itself checked by these ephemeral beings, who moved carelessly about, unconscious of their part in the drama, unaware of hatred or appeal. They were charming and impotent; the house was strong, forbidding, and enduring; Mrs Jones was stubborn. It was a curious conflict, waged silently.

She stayed for a week at Ostcott, and returned to her inconsiderable house in the suburb with a feeling of triumph, yet with a certain foreboding. She was up against something whose force she was not able to measure. She marvelled at herself, and was reticent with the friends who had heard of her purchase and were agog to discuss it, though they too had forebodings, and knew that one did not buy a 'place' in order to fill it with persons whose sole claim to distinction lay in the fact that they had, once upon a time, lived next door but two. They beheld Mrs Jones with reverence as one who had the means and the will to climb; and they respected her for the effort, while they mocked at her speech, and so much as was known of her origin. Mrs Jones was aware of their envy, as she had previously been aware of the patronage of the Furnivalls. She betrayed nothing. They admired her strength of purpose, and in their minds wrote her off as a social bad debt, strangely set down as a conversational asset.

Mrs Jones, with more shiny luggage, went at last from her villa, and caught the train which was to convey her to her ambitions. She might have driven in the car, but the car was still a toy to be carefully handled, and she was secretly intimidated by the chauffeur. She caught the train, changed, with the assistance of officials, at the right places, coming at last in the cool of a golden evening to the little station called by the name of the Manor. She was excited and happy. This lazy country pleased her, and she bore it no ill-will. With the house, only with the house, her quarrel lay. She drove smoothly towards it, saw with a quickening of her heart the grey sunken angles of the roof rise into view beyond the elms. As she walked into the hall she said to herself, with passionate satisfaction, 'It's mine now.'

She slept that night in the room where James II had stayed, so short a time before his fall, and as the tiny point of light died from the wick of her candle, she settled back among the pillows, and staring at the invisible tent of the bed that loomed above her, began to make her plans.

She would change it all. She would tile the mellow roofs, and widen the narrow corridors, pierce the thick flanks of the house for windows. She was absolute, her wealth was her power, and with it she would compel the house to her will, break down that remote intolerant pride.

She slept late, and in her sleep devised ways and means to victory.

All the next day the house waited, with a deathly stillness which only her deliberate footfall upon the oak disturbed. She went quietly about, sometimes fingering the carved panels, and the crested pillars at the turn of the stairs; the motto beneath the Gryphons crowned was 'Gardez'. She would sell much of the woodwork; some of the floors should be levelled, and the low doors, which endangered even her modest coiffure, should be cut to conventional height.

Malevolently she wandered about her house like a small stout witch, conscious of that breathless anticipation, despising it. She had known a builder, a friend of her husband in the old days. He would be glad of the job, and would do as she told him—tear out the place's very guts, thought Mrs Jones with an unusual freedom of expression. For the moment his name eluded her, and she cast her mind back, so that she could see the very house where he had lived, bought after some ignoble coup which had involved the building of a double row of yellow brick cottages. She could see those staring cottages, and thought warmly of the man who had constructed them, as of an ally. She would remember the name soon.

That night her sleep was troubled. She was disquieted, and woke from hour to hour to watch the changing shapes of curtains blown by the wind, and to hear the cracks and sighings and faint hollow noises of an old house in darkness.

Next morning she remembered the name of the man who was so necessary to her; Bowler it was, and he lived in Coningsby Road. She wrote to him immediately after breakfast, not stating definitely for what purpose she required him, but only asking him to come, with the usual suggestion about defraying all expenses. Her pen seemed to move unwillingly over the rough thick paper, which transformed her handwriting and even the turn of her sentences, so that they looked magnificent, rolling over the page. At the end she hesitated, and then was his faithfully; after all, he had only been her husband's friend.

When the letter had been sent off she felt triumphant and secure. The wet world outside her window promised a day of comfort and endless leisurely plans. She ordered a fire in the cream-panelled China Room, and sat stitching at a nightgown, whose interminably repeated seams were satisfactory to the need of her fingers for action, brooding destruction. In the pale firelight her hands looked coarse, reddish brown against the linen, and the walls seemed to recall patrician hands, with creamy idle fingers. Mrs Jones, suddenly angry, stiffened in her winged chair, and sat, defiantly busy, her face crimson with indignation and heat, conscious of mockery but stubborn in her resolve.

Next day Mr Bowler arrived, just at the mid-time of sun, when the house seemed to stretch and extend itself to take in the unexpected warmth. He was a good deal impressed, and his first words to Mrs Jones were concerned with the handsome approach.

'Foliage,' said Mr Bowler, 'I like that. I'd always leave a tree where possible.'

'I've got nothing against the trees,' Mrs Jones replied, 'it's the house—'

She was silent. The thing was so nearly accomplished that she was overcome by nervousness lest anything should prevent her. She had almost to stammer to get the words out.

'I want a thing or two done.'

'A bit old-fashioned,' Mr Bowler agreed, 'quite old-world. Not much what I call comfort.'

'There's been a lot of Kings stayed here,' said Mrs Jones, as though unwillingly she defended the house.

Mr Bowler laughed.

'Well, they were easy pleased in those days,' he said, looking at the spaced bare panels of the China Room. 'I suppose you'll be wanting a bathroom put in, and a few windows. I noticed the hall was dark.'

But there were bathrooms enough, and Mrs Jones was used to dark halls. She found it difficult to describe just what she wanted done.

'I want it all made a bit brighter,' she suggested; perhaps it was the clean pale colours that had managed to hold her aloof, in her place.

Mr Bowler had brought with him a book of wallpaper

patterns, and together they went through these. They were expensive papers, all of them, covered with luscious designs. There were blood-coloured papers in which branching lilies were steeped; huge roses, red, yellow, and even blue, climbing forever up a frail trellis; vast, glossy stripes; every device was there by which a house could be made brighter. Mrs Jones was determined to leave no single room as it had been; where, by reason of the panelling, paper could not go, she would have paint. And the odd little steps leading up and down into bedrooms, which had been known as 'goosey-ganders' to generations of Furnivall children, were to be levelled; everywhere windows were to be knocked in the thick walls, and filled with stained glass in those places where it would show. Mrs Jones went about tirelessly, continually finding opportunities for mischief, and continually assailing Mr Bowler with questions and demands. As the afternoon went by he began to droop, and then to become uneasy. Several times he looked at Mrs Jones with doubt. Finally as they sat having tea—this was her tribute to the friendship—he coughed and suddenly said, 'This'll be quite a job.'

Mrs Jones agreed that it would. Her top lip pressed down upon the lower until her mouth was set in a straight line. Mr Bowler continued, 'No end of a job. I don't know—I wouldn't like to say as the house could stand it.'

Mrs Jones looked at him with eyes that somehow matched her mouth.

'An old place like this, you don't want to go interfering too much. It all hangs together; take away one thing and down comes the rest. Now, these alterations you want done— they're structural. I wouldn't like to take on the job without you let an architect look it over.'

'Get one, then,' said Mrs Jones.

Mr Bowler seemed relieved, as though he had not expected this concession. Her savagery had frightened him.

'It's the right thing to do,' said he, 'there's one I know—'
He paused.

'Seems almost a pity, when it's been here so long.'

Mrs Jones got up, and stood facing him over her tea-table.

'Do you want this job, or not?' she asked.

'I do,' Mr Bowler answered, staring, 'I only passed the remark.'

'Well,' said Mrs Jones, 'I don't want any more talk about it. Architect! That means another nice bill for me to pay. Oh, I know; and I don't care. I'm going to have this house the way I want. It's my house. I paid for it. I'm going to live in it. There's plenty builders—'

'Now, now,' said Mr Bowler, 'when did I ever say it wasn't your house? I'll do what you want, and proud to oblige a friend. Only it seems to me you're going a bit far. What's the good of buying a house and pulling it to pieces? Might as well build a new one right off.'

'That's enough about it,' said Mrs Jones.

After the builder had gone, she sat again in the China Room, the nightgown now almost finished, on her knees. Her left hand held the stuff, and in her right was a threaded needle, but her hands were idle. She looked often into the fire, and laughed once or twice. She had enjoyed her afternoon.

Next morning as Mrs Jones went down into the hall on her way to breakfast a shaft of sunlight slanted through the long windows, making on the oak floor a square pool of brown, so deep, so friendly and gay, that she felt a sudden unreasoning happiness, as though she would have liked to caress that shining wood with her hand. But she was distrustful, and moved away; passing, her shadow fell upon the patch of light, destroying it. She did not look behind her. She was on her guard.

But from that moment the house continued wistfully to put forth its charm, shyly to woo her. It gave Mrs Jones sudden glimpses of its own beauty, like some inner room unexpected, revealed by a mirror tilted upon an outer wall. It hushed the commonplace swish of her skirt to mysterious silken rustlings, and suddenly crowned her white hair with a ray of sun from a high window. The attack was subtly, delicately made; but she perceived and resisted it. She knew that the house was fighting for its very existence with its only weapon, this rare quality of charm, which was the heritage too of its foster-children, the dispossessed Furnivalls. Against such impalpable thrusts she was proof, and it amused her to submit herself, and to allow the spell to be woven.

Friday, the sixth day after her arrival, was a night of full moon. It sent blades of light into the house through the uncurtained windows of the hall, and Mrs Jones could not resist the appeal of the silence, and the black and silver garden. She put on a pair of goloshes, which she preferred to call overshoes, and went out, fearlessly taking the path which went southwards through the woods, where it was dark, but with a friendly darkness quite different from the sinister gloom of paved unlighted streets. She twitched a branch from a lilac, for no reason, and walked on slowly brushing the flowers against her face. Stephen Furnivall had once brought her this way, and she had a vague idea that the twisting path found issue in a clearing which lay like a green standing pool amid the trees. She followed the track, but now and then she missed her way, for the branches overhead admitted none but splinters and tiny wavering circles of light; and when she quitted it felt the soft grass rise about her ankles and the coldness of the dew. So intent was she, staring down at her feet, that she came almost without warning to the little clear space, silver now, with dark trunks fringing it, and its northern edge dappled and tremulous with the shadows of leaves. So still was it, so lovely, that Mrs Jones halted, standing amazed in her overshoes on the beaten earth of the track, holding her breath lest she should disturb that silence, or intrude upon that loveliness; as though any movement of hers might set that round glass of silence ringing. She had never before been so close to trees at night. They seemed to breathe and murmur; they were alive. She did not dare to lay a hand on one of the dark trunks to steady herself in case it should be warm, carrying movement and life within it. The night held her closely, secret and wise, pleading with her, and she began to listen, abandoning her mind to the lure. She remembered how one night she had stood at a window, half undressed, thinking, I'm young; behind the triumph her thoughts were cloudy with wonder and sadness. That was before she was married, or like to be; and before she had known or cared what youth wanted. She drew her breath sharply, and closed her eyes now to feel that pain at the back of her thoughts; it was gone, not to be recaptured even in the quiet ecstacy of such a night as this. Because she could not feel the sadness she knew that youth must be dead. Oh, that first stirring and waking to beauty unrecognised! And the search, the silly treasures found which held their gold no longer than the autumn leaves, the forgetting, the dying down of the light that had led the search! Now, with the trees guarding her, leaning forward to stare into the pool of light, memories came darting, fantastic images of reality, thoughts from her childhood, figureless longings of youth. Her eyes coveted the plot of silvery grass in which, like a mirror, she saw that first self of hers pictured. She wanted to throw herself on it with outstretched hands, to possess it with her body and feel its touch against the bare skin of her feet. She was swept by a rush of emotion urging her to such delicious extravagances that she was almost overwhelmed. She forced herself to consider her age, her white hair, her ungainly hands, all the things which this disorderly folly of the moon would have had her forget. Vainly her reason battled against the temptation of the night; darkness covered her, her heavy body was invisible, her hair was silvery as the grass, her clasped hands were scented with lilac. She stooped to tear off the shoes that shielded her feet from the magical earth. In another moment she would have been free.

But in that moment came a sound which filled the quivering soul of Mrs Jones with horror; the fairy tinkle of a bicycle bell, and afterwards of footsteps approaching down the path where she stood hidden, her overshoes in her hand. She straightened herself instantly and stepped aside into the enveloping darkness, alive no longer to the night, scandalously aware that she was Mrs Jones of Ostcott, about to be discovered roaming at a preposterous hour in her own woods, and, but for the intervention of Providence, barefoot. She caught her breath; the footsteps came nearer. Before she needed to breathe again they had gone past her, and the man went tramping straight on across the open space. The sound of his steps died away in the opposite wood; only his footprints remained, dull upon the shining grass, and the thin sinuous track of the wheels beside them.

Mrs Jones put on her goloshes, and went quickly back by the way she had come, her heart thumping; confusedly thinking, amid the whispering mockery of the trees, 'He didn't see me. I believe I should have died—Thank God, nobody will know. Thank God!'

She ran the last fifty yards towards the house, and greeted its grave serenity, its twinkling windows, with a sob of relief. She let herself into the hall, and stood, while her heart's furious beating was quieted. Here was silence other than the treacherous silence of the wood, that had dismayed her with its dreadful rending of the decencies and proprieties of life. Here was safety from those half-ecstatic memories, and from the mad freakishness of nature. This was a kindly shelter made by hands, mellowed by living, a refuge, a place

7 Good Company

A friend of mine, Elizabeth, told me this.

It happened in Italy, where in a vague roving sort of way, she was spending the spring. She is a person who loves to be out of her own country. She will not go to good hotels. She deliberately chooses when she visits any place to be as uncomfortable as it can make her, and to disregard its more obvious treasures; this is because the treasures attract tourists, and the good hotels seek to accommodate them in large numbers. Elizabeth despises and hates other English-speaking persons who travel. They spoil canals for her, and pictures, and breast-shaped domes heaved up above a rabble of chimneys; they mar narrow streets with their neat inappropriate figures. Avoiding them, Elizabeth has come to know the odd corners of a good many countries. This is how she found herself, towards the end of the month of April, in Calabria, walking.

She went towards the little town simply because she liked the look of it on the map. She told me its name, but the unfamiliar syllables have slipped away from me, and I remember only that it was built where four hill-ranges met in the shape of a bird's claw; they ran, she said, west and west by south, with a shorter spur pointing due east, and the town standing on the top where they all came together.

She set out early in the morning from the station where the train had left her overnight, and a man driving a water-cart put her on the right road, which proved to be flat, straight and unshaded, an uncompromising Roman road such as impressionable walkers learn to dread. But she accepted it at its face value as the shortest way to her destination and stepped out upon it briskly. She had walked some twelve kilometres when the high sun forced her to halt, and her map showed that this was no more than half the journey. The hills facing her were tall, their shadows thrown eastward must early darken the valley. She understood that she must make haste, rose to her feet again, and found an easy but quicker stride. Soon the road began to climb, tacking left and right across the rising ground, with perpendicular mule-tracks creeping out of it like tributaries. Elizabeth distrusted short cuts and kept to the main way, which went looping on, very slowly rising till it reached a broad ledge of rock from which she could see the remaining couple of miles running diagonally, straight to the topmost point where the town was, with the tiny sharp angles of its roofs silhouetted, and the belfry of its church.

With the goal in sight she went on more strongly, refreshed by a wind that had risen and was blowing down from the summits. It brought with it the sound of bells rung madly, not in organised peals, but frantically clashing together. Sometimes a single bell would make itself heard for a moment alone, and then down would swing the others in full cry after it. A feast-day, Elizabeth thought, and thought too that this might be the reason why the road was so deserted. At this hour it should have carried muleteers and men with laden donkeys going home from the fields; but it was empty. The rare houses were silent, and when they joined on either side to form a street, still there were no signs of life, so that she might have thought the town deserted but for the lights, and a tethered mule or two, and the yelling bells.

The street mounted steeply towards the church, near which the lights seemed to be gathered. Elizabeth had been climbing for the last hour, and she was tired. She sat down to rest for a little on the steps of a house, idly looking about her. Directly opposite, an alley ran into the street, and along it she could see a group of men advancing. They kept close together. One of them, a young and fattish man, was carrying what seemed to be a huge doll draped in white. This he set down in a doorway just by the corner, and wiped his face. The other men stopped, and stood crowding about the doll in the narrow mouth of the alley, taking care, Elizabeth thought, not to allow themselves to be seen from the street by any person ascending or descending. They were marshalled by two priests, who talked together in whispers that sounded angry, or from time to time peered round the angle of the building which sheltered them, looking up always towards the church. The men were restless; they moved incessantly, but did not talk much, or smoke. They looked at each other with gleaming naughty eyes, like children in hiding, waiting for the seekers.

Quite suddenly the bells stopped. As though this had been some signal the men broke into a gust of talk, immediately silenced by one of the priests, who advanced to the viewpoint at the corner, holding up his hand. Abruptly he withdrew, and Elizabeth heard him say as he turned, 'Vengono.'

She looked up as he had done, and saw that a light was beginning to glow and tremble against the white walls of the farthest houses. It increased until they were altogether reddened, save for the black slots of shadow marking windows and doors, so gradually, so calmly, that when the first of the torches came in sight she felt as though the little naked lights had pricked her eyes. Their bearers came together by groups of two or three until perhaps twenty were gathered; they stood in a bunch, hesitated, and then began to descend the hill, tossing the flames high, and searching every crevice with their light. A procession followed, a great number of women walking about a gilded chair that was carried on men's shoulders. The shape of a cross shone once, and disappeared as the torches swayed. She narrowed her eyes against the light, and so made out a figure dressed or painted in gold, sitting stiffly upright in the chair, with a gilded flower or twig held unnaturally, as though it were tied in its hand. A feast day, of course, she thought, and this is the patron saint. But the silence disconcerted her, the odd silence that advanced with the women and took no account of the inarticulate noise of their footsteps. In the alley the men too were silent; nobody moved. Elizabeth returned her attention to the women, following patiently behind the restless questing torches, which by this time were abreast of the hidden men. A moment later the light discovered them. There was a shout. The torches yielded, forming a double fiery line through which the seated figure pushed on until it came in sight of that other figure, recoiled as though in an ecstasy of joy, then went swiftly forward till the two were face to face. The chair-bearers lowered their poles so that a child reaching up to the draperies of the saint might pull apart the thick folds, and from between the carved breasts two birds flew out, to hover above the lights making faint sounds of amazement and dismay before they mounted into the darkness. Everyone watched them, and when they could no longer be seen, one of the priests started to sing, very loudly and roughly, in order to be heard above the voices. The men took it up and sang a verse, preoccupied with lighting their candles, a dozen matches flaring blue at once. Elizabeth could hear the words of the hymn quite plainly as they passed her.

> Terraemotum, pestem, bellum,
> Procul pelle, et flagellum
> Appropinquet civitatis
> Quae tuae fidit pietatis.

The tune paused and leapt forward to where the women were standing; it became thinner, more vague; she could only catch a word here and there:

... o virgo gloriosa
... laudens ...
... audi vota ...

While they sang, they began to walk up the hill again, and the men with the two images followed.

Elizabeth was delighted. She was filled with selfish joy because she was alone, the only strange witness of their childish but impressive rite. In the hope that there might be more to follow, she rose from her doorstep—rather stiffly, for the warmth of the long climb had gone out of her—and went after the procession, walking to the quick rhythm of the hymn. By the time she reached the top of the hill half the people were already inside the church, whose great west arch was wide enough to admit the marchers in their ranks of four. The church gathered the voices and lent them sonority, so that when the men had crowded in and took up their verse in turn the sound was terrifying, and the candle flames on the altar could be seen training this way and that as though to escape. There was no seat for Elizabeth, or for anyone else, not even a straw-bottomed chair. Most of the women knelt on the floor, while the men stood or leant against the walls. Elizabeth took her pack from her shoulders, mounted it, and from that elevation, the pillar solid at her back, she was able to watch the doings of the priests and ignore the curiosity of her neighbours.

Three of the priests were kneeling before the altar, motionless for once, so that the blood-red brocade of their copes was piled on the steps in stiff folds like stuff in a picture. He in the centre was reading from a card which the others held for him, fluently and loudly, all on one note; occasionally his voice dropped a semitone, and then his assistants would quickly slip in an Amen, which at once set him off again.

Elizabeth could not hear. She was interested, but tired; moreover, though she kept her eyes above their level, she was conscious that the men were finding her worthy of attention. She examined the smiling, gesturing saints in their niches, the little bunches of lights before each, the flattish Romanesque arches. When at last, her exploration finished, she glanced at the altar, the reading priest had ascended the steps and was holding out towards the people a little square gold box, rough with gems. He displayed this, set it on the altar, knelt, and called three times in a voice which exacted response, '*Sancta Canidia!*'

To which all the kneeling, standing, suddenly attentive congregation answered, '*Ora pro nobis.*'

Only Elizabeth said nothing, not because she disapproved, but because she was feeling ill; or perhaps not ill, but completely tired and indifferent and weak. And she could not take her eyes from the gold box on the altar. She wanted to sit down, for she felt as if she must very soon faint. All the candles stooped towards her; she heard sounds that should have been meaningless, while her excellent common sense remembered with anxiety the heat of the noon road.

The priests paraded away with the gold box and hid it somewhere. Elizabeth found that she could move, and reminded herself how she had always heard that people could be hypnotised by staring at a shining object. She felt some relief, took up her pack and blundered away to the door. Just outside the church she came to a halt, with a white wrinkled face of disgust and fear; the people coming out found her standing, looking down at one of the torches, thrown on the ground still smoking. By good fortune the first woman to reach her was the landlady of the inn, who led her away and paid no attention to the voice that said, a dozen times over in English, 'My God, the stench! What is it?'

The landlady put her to bed, and gave her some warmish nasty liquor to take, which cleared her head so that she found her Italian and was able to explain about the sunstroke. The landlady was sympathetic. Elizabeth asked her about the saint in the gold chair.

'Ah, the saint,' said the landlady, nodding in a very expressive way, 'she has enough to do, getting the people of this town to live like Christians. It would puzzle the good Jesus himself. It is too much for one woman alone.'

'Who was she?' Elizabeth asked.

'She was of this country,' said the landlady proudly, 'and a great prince from Rome married her. All the girls in these parts are pretty; good-for-nothing too, but a lot the men care for that. Not that I grudge them. I like to see them happy while they're young; it doesn't last long.'

But Elizabeth wanted to find out about the saint.

'Oh, yes, she lived here,' the landlady went on, 'before she was married, if you can call it married. She ran away on her wedding night, and never slept with her husband at all; he was a pagan, so she's not to be blamed. Ah, she had spirit, like all these girls. So ran she away into the desert, one of these deserts near Rome that was full of Christians like herself; but the soldiers came after her, and took her away to be martyred. Virgin and martyr, she was.'

She described at unnecessary length the torments which the saint had endured, and her final throes.

'And what does the ceremony mean?' Elizabeth persisted.

'The statues meeting?'

Apparently it meant the saint's search for Christ in the desert, and her triumphant ascension with him into heaven.

'And the birds?'

The landlady did not know. They were pretty. They always hung like that for a moment above the lights; according to the direction in which they flew away the faithful might make a guess at the weather that was likely to prevail during the ensuing year.

Ordinarily Elizabeth would have triumphed, thinking with disdain of the tourists with their Easter week ceremonies and the sophisticated pageants of Rome. To-night, however, she could not triumph. She was too busily explaining to herself more personal things, attempting to reason away that horror which had overtaken her outside the church, when the smell of the burning resin, which hitherto she had savoured with pleasure, had seemed to her nostrils bitter and threatening. Her common sense was baffled. She was apprehensive, aware of something approaching, unhurried, to which her common sense could oppose no barrier, and which rejected all sensible explanations such as sun, and fatigue, and the crowded air of the church.

When the landlady left her, Elizabeth lay awake above the cheerful noises of cooking and drinking, quietly, in the dark. The noises grew less, were finally still. A patch of moonlight climbed onto the bed, and began to creep across it, making icy valleys and dark crests on the coverlet, beneath which her limbs lay at ease. As she watched it, Elizabeth had a pang of fear; hesitated; was sure. She sat up with a quick start that convulsed and re-shaped the moonlit ranges, and said aloud, 'Who are you? What do you want?'

She heard the answer, and felt suddenly like a person drowning, sinking quick into unimagined space. She was herself, but dwindled to a speck, a mere pin-point of consciousness about which great shining worlds revolved, alone, and naked to the suns that flared above her. The strong light was terrifying, unbearable. She thought to escape from it by abandoning herself to the darkness that lay somewhere below, and began, of her own will, to fall. The suns rushed upwards from her, trailing their fires; they circled above her like coloured birds, wheeling as they swung to and fro in their orbits. They grew smaller and vanished; the clear torturing light remained. She felt herself screaming soundlessly, powerless to trouble the luminous infinite silences that gathered round her as she fell.

The terror withdrew, or rather she twisted away from it as a diver turns his hands to the surface and comes slowly up through the yielding pressure of water. She lay face downwards on the bed, her mouth writhed open, feeling her heart thud against the mattress. After a time she had breath to think of other matters, and to remember moments of fear, of insistence, of acquiescence, of possession. Vaguely understanding the impossible thing that had happened, she fell asleep at last as from a high tower and did not wake until the day noises were in full swing about the house.

She had planned to stay in this place for a day or two, but now that was out of the question. The landlady, to whom strangers were like manna, did what she could to scare her guest, reminding her of last night's seizure, and declaring that only a mad person would choose to walk who might, for a nothing or so, sit all day under an ample pergola of vines. Elizabeth was firm, and in the end was allowed to go, with the landlady watching under her hand from the door.

It was a pleasant morning into which she stepped, no longer alone; and since the hills fan high she was conscious of the air standing cold about her. Further hills lay ahead, the lower slopes of them misted, so that they seemed to be floating. To Elizabeth's mind, which since waking had shrunk from any contemplation of the future, came the thought that perhaps, since she had to go through with it, it might not be so bad. She had been surprised out of her ordinary prudence. She knew neither what to expect nor what to fear.

She began to consider the whole thing in the impartial manner made possible by movement and the morning light. She knew, in some inexplicable way, that she was possessed, and by whom; but she did not understand the terms of agreement. She supposed that it would be made clear to her as they went along, two persons crowded into one body, drawing as they walked great breaths of high sweet air. There was the question of communication, too; but this began, almost immediately, to answer itself.

The saint had something to tell, evidently. During the hours of marching she assailed Elizabeth with words and fragments of Latin, passionately explaining something; but Elizabeth was familiar only with the dog-Latin of the Church, and this dead lion of a tongue baffled her. Still, there was a friendly intention in those phrases she could understand, and the saint, aware of her difficulty, was beginning to shift into another medium, the coarse Italian of the south, when they came unexpectedly upon a village that clung like lichen about their downward sloping road. It was a poor place, but it afforded wine and bread which they ate gladly, and afterwards climbed to the church which stood a little apart from the houses, not from motives of curiosity or piety, but simply because it was sure to be cool inside. The priest was there, taking down the crucifix from above the tabernacle, and preparing for the Friday evening Benediction. He was happy to see a stranger, and at once came forward to talk. He showed his treasures, a fragment from the cross of the Good Thief set in a round crystal reliquary; an old silver censer with the beasts of the Apocalypse twisting upon it, cut so that the smoke must come pouring from their mouths and nostrils; finally, two bones of Saint Apollodonis himself, to whom the church was dedicated. He told the history of the saint, from his conversion as a young officer of the Twentieth Legion—the

'Victorious Valerian'—to his death in the arena; spoke with awe of his patron's steadfastness and with confidence of his influence in Heaven. As the anecdotes succeeded each other, Elizabeth began to feel tears prickling her eyes. They were not her own tears; she was prepared to consider Saint Apollodonis with reverence, but without emotion, and the impulse surprised her. She resisted, but that other will was too strong for her, and the puppet they shared began to jerk with inexplicable sobs that relieved an inner burning feeling of shame. The surprise of the priest was very evident; he was too experienced to suppose that such sensibility could be due to any but physical causes, and made the hysterical Elizabeth sit down while he fetched a glass of water from the sacristy. She obeyed him without protest; that part of her mind which remained her own property at once set to work to scold her for the imbecility she had displayed on the previous night; not to have insisted, not to have bargained, not to have realised the immense advantage which had been hers, that working dependable body which she had abdicated. She was too angry with herself and too much ashamed of the tears to enquire their reason.

When she had drunk the water the priest made her lie down on the flat top of a stone tomb that stood at the west end of the church, and left her to make his own siesta. She would have been glad to sleep, but Canidia was restless; she began to murmur, and to invade Elizabeth's consciousness with disconnected phrases; the word fire came very often. Elizabeth could not understand it, for the martyrdom had been stated by the landlady in terms of wild horses. And there was that feeling of sinking, of utter abasement; strange sensations to come, second-hand, from the eternity of the blessed. She wondered if the saint had known Saint Apollodonis, and why she had elected to come wandering out of her parish in the body of a perfect stranger. A verse of the hymn came to her mind, something about the lilies and roses of Paradise that were the virgin martyr's crown:

> Nunc te lilis, nunc te rosis
> Sponsus ornat odorosis.

She could not remember it all, and while she was searching for the words that had escaped her the saint, with a gesture like the outflung hand of a man in agony, struck their minds apart. There was no more to be done; she would not respond. Elizabeth went out of the church and towards the road again. They walked on, dissociate, and held no other communication during the afternoon journey.

The village to which they came just after sundown had a sea smell in its air, and by the map the Adriatic was not far away, due east. Looking from her window in the morning Elizabeth could see a blue distant line, and was glad, for she loved the sea. As she stepped out on the road striped with long early shadows, going towards it, she was happy.

But the road was long. After an hour of delicate air, the coolness withdrew; the road became hot, unshaded, and straight, and as the day drew towards noon, and there appeared no place in which she could possibly rest, Elizabeth began to be impatient. A dozen miracles occurred to her memory, practical miracles such as fill the Golden Legend; springs of water, cooling showers, the scent of unearthly roses—little tender gifts from God to his chosen. What use was a saint, she thought, who could not command such graces? And again she wondered why Canidia had quitted her tall church to come tramping in the heat. The other disregarded these hints and queries; no streams appeared; but, as though it had been spoken at her ear, Elizabeth heard a sentence.

'I have been exalted on men's shoulders; now I sink low, that God may be tempted to raise me.'

And then two fragments—'No crown yet,' and 'The same journey'.

Elizabeth could make nothing of it; for how can a saint be raised, unless it be to some other heaven? And what need could there be, after so triumphant a death, for further humility? As for the crown, it was fantastic to suppose that the saint was no saint at all. And yet the word fire remained without explanation, and the tears in church, and indeed the whole pilgrimage. Elizabeth listened, hoping to hear more. Nothing came, and she walked on, distracted by guesses and elusive improbable truths, through the throbbing day.

The road was straight now as the pike of a legionary, the sort of road that could only lead to Rome; it stood up before her to the horizon and dipped to the horizon behind her. A quarter of a mile away, to the left, she could see a clump of trees and men working, moving about in the shadow; so oppressed was she by the interminable promise of the road that she had deliberately renounced all her walking principles, quitted the direct way, and made for the wood.

The men greeted her without surprise. There were two of them engaged in stripping leaves from the young trees and cramming them into bags to serve as fodder. Along the branches of the trees vines grew, which had been grafted on to the trunks, and the men as they packed the leaves away took care that the clusters of young grapes should be laid open to the sun. They said, civilly, that she was welcome to sit in the shade, and took no further notice of her. They looked decent, elderly men. She wondered if it would be safe to sleep, and while she sat thinking, propped against a tree with her pack making a cushion behind her, the decision made itself. Sleep tempted her, lay before her as a depth, a cool chasm; she could feel in imagination the quiet tides advancing in which herself with that other petulant half-self might sink and for a time be one. She allowed the tides to approach until she could feel the light spray, the wind; told herself that she must be careful; and was out of her depth before she knew. She woke to find the pack missing and the men gone.

At first she did not understand. She thought that she had made a mistake, and that the pack had never been at her back but beside her, behind the tree, somewhere else. She did not want to admit that she knew it had been taken for fear of the panic which would come upon her. She searched the vineyard tree by tree, and was rewarded by finding the pack itself cast aside, gaping, and holding only two crumpled handkerchiefs. Stockings gone, shoes, the rest of her money, the map, gone all of them. Her passport she always carried in the breast pocket of her coat. That was safe, and a comb, and a couple of lire, and a little notebook in which she was always meaning to write her impressions. These were all that remained.

Elizabeth had never contemplated anything like this. She was accustomed to use her money frugally, but it was always there, or some means of getting at it, and she had never before been stranded so far from headquarters. She had nothing about her that could be turned into cash, not even a wristwatch. She despised walkers who wore stealable things, and considered that they were asking for trouble; she had not bargained for trouble which comes unasked. She approached the saint for advice, but Canidia was distant, unwilling to be disturbed, and remained tranquilly meditating in the very middle of Elizabeth's own mind, like the blind spot of calm at a tornado's centre. Elizabeth quitted the hope of her intervention with a shrug and began angrily to make plans.

She trifled for a time with the idea of following the thieves and demanding the return of her possessions. This, however, could hardly take rank as a plan. It was a wish, the momentary solace which she permitted to her outraged self-confidence. After she had allowed moral force to prevail, and had looked with her mind's eye, a stern one, upon the humiliation of the thieves, she returned to her practical self. This country was wild, of which her despoilers were natives; they would probably find it a very simple matter, if she made a fuss, to despatch her in spite of her passport and her nationality; and in the diplomatic incident which might ensue she could have no interest. She abandoned the hope of restitution in its turn and began to consider her real course of action.

As bad as the loss of the money was the loss of the map. She had not bothered when she had it to memorize the names or positions of the larger towns where she might hope to find help; a consul perhaps, or a compatriot. The village to which this unfortunate road was leading was so small that probably it was without a post office. Even if it had an office, there was the question of how she was to live, after she had bought paper and a stamp with her two lire and before the return letter could come. Bluff, Elizabeth thought. I'm English, they will believe me. If I stuff my pack with leaves and roll my mackintosh over the top they will never find out. How long would that letter take? Five days, six? Say a week; a week spent hanging about a place of which I know nothing, and which may be uninhabitable, for no apparent reason and with nothing to do. If it takes longer, and they ask for ready money—But she would not allow herself to dwell on that.

She strode on, contemplating ways and means, and when next she looked at the road with seeing eyes a village was beginning to gather in its sluttish southern way on either side; high, but with the sea so close below that she might have flicked a pebble into it from where she stood. The sea was very smooth, but further out, where the sun caught it, a patch of silver shivered and danced. No breath of that faint distant wind reached her.

It was a beautiful village where blue and green nets hung

drying between poles; a mere lovely desert, since it had no post office.

'But I can buy a stamp and send a letter?' Elizabeth asked.

Certainly she could do that, or at least she could give the money to a youth who undertook such commissions, and who walked twice a week to the town farther along the coast to fetch letters and carry them. In the old days, before there was so many letters, they had used pigeons as messengers; that was long ago, before the government had begun to interfere.

'How far away is this town?' she asked hopefully.

It was thirty kilometres off. The boy walked there in a day, stayed twelve hours, and came home the day after. She gathered that in addition to the money for the stamp it was customary to give him a lira for his trouble. Elizabeth wrote the letter to her bank under the eyes of half a dozen persons who had gathered to help and advise, and began her career of bluff by giving the boy her two lire. The envelope was received with reverence and borne away, after she had exacted from him a kind of receipt; and she settled down, rather grimly, to a week's waiting.

At home in England she was accustomed to say that one could get on perfectly well without money in any country if one knew the language. It was one of those things that are said. And now she discovered, when at last her statement was put to the proof, that it was nearly a pure lie. At each minute of the day little expenses cropped up, extra-mural, outside that wall of credit which stood between Elizabeth and hunger. There were cigarettes; there were beggars; and odd civilities such as bottles of wine which seemed to be expected here and there. Her nationality, while it maintained her richly in the unsavoury best room above the wine-shop, brought with it expectations and responsibilities which she was not prepared to satisfy or to accept. She was the wealthy and eccentric foreigner. She was nobility obliged to keep up the illusion of prodigality and disdain. And all the time she had not one centesimo, actual cash, in her possession; her pack bulged with dying leaves; and she was completely uncertain when, or if, her release was coming. She was reminded of those endless centuries during which Canidia had sat lifted above the crowd in her golden chair, clamourously petitioned; powerless perhaps; sitting there like a starving man in King's robes. She began to suspect the irony of that recurring ceremony with its chanted praises.

For five days Elizabeth dwelt in outward splendour above the wine-shop, with all her thoughts running ahead to the day when the answer to her letter should come. She was preoccupied by this expectation to such a degree that on the morning of the fifth day she forgot her knapsack. As a rule she carried it with her everywhere, never once losing sight of it, but on this day, when it had become humanly possible that her answer might arrive before night, she was negligent. She walked out of her room and downstairs into the sun, leaving the pack where it had lain all night, beside her pillow. She went along the beach, a walk made vivid by the hope that when she got home something might have happened. The sun lay warm on her shoulders, tempered by a breeze not too impetuous. The saint held apart, so that Elizabeth had her mind to herself. She wondered, as she walked slowly along kicking at the sand, how long the saint proposed to remain with her, and whether it would be possible to have her in England. She had, on the whole, behaved with restraint, during these past days especially. She seemed to have out-worn the exuberance which at first had been distressing, and in spite of her confused confession and deliberate search for occasions of humility, Elizabeth felt that the loss of the money could not have been her fault. That thought recalled the pack, and Elizabeth's mind, which had been a wide expanse upon which images, towering cities and hills, were pictured, instantly narrowed to a single anxiety. She had been walking for over an hour, she could not return in time to forestall the woman who tidied her room; the secret was out. She walked on, trying to find consolation in the hope of the letter which was to make human relationships simple again.

When she returned to the village the woman spied her and met her at the door with a certain relief, for after all, so far as the woman knew, there was nothing to prevent Elizabeth from walking away into the outer world, leaving her hosts to regret their simple faith in her. Elizabeth walked up to the door bravely enough, with a beating heart, and made some civil remark to the woman, who answered civilly, but with a question in her eye. She turned as Elizabeth went towards the stairs, and the question found words.

Would it be convenient, the woman asked, for the lady to pay something? It was almost a week since she had come. There was a carrier going into the town next day to bring provisions, and he had to have ready money, naturally; they needed a good many things, things for the guest to eat. The woman was polite, for it was still possible that the foreign lady had a pocket full of hundred lira notes, and madly carried leaves instead of ordinary clothing about with her in a capricious search for some paradise lost. But as soon as she met Elizabeth's eye, she knew that this was not the case. She knew just what Elizabeth would say.

'I'm afraid I haven't enough money with me. I'm expecting some in a letter from Rome. It will come soon—to-day, perhaps.'

'A letter?' said the woman, rather less politely. She knew nothing about that. Could the lady let her have something to go on with? The lady had been given the best of everything, and the best cost money. Something—twenty lire—to go on with?

'I'll see,' said Elizabeth feeling in her breast pocket. There was nothing in it except the passport, but that had gilded lions and crowns on it, and looked rich and bulky. She pulled it out and affected to search its folds, and even to turn over imaginary notes of small worth. She put it back.

'I'm afraid I can't manage,' she said, 'I must wait for my letter. I'm sorry to inconvenience you.'

The woman dropped her previous manner like a cloak that suddenly grows too hot, and answered, certainly that it was a pity. And a pity, too, that ladies should go wandering by themselves without any money, because honest people expected to be paid for what they did, and didn't take it as a favour when ladies came and ate their food, and then said, to-morrow, to-morrow, and talked about letters from Rome. Other people could talk, and talk about magistrates if it came to that, and the law, which was always ready to protect honest people against cheating foreigners.

Elizabeth began to be angry.

'I have told you that I have no intention of cheating you. My money was robbed from me on my way to this place. I have sent for more, which possibly may arrive to-day. Be good enough to tell me when the messenger arrives.'

The woman replied with decision that she would do so by all means, and withdrew. She had been a little awed by Elizabeth's manner, which was that of the mistress of an English household. Elizabeth went upstairs in a leisurely way, and even when she saw that the woman's husband had come in and was listening, she did not hurry, though her heart went faster. She climbed to her room and lay down on the bed, admitting to herself that the husband frightened her. He had come home two days before on leave, and still wore his uniform, the dull greenish grey of a sergeant of infantry. He altered the feeling of the place. He made Elizabeth self-conscious, sex-conscious. When, standing in a group of men, he turned his head slowly to look at her, she hated him, though there was no insolence in his eyes. When he poured her wine for her at meals, he did it deliberately, taking his time and looking at her, while she watched his hands, covered thickly with hairs except where there were small square clearings for the knuckles. Slimy, she called him, and with that word was continually shaking him from her mind, but it was not the right word, as she knew very well. He was not greasy and fat, but strong and knotted like a tree. She thought of him as slimy because that was the sort of man she disliked, and she wanted to dislike this man.

A single knock came at the door.

'What is it?' she asked rather shrilly.

There was no immediate answer. She got off her bed and went to the door in her stockinged feet to ask again, 'What is it? Who's there?'

When she heard him say 'the messenger' she forgot her terrors and opened the door at once; but he had nothing in his hand.

'Has my letter come?' she asked with confidence, for it seemed incredible that she should be left any longer without power to leave this house and its perplexities.

He shook his head, staring down at her feet.

'Nothing at all?' She persisted, 'Are you sure? Can I see the messenger?'

He was sure; the boy was gone. There was nothing for the lady.

Elizabeth pulled herself together, smiled to prevent the corners of her mouth from going down, and prepared to withdraw. But he kept his hand on the frame of the door; if she shut it his hand would be crushed. She was obliged to wait while he spoke.

'The lady must not be upset. She is welcome here. Money for food, says my wife; as though the priest had to keep us, out of the box in the church. There is food enough, thank

God. In a few days the letter will come. The lady shall do as she pleases, whatever my wife may say.'

Elizabeth could only thank him and make a little movement as though she were about to shut the door. He disregarded this and stood facing her.

'There is no reason why the lady should have a thin pocket. We are Christians here. If we have enough, we share—'

He took a little bundle of notes out of the breast of his shirt and held them towards her.

'The lady can repay when her money comes.'

Elizabeth found her pride at this, and her courage. She answered stiffly, 'Thank you. I have no need to borrow. You are kind enough to allow me credit, and I shall, of course, repay you.'

And shut the door firmly, without caring if she caught his hand in it or not. She heard him turn away at once and go downstairs; then she sat once more on the bed and listened to the troubled questioning of her mind.

'Now what are you going to do?' she asked herself. 'Is this definite enough for you? Do you see what it's going to be like? It's the worst thing that has ever happened to me. It will be days before that money comes, and I'll have to keep him quiet. He wouldn't mind snubs. It's the worst possible ill-luck. Too humiliating.'

She thought of her companion, and at once her temper veered in that direction. 'You're no help. Ever since you came I've had nothing but disaster. Why don't you try to speak to me? What are you doing, hidden away where I can't get at you? I know you must be there, because I haven't room to think with the whole of my mind. I wonder if you have had anything to do with this?'

Suddenly she remembered that she might consult, and, if necessary, take refuge with the priest. It was a perfectly simple expedient which had not once, until now, entered her head. She laughed at herself, put on her shoes, and went out immediately, though it was getting dark, for she needed to be reassured. She knew where he lived, and went quickly along the road that ran inland, till she came to a kind of narrow lane which led up to the small white house. The house was very small indeed; clearly it would be impossible for the priest to take her in, and she must be content with moral support; so she told herself as she knocked at the closed door. There was no answer, and no answer still after she had knocked half a dozen times. The front door, the side door, all the shutters were closed, and would not yield. She turned away, depressed but not hopeless, thinking that she might return in the morning with a note, and secure in the knowledge that she was not altogether cut off from help.

The man was standing by the door when she reached her lodgings; she was no longer afraid of him and said carelessly, 'I walked to the priest's house.'

He looked at her, smiled, and answered, fingering the metal figures, the two and nought on his high uniform collar, 'The priest is not there.'

'No,' Elizabeth said, 'I found it shut. I suppose he's at the church.'

'The priest has gone away—'

'That's not true,' she said, before she could stop herself. The man smiled and continued as if she had not spoken, '—to a meeting at the Bishop's house in the town. Crocifissa, that looks after him, has gone home for a week. They won't be back till Saturday.'

'Oh,' said Elizabeth, recovering a little, 'what a pity.'

'Yes,' the man agreed, quite seriously, 'no one can make his confession this week.'

Then, with a movement that seemed sudden because it was unexpected, not because it was quick, he put one of his dark hands on top of Elizabeth's narrow smooth hand that held her stick. She was horrified because the touch did not shock her, so angry with herself that she forgot her dignity and hit out with her right hand as hard as she could. He drew back his head and her knuckles grazed his chin. They stood in the half-darkness, but Elizabeth saw herself very clearly striking that ineffectual blow, weakness trying to meet strength on its own ground. She was ashamed because she had behaved like the sort of woman he was accustomed to, and this lent a sharpness to her voice when she said, 'Take your hand away at once.'

He obeyed her, and as she went into the house she thought she could hear him laughing. That laughter made her twist and crush her hands together like a woman in physical pain. She would not go downstairs to eat anything. She sat motionless on the bed, looking at her knuckles that the stiff hairs on his chin had made bleed, and trying to find a way out.

In the middle of the night she woke, for no reason; she was used to the thud and wash of the sea outside her window. The house was quiet, but only for the moment. She knew that there had been movement, which now was still.

She listened, her heart quickening, and hoped that the wedge of wood which served to fasten her door would hold. Soon there was a sound outside the door, a crack such as the bones of a foot will make when the foot is lifted from the floor and pressure on it ceases. She heard that, and afterwards the creak of the latch, followed by a tiny shifting noise as though the wedge had given a little before it gripped again. After that came a very frightening silence which seemed endless, until at last the crack of the lifted foot sounded farther away.

Elizabeth lay down flat again—she had been straining up with her hands on either side, propping her—and whispered 'Thank God'. But when she had done this lip-service to the proprieties other thoughts came. She found herself wondering what would have happened if the wedge had not held; what would she have done when she felt those hands on her. She knew that she might have lain there in silence and allowed things—different things, that belonged to the breathing night outside, and the sea smell, and the youth of her body.

'Oh, God,' said Elizabeth aloud, with quite another intonation, and turned on her side, with her right hand under her cheek and the left clenched against her mouth. She struck her mouth once, very gently, to punish it, then twice, very hard; then again became gentle and let the hand go to gather the bedclothes up to her breast. She lay there with open eyes all night.

In the morning it was difficult not to betray when she saw him that she knew the door had been tried; and the woman, who had a new bruise on her cheek, stared at her in a curious way. Elizabeth had a feeling as though something were closing in on her; something strange and quite new, which might be freedom. She shook herself like a dog, took her stick, and began to walk out of the village at a great pace. She might go on to some other place, anywhere, and tell her story, get money somehow, borrow it, and so find her way back to Rome without setting foot again in that cage of a village. She knew that it was only necessary to have a little courage in order to carry this plan through. She walked on in the heat, planning, almost determined, while her innermost self noted the passing of the miles and told her that it was not too late to go back.

Her new resolve had really no chance. There were reasons innumerable against it, besides something which Elizabeth could not recognise and would not admit, but which lay deep within her and was powerful. She gave battle, and was defeated after she had gone almost too far to retreat, so that it was quite dark when she found herself back on the beach road at last, and quiet except for the sea. Suddenly she was unwilling to enter the waiting house, and sat down on the sand to be alone for a while with the soft perpetual sound, watching the faint arcs and sinuous lines of the waves outlined in phosphorescent light; the wash of ripples on the shore was like the translation of that light into sound. She was tired enough to be soothed by it, and to find pleasure in the eternal re-shaping of the patterns, the unvarying hush of the poised water breaking and withdrawing. There was no moon. The stars burned, not with the frosty twinkle of an English sky, but steadily. In an unreasoning way Elizabeth pictured Heaven lying beyond those glowing sentinels at a frightful altitude, and supposed that it would be desirable to know it one day. This aspiration was mere sentiment, towards which the sounds and shadows of the night had contrived to lure her mind; she was laughing at herself, when she found her mind overtaken by a tumult, a furious shudder of longing that rose in her like a flame, and said aloud, wondering and sorry, 'Is it like that? Do you want it so much?'

When it was over she got up, aware that it was late, and that she must go indoors to bed.

The only lighted windows in the village were those of her lodging. As she approached them she halted. Voices, snarling, ugly, were loosed inside, and she could hear, but not understand, all the words that were flung like clots of spittle between the man and woman. The sounds came from a room on the left of the open door; she might have gone past it and upstairs. Instead she went towards it, and looked in.

The woman stood by a table, her hands clutching her breasts, her head forward, yelping at the man, who regarded her sullenly, backed against the stove. There was wine on the table and a litter of dirty plates; no movement in the room, only noise. Almost at once this ceased; they had seen her. The woman looked away, after one glance like a thrust; the man's eyes rested on Elizabeth with an expression that was not insolent because it was so sure. The woman screamed some challenge; he withdrew his eyes, and gave an abrupt laugh and caught up something from the table. For a second a thin line of light showed, lying along his palm, before the hand shot forward with the fingers doubled to the shape of a snake's head when it strikes. Elizabeth knew what came next; the sound of a whimper and a fall; afterwards footsteps advancing, a face half-lit, and her terrified eyes staring, as though it mattered, at a number written in metal, the same number but differently wrought, two X's together; she knew that she screamed and pushed with the flat of her hands at a strength which disregarded her and by which she wished to be conquered. Something in her failed, something else laughed and was triumphant; then darkness, and yielding. Elizabeth knew with nightmare certainty that it must happen and how each step of it must go, but she fought desperately while she waited for the two sounds that were to be the beginning of the end. Her will rode shouting against the invading desire, and fell back; tradition was as easily overthrown. In her despair she found means to loose the hold which she had kept upon her mind, let pride go, and began the soundless, endless dwindling fall with naked suns about and within her that she knew now was prayer. Even in the abyss of light she waited for the two sounds.

They did not come. Slowly, as her soul ran murmuring back into its house, she became aware that something had happened to check the inevitable. Holding to the sides of the door she opened her eyes and looked.

The two stood as before, but as though they were posing, one with a hand stretched out in the act of throwing, the other with a hand held stiffly across her body to guard it. Both stared down at the floor, where lay a twig of olive that had gently touched the ribs of the woman and dropped at her feet.

'But,' I said when Elizabeth came to this point in her story, 'I don't understand.'

She went on, paying no attention.

'And next morning the whole population of the village went off to church to give thanks for the miracle. There was a statue there, quite black, all pierced with swords, that everyone thought had done it. The man wanted to give it a silver-gilt olive branch, but they couldn't find anything except a brooch shaped like a fern. He thought that was good enough, and put it on the statue's cloak. Afterwards, when they all came back, he gave me my money.'

'Had it come, then, after all?'

'Yes, and he'd been keeping it. So I was able to get away.'

'Your poor saint,' I said, 'she must have felt rather out of it.'

'I don't know,' Elizabeth answered, 'She'd gone. It was her miracle, of course. She'd got into heaven.'

'Wasn't she a saint at all, then?' I asked.

'Officially she was; they couldn't allow the Church to seem to be in the wrong. But actually, no. That's where the fire comes in. Purgatory. She wanted, you see—she let him— And she hated being martyred.'

'But why should they canonize him, too?'

'I suppose he got converted afterwards. My man did. I don't know. It's the way these things seem to go.'

'It all sounds very real,' I said, to please her.

'It was real,' Elizabeth answered; but her voice tilted it into a question.

8 A Curious Story

'Yes,' said the poet slowly, 'that's a very curious story.'

'Curious?' the author repeated, 'is that all? It's damnable. Why should it happen to me? I don't understand it. It's not as if I were one of these imaginative fellers. I don't drink, either.'

He pushed his glass away as though repudiating it; then, staring out of the window, fine brows drawn down and eyes fixed, he took it again and slowly, unconsciously, tilted it to his mouth. The whole gesture was magnificent; so might Tristan have looked out over the rim of the treacherous cup. This occurred to the poet, and amused him, but he knew the actor too well to smile. Instead he asked, 'What's to be done?'

'How should I know? I don't understand these things. Why to me? When I say I'm not imaginative, I don't mean to say I've no imagination. A man can't play my parts without it.'

'I know,' murmured the poet.

'What I mean, though,' the actor went on, searching painfully, after the manner of a man unaccustomed to finding his own words, 'what I mean is, I can imagine people; how they talk and move and look; give me the lines, and I'll tell you how such and such a man would say them. I don't understand how people feel, but I know how they show it. That's imagination, isn't it? Of a sort.' He spoke almost wistfully, and the poet nodded. 'I'm always watching, and remembering little things; tricks of the hands or the intonation of words. Then I make something out of all the things I've observed. That sounds like patchwork, but it hangs together, doesn't it?' Again the note of wistfulness, and again the poet nodded. 'But, of course, I'm practical. And I've got to keep my eyes open. Now-a-days a man who doesn't keep his eyes open in London—in a London theatre—is damned. Perpetually damned; and deserves it.'

'Yes, I understand all that,' said the poet, 'but come back to the problem.'

'That is the problem. Haven't you been listening? Here am I, a man of—talent, shall we say?'

'By all means.'

'Anyhow, a man of some ability in his profession. A practical man, too, as I said before; business man as well as artist. I'm healthy. I don't drink. I don't overdo myself in any way. I've a useful imagination—not your wandering kind. I apply it only to my work. It doesn't worry me. And yet in spite of all this I see things which are invisible to other people. That's the problem, isn't it?'

'I don't see how I can help,' the poet said, slowly.

'Well, you're used to these things. Look at that stuff of yours, full of fantastic happenings. You might be able to interpret.'

'Do you mean you want me to come and try to get into communication with her?' the poet asked, flattered by the reference to his work from a man who boasted that he read one book a year.

'That's it. Come and see for yourself. You're the sort of man—you might have more in common. She might answer you.'

'You've spoken to her?'

'I told you I had. Spoke to her—thought she must be one of my own people at first, in spite of the dress. Asked her what the hell she wanted; what she was doing hanging about outside my dressing room. Then she went away round the corner of the passage.'

'And it was there you noticed about the shadow?'

'It noticed itself. There's a big light, hung low just round the corner. There are corners and turnings everywhere, by the way. It's one of the older theatres. Well, this light throws a long shadow of anyone passing right into my room if the door's open, as it always is. But she went away, and—nothing.

Nothing at all. Gibbons thought I'd had too many, talking like that to somebody who wasn't there. It's annoying. I value Gibbons' opinion. That's why I didn't say a word the second time. She looked ill, too, poor little soul; her face was chalk-white. There were two moles just at the left corner of her mouth.'

The poet, who had lighted a pipe, sat for a moment in silence, gravely considering the clouding whorls of smoke; he was inclined to accept the challenge and put his principles to the test, for he held and proclaimed that the function of poetry was to tackle the problems of the man in the street. Moreover, this was something in his own line.

'What's the time?' the actor asked, breaking in upon his decisions.

'Close on seven.'

'Well, it's no use talking. Look here, will you come back with me now? I've got to go.'

'What about dinner?'

'I'll give you some sandwiches and a whisky and soda at the theatre.'

A little reluctantly, for he enjoyed his dinner, the poet agreed. They went out together and down the steps of the club, the actor walking easily, the poet's thin shoulders huddled together as the night wind came shrewdly. Both loved this October hour; but while to one it was a prelude only, to the other these gleaming corridors of the streets themselves made the song. They walked silently, their steps falling together, and when some eddy of traffic made them pause, the rhythm between them was unbroken; both were thinking of the woman who had lingered outside the actor's dressing-room two nights ago. The actor violently told himself that such things did not happen to normal people, and tried to believe that his nerves had tricked him. The poet pictured the woman, and heard already the distant voice which revealed the reason for her coming; he heard his own voice, too, splendidly talking.

They came soon to the theatre, whose dingy but impressive facade shone with the actor's name. It stood on the site of an historic house, whose original building had suffered the common fate of theatres, and had been burned to the ground less than a hundred years ago as the result of a daring experiment with gas lights. Nobody experimented now. The lighting and accommodation were modern enough, the plays were the plays of the moment. The public knew what to expect, was satisfied, and at times enthusiastic. Receipts were steady. It was a business-like, traditional, creditable house of public entertainment, to which its lessee came daily with a little stir of pride and a feeling of continuity, for Charles Makebody, his grandfather, had played here for a time in the late sixties. He loved his theatre, and was angry that to-night, instead of pride, a feeling of apprehension and distrust invaded him as he went in past the doorkeeper. The poet, for whom a theatre was still the mysterious temple of joy he had known as a child, followed eagerly, staring at the shirt-sleeved men, recognising in the tall silhouette which for a moment blocked a narrow doorway the actress who shared with Makebody the chief opportunities of their polite, intelligent plays. When at last they reached the dressing-room he was almost afraid to enter, so crowded did it seem, so disconcerting were the mirrors which reflected him from every angle. He looked about him, sitting awkwardly in a low chair, and no longer wondered at the grace of the actor's carriage, nor at the ordered perfection of his clothes.

'Do you find it stuffy?' the actor asked. 'People do sometimes. I'm used to it.'

'You're at home here,' said the poet, 'it's your setting.'

'It ought to be. I was born on the stage—well, in the wings, anyhow. And my people have known this house pretty well for the last hundred years or so.'

'So long!' said the poet, seeking in this an explanation of the perplexing matter of the woman.

'We're an old family, as stage families go. As any family goes. And we've got our tradition. We're better than half these little straddling squires without half an acre of land to their names. My great-grandmother played with Siddons once in *Venice Preserv'd*. And yet these mountebanks in the papers talk as though I were some kind of performing monkey.'

The poet laughed and suddenly looked away towards the door. The actor saw the direction of the glance and nodded.

'That's the place. Just outside.'

He slipped out of his coat, and said to the dresser who held it, 'Now we'll see. Thought I was off my head, didn't you?'

'Oh, no, Mr Makebody. But sometimes a gentleman gets these what I call notions.'

'Oh, no, Gibbons. I wasn't drunk, as you so politely hint. You've never known me drunk two nights running. We'll see what Mr Dering makes of it. He's used to such things. He knows how to deal with them.'

Gibbons looked doubtfully at the slight figure of the poet, uncomfortably huddled in his easy chair. The actor proceeded to his toilet, sitting full in the light before the dressing table. Gibbons stood behind, and the poet watched the man's thin fingers rubbing grease into cheeks and chin with a caressing circular movement. They were silent, all three; and suddenly the poet remembered how as a boy he had lain for an hour by a hedge, waiting for a shy swift bird to return to its nest in the leaves above him.

The face was prepared. Gibbons opened a wooden box and took up a hare's-foot from the table; the actor, gazing steadily at his own reflection, inclined his head so that the strong light fell upon his right cheek; Gibbons dipped the foot in brownish red powder and began to touch the lighted cheek with colour. The poet could see both faces in the glass and watched them there, a little distorted by the angle, idly watched, forgetting why he had come. But he was recalled by a gesture. Without any warning the actor put up his hand and caught Gibbons by the wrist, holding him still while he leaned forward, staring into the mirror. He spoke, very softly, as though he feared to alarm some hovering thing.

'Look there; in the door.'

The poet shifted his eyes to the doorway. It was blank and empty, and the wall behind it betrayed no shadow. He looked back at the actor, who had risen, still clutching by the wrist the hand with the reddened hare's-foot, his eyes still fixed upon the mirror; saw his lips move and heard the breath, 'Speak to her. She's going.'

Gibbons took a step backward as though to go to the door; instantly the clasp that held him tightened.

'Quiet. Dering, speak to her.'

The poet obeyed. He saw nothing; but he knew that Makebody was gripped by some power that was neither drunkenness nor fantasy. He spoke towards the empty space of the doorway.

'Why have you come?'

There was no sound. The poet spoke again into the silence.

'Who are you? Can't you speak to us? We don't understand.'

They waited. A minute passed. Then the actor dropped back into his chair, saying, 'Gone.'

He released the man's wrist; Gibbons went at once to the door, and noisily banged it shut. He returned to the table and spoke briskly in his clipped London voice, 'Now then, Mr Makebody, if you please. Don't want to miss your entrance.'

The actor lay back in his chair, and with closed eyes endured the application of the rouge, the bronze, the blue eye-pencil, the touch of white at the temples. Then he rose. In silence the exquisite trousers were donned, the coat so delicately adjusted to shoulders and waist. He stood without self-consciousness before his mirrors, surveying his back by means of a hand-glass. Satisfied, he set it down and said with indifference, almost with gaiety, as though he had forgotten, 'I must be on in two minutes. Wait, if you like. Gibbons will find you a spot of whisky.'

Once more he studied his clothes in the long glass, and went out, walking quickly away. The poet did not move. He felt a little foolish. The dresser caught his eye, grimaced, and jerked his head towards the sound of the footsteps.

'I didn't see anything,' said the poet.

'Nor anyone else,' the man answered, setting the wooden trees in a pair of patent leather boots, 'well, I'm sorry. I didn't think to see Mr Makebody go that way. But you can never tell.'

'No,' said the poet.

'He's what I call a real actor,' the man went on, 'born to it, as they say. It'll hurt him bad to give it up.'

'Why should he give it up?'

'He'll get worse,' said Gibbons briefly.

He began with quick mechanical movements to tidy the littered table, and talked on, his back to the poet.

'He's not, as you might say, a great actor. Hasn't got the temper. More like an ordinary gent. Yet he goes over the edge just as if he was one of these geniuses. I'm not saying they're all mad; not by no means. But they've got, as it were, a kind of a right to go off it a bit now and again. It don't mean anything to them. But Mr Makebody, he's ordinary, like you and me.'

'This isn't an ordinary delusion,' said the poet.

'You didn't see anything,' the man answered, as though he were sure.

'No,' said the poet, 'and yet—'

The poet sat holding his pipe, grateful for the warmth of the bowl against a hand that had grown chilly. He was puzzled, and sorry for the actor. It was possible that something had stood there in the light; but whether it existed of itself, or took shape from the brain of the man, he could not be sure. Horrible, he thought, for a mind so to make its own agony visible; to see pain walking, moving in familiar places, making of this everyday passage something alien and forlorn. But if Makebody were sane, what then? He found no answer, and sat withdrawn in thought, while Gibbons folded and hung and concealed trousers and coats and handkerchiefs.

Twenty minutes later the actor returned. He looked normal, save for an astonishing brightness of the eyes.

'It's going well to-night,' he said.

The poet stared at him.

'The play?'

'The play. There's no doubt this game has its compensations; but you've got to be tough.'

He took the drink that Gibbons had prepared, a weak mixture, as the poet noticed.

'For the last week there's been something wrong. It comes like that, in patches. It's like playing to lumps of dough. No life. No sympathy. Then, one night, God knows why, it's all real. They understand. That's the public for you.'

The poet wondered where this led. He was afraid to refer to the matter between them, and sat caressing his pipe, disturbed by the other's tranquility and apparent forgetfulness. The actor, sensitive to atmosphere, guessed at his difficulty.

'I'm sorry for having brought you here,' he said abruptly. 'Of course, you saw nothing. It must have seemed as though I'd wanted to fool you. I'm sorry. It must have looked like that.'

The poet murmured a disclaimer.

'It's a funny thing, though,' the actor went on. 'Funny that I should have been talking away about tradition and so on, and yet not have understood. I ought to have seen. And of course, that puts you and Gibbons out of the question. It's not your affair. She saw that.'

Still the poet would not ask, for it was evident that Makebody had made some discovery which he would, in his turn, reveal to these inhabitants of another world than his. But the poet, in spite of the published works which attested his own strange beliefs, felt horror at the sight of this madman sitting comfortably in a chair, discoursing between sips of whisky of the unseen.

'It's not your fault,' the actor continued, following out his thought. 'It's not a thing you can explain. No outsider can know how you get to long for the stuffy smell, and the flare of the lights in your eyes. But it's in our blood. Even now, she couldn't keep away. It's our breath. But I ought to have understood before.'

He was silent for a moment, and then very gently said, in his smooth deep voice, 'She must have died so young.'

As the poet sidled his way through raging streets half an hour later, thrusting his big head forward from his shoulders, he thought, with a humility rare in poets, 'We don't know so much of life, after all. We make little figures, and sweat out our very souls to make the pasteboard look like flesh. Then the thing happens, but not to us. It comes to some dull clay like Makebody, and he knows how to hold it. We can't. It gets lost in words. It slips past us. Damn him!'

The mood lasted no longer than his walk; and when he entered his room and saw it warm with light, the big table scattered with papers, his own latest book showing its pale covers beside them, he took heart again. After all, a poet has the telling of the stories.

But what was there for him to tell? Nothing had happened; Makebody might have been drunk. His published fantasies were more full-blooded. They began, and ended, and had stuff in them, for all their delicacy, more tangible than this incident could offer. He put away the idea, and months later, when a paragraph which had been lying in wait for him brought the matter again to his mind, he gave it only a moment's attention. The sentences occurred in a facetious guide to London's amusements published in 1827; the author, surveying the players of the Olympic Theatre, wrote:

'We shall touch upon the ladies as the butterfly deals with flowers—briefly sojourning with the honeyed hyacinth, and kissing long the lowly and unnoticed marguerite.

'The first kiss shall be for little Barnet. How roguishly she looks as a Somersetshire wench! How felicitous is her Taunton diction, and how dark appear her tresses beneath a white satin hat! Some may cavil at the two moles which point the way to her lips—"those pearly gates to Cupid's rosy bower"—but for our part we would dub him a poor creature who neglects such an invitation, given under Nature's own hand and seal.'

A star followed, directing the reader's eyes to the foot of the page, where a line of heavier type continued, 'Alas! Even as we write comes the sad intelligence that Miss Amelia Barnet's "hour upon the stage" of life is ended without warning. Let our words stand, for "flowers to strew her corse".'

The poet paused, thinking, 'No wonder she came back; no wonder she tried to catch some echo of it all. How could she think herself so utterly forgotten? They don't realise, it's too enormous while it lasts. Direct contact. Her will to please, and their delight in her. By God, it must have been hard to leave it, just in the flower—'

For an instance he wondered at the young glowing life, the brief candle; and then there was the rest of the book to read.

9 The Man Who Had Great Possessions

'I've often been sorry I didn't go on with it,' said Philip. 'There's something about writing—a faint aristocratic haze, left over from the centuries when it meant something. Knighthood, the same; even now the glow hasn't entirely faded.'

'It can't last much longer,' Anthony answered. 'We're a democracy already, and going down the slope at our best pace towards whatever more ignoble depths there are. What do you suppose the aristocrats of letters will be doing in fifty years time? They'll be writing captions for films, and glad of the job. If there were anything else I could do I'd get out of it myself.'

'Why's that? Competition?'

'No; I can do my selling all right when there's anything to sell.'

'There's no lack of material, surely. I never pick up a paper without seeing some paragraph that would make a story.'

'That's no good to me.'

'What is?'

'I don't know. If I did I shouldn't be sitting day after day in front of a blank sheet of paper.'

'Nothing doing?'

'Not one crimson thing.'

'Is this some high falutin about only giving your best?'

'It's six months since I've sold anything; any slight tendency to high falutin has long since gone by the board. I'd write any muck you like, for any money. But there it is.'

'I always thought that after you'd got the technical hang of it you could dish up your stuff more or less to order. I don't mean the good stuff, of course; but the ordinary stock-in-trade, surely—'

'You don't see what I mean. When I say I can't write I mean that I am physically incapable of getting words down on paper. The ideas aren't there; there's nothing to hang words on. It's a pathological state, like being struck dumb; the usual processes won't proceed. The moment I sit down with a pen my mind goes blank, so that it's an empty space with my will driving furiously about in it, slashing at air. That's the best description I can give. It's pretty awful, I can assure you.'

'Would a doctor be any use? They can do all sorts of obscure things nowadays with nerves.'

'It's nothing they can get at. It's something in me—something secret.'

'Have you any idea how it started?'

'Yes. But it's only a suspicion. Too absurd, too wild to state. Let it alone now. Can you drink beer?'

Philip could and did drink beer; they talked for another half hour before he rose to go. As he put on his overcoat he said casually, 'The law offers a good many opportunities for swindling, and I've availed myself of most of them. Just now I'm crusted with money. Does the fact interest you?'

'Not at present, but I'll bear it in mind.'

Anthony helped with the coat and added, 'It isn't the money; it's this feeling of being out of work, willing to do my eight hours a day and not being given the chance. It's the utter impotence that's such hell.'

'Well, the money's there if you want it.'

'I know. Thanks, Philip. Good-night.'

Anthony shut the door on his friend and stood thinking. He thought, 'I'll have one more try, but it won't do any good. She's got the whip-hand now; she'll be too strong for me. And I made her.'

This last idea amused him. He laughed and said aloud, as he went to his room, 'God! It's ludicrous.'

On the table that was his desk lay a heap of foolscap, the sort of paper he liked to write on, on whose surface the ideas seemed to grow and run of themselves; light fell softly on it, shaded to the very texture of his choice; the house, and the street outside, were silent. He sat down at the table, took his pen in his hand, and waited. He had been used to find the silence richly filled with thoughts; some of these he could take in his hand and hold, to examine them; others escaped. Sometimes not one came within his reach, but he could always feel that they were there, alive, and near enough to his grasp though it could not close on them. To-night, as on every night for six months, the silence was blank; no pulses stirred in it. He waited, giving the thing every chance, sitting very still, looking steadily at the paper that appeared like vellum in the shaded light. The house, which often held small noises and movements until quite late, was altogether quiet. The street, too, was deserted. A light wind lay to the west, so that he could hear the bells of Big Ben developing their tune through the hour, and finally the hour itself, like two strong waves breaking against a rocky coast; just like that, the boom, and the following hush.

As time went on he became restless. He lifted his legs, crossed, stretched, crossed them again; drove his left hand through the hair on the back of his head, upwards against the growth; squared his shoulders, arched his whole body in the chair; drooped, letting his stomach muscles go slack; slipped down in the chair until its back pressed his head forward and his chin down on his chest; righted himself, straightened, and leant over the rectangle of paper before him, staring as though it were a pool and he Narcissus; but all the while his right hand lay motionless, holding the pen aslant at the edge of the sheet. At three o'clock this hand moved. It threw the pen sideways, with a violent turn of the wrist, on to the floor. This was the only outward sign that he had gone in despair to the different place to find and implore her.

Half his waking life had been spent in this place, and so well did he know the geography of it that he could enter without preliminaries and be at home. He had built it stone by stone, consciously grouping the houses and trees in his mind, so that they were fixed and stayed as he had imagined them, untroubled by the seasons. The landscape in which these were set was changeless too; a warm sea to the south; inland a moor, colourless with misty rain, and solitary; hills in the far distance that were always clear and green, as though the weather soon would break over them. The towns were small. They lay on the sides of naked windy rises, or curled in the valleys indifferent to storm, and he visited one or other as the mood drove him.

He had begun with a single house, a low, half-timbered building with dark mellow rooms, and the smell of wood-smoke and burnt lavender hanging in its passages and stairways. He was not quite sure if he had built it to please her, or if he had found her standing there when he first entered it. She was the centre of this different world; its other inhabitants had come into being because she must be served and cared for and provided with picturesque opportunities; they were necessary, too, in the towns, which otherwise might have seemed forlorn with their narrow streets empty, and no heads showing in their overhanging windows.

These other inhabitants were, as was proper, entirely obedient. They wore uncomplaining the faces and clothes which their creator assigned to them, and moved at his bidding with a spontaneity which gave them a very creditable semblance of life. They knew their places in the background.

It is true that he could not always maintain the streets themselves in subjection. They had more character than the people who walked them, and sometimes would twist into unpremeditated shapes under his very eyes. He would correct them, and for a while they would heed him; but when he was not looking, or when a different pleasure engaged his attention, they would slink back to the appearance they preferred. This happened frequently after a visit to Spain, and when he saw that it was not worth while trying to keep the streets English he let them have their own way, with the result that one or two aspired to be arcades, or rose high and white, windowless, but with doors of iron filigree through which a fountain could be seen, or a mass of purple flowers crowding on a wall. It was odd to find such streets leading to an English market place; they spoilt the homogeneity of the towns; but he understood how difficult it must be for streets to be docile, vessels through which flows the blood of cities, the unsatisfied, wistful, inconstant multitude.

Until lately she too had obeyed him. He could be sure that if he wanted to find her she would be waiting in whatever setting his caprice might commend, always lovely, and intent to please him. Then, suddenly, her personality, which had been no more than the exquisite mask of a woman set above his own tastes and prejudices, became vivid, disturbing, and cruel. The body still kept its long lines as he had moulded them, the hands were as gentle; the face, somehow, had changed. It watched his coming with the smile he had contrived for it, but the eyes held apart from welcome. And once or twice when he had not summoned her, when he was not thinking of her, she had come, against all the odd laws and conventions of the place, to stand behind him and watch with cold eyes, not speaking. This dismayed him, for it was understood that the things and people were only real when he wanted them; they were permitted no life except in his thought; he called them out one by one as a conductor beckons to his instruments, and when he forgot them they were non-existent. Her unbidden coming dismayed him.

The vague beginnings of revolt had first come to light just at the time when he had discovered that he loved his work. Before, there had been the war, and after the war the feeling that there could be no employment that would not seem trivial or wearisome. He could write, and did, but it was a task which gave him no pleasure, to which he dragged himself always with physical unwillingness. He forced himself to work, so many words a day, good or bad, written in snatches between cigarettes and chapters of other men's books. Writing, to him, was mere labour, and he found his pleasure only when he spent the money it brought him.

Then came the feeling, after six years. At first he did not understand what was happening, and imagined that he put off till evening the obligatory pages because he wanted to have his day free. But he came to know that he had set apart these calm, warm, and enclosed hours in order that he might have the fullest assurance of pleasure. The things that he wrote during this very short period were neither better nor worse than those which cost him such mountainous pangs; the difference was that he lingered where once he had hurried, and the sense of achievement was constantly with him. He went less frequently to the different country because now happiness came running to him in the sunlight, and there was no longer any need to seek it by the light of torches in the friendly cities of his mind.

However, there had to be intervals. He could not sit always at his table in the window, and even though he was constantly preoccupied with thoughts of his work there were gaps, joints in his armour of preoccupation. He found that the different country had become a habit; he knew the way to it so well. If he shut his eyes for a moment to rest them he was pretty sure to find himself standing in the low dark room of the manor, calling for her; the first sign that she had ceased to obey was her failure to answer that call. He could bring her dress under his hand, but she evaded him, and it was evident that she had begun to have a life of her own in which he counted for nothing and whose movements were hidden from him.

That first absence or withdrawal perplexed him. He reasoned with himself in good set terms, pro and contra, hoping that she might be listening in some corner of his ego, and might, when the moment came, put her finger on the string of the thought to make a true note. He began, arranging his arguments in order.

'One. I made her. She is as much mine as the people I put in my books; they don't go on having lives to themselves outside the covers, and she was created by the same process as they.

'Two. She has remained with me now for—how many years? It began when I was about sixteen, and she came a little later. Say fourteen years. She's still the sort of woman I want. I was content with her. I haven't changed. Why should she?'

He waited, but she had nothing to say. He went on.

'Very well then. Three. She has become a real person, having individuality and will of her own. She has begun to dislike me.'

He waited again, and thought he felt a murmur that confirmed the last words; angrily he caught up the argument again.

'But that's ridiculous. That means the flat contradiction of my first statement. How can she be real, how can she belong to herself apart from me? She's only a thought. If thought is not let loose, if it's kept pent up inside a person it can only live in, by, with, and from that person. It can be real only to him; in this case to me.

'Ah, but there's your answer. She doesn't matter a pin to anyone else. No one else knows. So she exists in me, and she can feel all the emotions of which I am capable. And she is jealous, I think, because I could find satisfaction apart from her. Well, anyhow, I can fight her.'

It was a dreary battle. She knew her way about his mind, all the tricks of it, the very springs of its motion. He tried in a dozen ways to free himself.

He got drunk very deliberately, and deliberately, one by one, watched his faculties go. Movement went first, and that did not matter, since he had taken the precaution of seating himself at his table before he began; he knew that his legs were not dependable after the whisky had sunk half way down the bottle. Hearing followed, until the sounds in his head became indistinguishable from exterior sounds; connected speech; vision. His power of criticism remained till the end, a small thing watching from an incredible height; an intelligent gnat, surveying confusion and upheaval with a dispassionate eye. Vague and majestic thoughts assailed him from all quarters as in the days of his freedom. He told himself that he would remember and record them in the morning, and happily fell asleep with his head on the pile of blank paper and the ink from his fountain pen soaking into his hair.

He tried women. ('Jealous, my lady, are you? Wait a while. I'll give you something to think about!') But these were too easy or too difficult of access to succeed in distracting him. Besides, he despised the pleasure they offered, of rolling a stone up a hill for ever, still knowing that it must fall. They were unsatisfactory, the touch and look of them. He confessed as much to himself, and twisted a little as he thought that perhaps she might be laughing at him.

Finally, he tried waiting. There must be times, he supposed, when she would be off her guard. He went to a doctor to ask for a stimulant which should keep him awake on the pretext of urgent work to finish, an all-night sitting; obtained it; and going home began preparations for his vigil. Tobacco, matches, pens and paper were arranged so as to be within reach. The machine for coffeemaking, which he never used, was cleaned and made ready; he brought in a clock from his bedroom. At nine o'clock he sat down at his desk with his hand holding the pen slanting across the sheet.

He made no effort to concentrate. He knew very well the value of direct assault, that it was no more than the beating of naked hands against stone. This was siege, a test of endurance. One thing he had not realised, that his idle mind would so plague him; he found himself counting, making odd combinations of numbers, doing all the arithmetical jugglery which he had abandoned since his early school days; listening to his own pulses; marking with the fine point of the nib the root of each hair on the back of his left hand. All these obsessions he treated as enemies, her servants, though in the normal course of things she let him alone. She forbade his mind to obey him in one important matter, but she did not distract him by irrelevant onslaughts such as these. During the times when her writ ran in his consciousness he was left like a man warily sleeping, equipped, but for the moment powerless, with his senses lying like a sword ready to his hand.

The hours passed slowly. At three o'clock he rose and stretched himself. He was not sleepy, but he yawned at the thought of sitting there till dawn, past dawn, on into the morning, into the next night. He wondered how long he could hold out, and calculated that if he did not eat much and drank only coffee and his stimulant he could keep awake for about fifty hours. He had done as much during the war, and he remembered how on each occasion he had fallen, not sure if death or sleep were upon him until he woke ten hours later. He resisted the temptation to have a drink for the sake of having something to do, and told himself that he had better do without as long as he could; the things might lose their efficacy if he started on them too soon. He looked out on the dead street for a while, and went to his table again, slowly, to wait.

Altogether, his vigil lasted nearly sixty hours, and ended as the previous experiments had done. Before he let go his hold and allowed himself to sleep he perceived with unsparing clearness that he had been a fool. For was it likely, he asked himself—aloud, that the effort and the sound might hold him from sleep—was it even possible that he could have hoped to surprise her, who had her being only in his waking thought, whose watching and fatigues were his own watching and fatigues reflected.

'I cannot imagine,' said he aloud to the room, stuffy with smoke, 'how I can have deluded myself into attempting anything so absurd. It reminds me of that lunatic's game when one inserts the forefinger of the right hand into a circle made by the forefinger and thumb of the left and tries to catch it with itself and its thumb before it can withdraw. I am a very profound idiot.'

He pronounced these words very distinctly, stared for a second as though he challenged himself to deny them, then let himself go gently forward, his head turned sideways so as to rest comfortably on his folded arms.

He woke in time to have a bath and greet his friend Philip, who commented on his appearance, which was still extremely haggard. Anthony allowed his friend to suppose that his condition was due to the extravagant claims of a lady, which in a sense was true. Philip accepted the explanation and let it alone. They talked till late. Anthony was tempted by the other's easy companionship to confide his trouble; but when he had told half he was suddenly unwilling to tell the rest. This was not because of any secrecy or restraint to which his tormentor obliged him; his reluctance was nothing more than habit. He had told no one of his life in the different place, and he realised how paltry it might seem and how unreal, told in that atmosphere; even she, the strong warrior, the enemy with whom he struggled only to possess her more completely, must appear a delusion to be treated by doctors. He could not make Philip see her as she was, glorious and desirable; Helen, in steel, leading out the Trojans to battle against her avenging lord. So he let the matter drop with a half confession, and when his friend had gone and he had failed with a last attempt to beat down her guard, he went to the low dark room in which it was still daylight, and stood there with his head hanging, waiting for her.

He had played the hero so often in this room; here so many exquisite scenes had unfolded between them, unreal yet oddly satisfying scenes of passion, tender quarrels. It was humiliating that now he should stand between walls that remembered his triumphs, waiting until it should please her to come, too wretched to take up an attitude. He was no longer gracefully strong as the room was accustomed to see him, for he had forgotten to adjust that other appearance which here was his, and the clumsy and angular figure with which his mirror in the real world was familiar had leave to show itself. Perhaps his defencelessness and the eclipse of his vanity appealed to her; when he lifted his eyes she was there.

He made no movement to go to her. She stood as though she were prepared to listen, one hand flat on her hip, the fingers pointing down. He could not fix the outline of her face, which eluded him even when she turned towards the window. Disturbed, wanting to make sure, he took a step forward; the shadowy face smiled, the right hand lifted to forbid his approach. He wondered if this were part of her vengeance and halted, hoping that she would speak. As she did not he said, humbly, his head drooping, 'I want to talk to you. I want to talk over this whole business. It's been hell for me.'

He tried to make her answer 'And for me too, since I love you,' but she was free now and would have none of it. He knew that she was smiling. He said furiously, like a child, 'Can't you see it has?'

There was silence again. He went on, more calmly, 'And I want to talk it out. I can't stand this much longer. We've got to get down to something definite. I must know where I stand, what I've got to give up. First, why don't you want me to write?'

She smiled once more, as though that question were not worth answering.

'But I've got to live by it. I mean, live—stoke myself, warm myself, house myself—so that I can have my life with you. What does it matter if I enjoy my writing? That's a side-issue.'

She watched him, gravely now.

'And as things are, don't you see, it's not fair. You won't let me have either life. I can't write, and when I come here you don't show yourself, or you make me feel unwelcome. It's no fun without you, you know that. The whole thing came building up around you. Do you want me to get out, is that it? Do you want the different country for yourself?'

She shook her head. He cried out angrily, 'Well, then, what am I to do? This is the final irony. Go on; give me my orders.'

She said, the words coming with difficulty, as though she had been used to have them dictated and could not easily assemble them to fit her own thought, 'Not to write.'

'And starve. Yes, go on.'

'Other ways.'

'What else in all the world can I do?'

'With your hands.'

'What could I do with my hands? Make roads, I suppose. That would look well; that's a comfortable living. What's the idea, for God's sake?'

'Discover.'

'How? How can I tell what's going on in your mind?'

'You made it.'

'And yet I know nothing of the way it moves. I'm powerless.'

He paused, and softly laughed.

'Poor God!'

He had forgotten to arrange the daylight; it sank, and now they were talking in half-darkness which hid, perhaps to his relief, the uncertain outlines of her face. It gave him courage.

'Why should I work with my hands? Why do one thing badly when I can do another well enough? Are these the kind of muscles a man can live by?'

He clenched his fists and lifted his arms; even under the thick folds of the coat his muscles made a poor show. He looked down, forcing himself to realise the poor height, the weakness of the whole machine.

'I'm not built for a navvy. Explain to me what you mean.'

'Thought is alive. Things made with hands don't matter.'

'Are you jealous of life? You fool! Do you imagine that you can put up your hand and stop life as a man catches a ball?'

'Your lives.'

He had to think it over, frowning.

'You mean that I may create someone who should rival you; and then others; a whole host of striving creatures. No; it won't happen twice. Look at the people I made to put in the towns. They're obedient.'

'So far. You don't love them. Remember the streets.'

'You're threatening me.'

'You try to have reality both ways.'

'Neither way. You're inaccessible, and you've made writing impossible.'

'Give it up.'

'Are you to be my only reality? Am I to have only one thing in my life?'

He heard her laugh in the darkness before she answered, 'That's happiness. It frightens you.'

Bewildered and angry, he began to declaim his grievances, and to set forth the logic of his case as it appeared to him.

'My imagination's my stock-in-trade. I have used it for two purposes, to live the life that pleased me—this life, as it was six months ago—and to provide myself with the means of keeping the breath in my body. That's excusable, surely; reasonable, surely. I didn't aim very high; to make a decent living in the best way I could; to provide the little luxuries which keep a man just above the mud; and afterwards to have my happiness in this place that I've built, that's mine as much as if I'd made it with nails and a hammer. I'm ugly, I'm difficult. How could I look for happiness in the sort of world I write for? But you don't see that. Practically, you tell me that I've got to give up all the joy and life of my body if I want the other. That's too hard a choice, when I don't see the reason for it, and I won't agree to make it. You can't force me.'

He knew before he came to the end of this tirade that she had gone. He paused for a second to make sure and then screamed after her, towards the door through which she must have passed, 'All right! You'll run my life, will you? I'll fight you till I'm dead; I'll kill myself and you. That's a third choice, you hadn't thought of that. You'll forbid me to write. You'll drive all my ideas into the enclosure you guard. All right. But there's one thing you can't keep from me; memory. I'll get you down on paper, like a stuck butterfly, with a pin through your breast. Do you hear me? I'll do it. I will do it.'

She made no sign, and he, becoming aware of the emptiness of the room, the living, noiseless suspense of it, like a man fearful of discovery who holds his breath, wondered if he had stumbled on a way out. He opened his eyes to the lodging-house room. This time, he thought, the idea would keep till morning.

Morning was grey, full of the steady sound of rain, an admirable day for writing. He was curious to know if he would be able to carry out his design; she might have power over words as over thought. But his memory brimmed with her, and when he began his portrait he found that the words came easily and steadily as the falling rain.

'I don't suppose this story will ever be read; certainly it will never be published. It is not, strictly speaking, a story at all, but rather—well, what? An attempt at exorcism, an effort to shake myself free. I would rather not write it. She has been my world since I was sixteen. But if I accept her alternatives I shall simply cease to be a man. The whole thing is so strange. She has been mine in secret for so long, and when I have written her down that security and hidden joy of possession will be destroyed. It will be as though I left her naked in a room with an open door, through which at any moment strangers may walk and find her. She knows that I have this feeling, and has tried to use it in order to keep me; I can't allow that. This is my chance, and I must go through with it.'

He described very shortly the growth of the different place, how it had come, deliberately chosen, and yet so gradually; and how, when it seemed to have taken its final form, he had mapped it. The towns were made of all the streets he had liked, and the country surrounding them had been assembled in the same way, bit by bit, like a patchwork quilt. He described the manor house and how he had found her there, evoked by a longing that seemed purposeless and vague.

'I will try to tell as clearly as I can just how she looked when I saw her for the first time. She was standing by the window in the room that faces west; I had not expected to see her, and I stared so long, in order to remember her, that this is the picture I can most easily recall.

'She was tall, I thought. I allow myself a few extra inches in that country, and her eyes were on a level with my mouth. The effect was that of a tall woman, thin, and not so very young. That phrase does not give my meaning. She was ageless; I have never thought of age in connection with her, but her face had a certain maturity, an experienced gentleness very different from the timidity of a young girl. She was dressed in a mediaeval sort of thing, long, and of the reddish-purple colour we call wine, though it is quite unlike most claret; there was gold on it somewhere, just darker than her hair. Her hands were the colour of new ivory, and they felt like ivory that has lain in the sun. Her whole body felt like that, just warm, and unbelievably smooth. Of course, that was afterwards. This first time I did not touch her. She stood quite still, looking at me from under her eyebrows, which hung straight and low above her eyes. We stared at each other and then she laughed and came towards me, holding out her hands; her gestures were as smooth as her skin, and she walked as though her body were glad to obey her. That was the beginning, when I was just sixteen.'

He gave the first interview in detail, remembering without difficulty each moment of it; and tried to give some explanation of her coming.

'I suppose no effort of imagination can be entirely creative. It has to have something to work from, straw to make bricks of; unconscious memory, probably, is the chief source from which we draw. And so she cannot be altogether mine. I must have jumbled together a number of fairy princesses and faces in pictures to make her, with one or two Roman ladies besides—for the boy who can read Virgil will go night-prowling among the other Latins—the Circe of Petronius, or Lalage, "her candid shoulders gleaming like a moonlit sea".'

This interior life of theirs was so perfect that he had not troubled to form other relationships. He had few friends, and, except Philip, they hardly counted; he was glad to see them and glad to say good-bye. He did not set off on the usual wild-goose chase of an imaginative and sensitive man in search of the ideal woman who would content him physically and preserve his illusions. He let women alone, except during the short time, a few weeks, when he had frequented them to spite her. They were cynical, and had eyes for his shortcomings. She was the unchanging companion, who did not perceive that he was little and ugly and not very lovable. He insisted on this, and was rather proud, in a way, of her new jealousy, flattered that she would not share him, even while he defied her.

'When I think of the things we have done together! the storms on that sea; not, of course, where it is sheltered by the headland, but further out, in the wide strait you have to pass to get to the islands. There's nearly always a wind there, blowing from the south, and when it meets the tide coming down you may find yourself in as much trouble as is good for a small boat. I've seen her then in a soaked blue jersey, facing what for all she knew might be death, and smiling. (I might have let her die, and have brought in her body by superhuman swimming, not understanding that she was dead until I got her to shore. That would have been a tremendous scene for me, and once or twice I had a mind to do it, but I saw a drowned woman once, bloated and greenish, and that might have got into the picture.) We used to walk a lot, too, on the moors, with the heather crackling and twisting under our feet. That was the marvel of her, that she was exquisite and right in every setting as no flesh and blood woman could ever be. Perhaps it was in the house that I loved her best; I've told what she was like there. There are scenes we must have played out a hundred times—'

He wrote them down, word for word, all the absurd intimate talk. It hurt him to do it. When he had written enough to satisfy his honesty the portrait was nearly finished, and what remained to be said was more in the nature of soliloquy than appreciation.

'She is adorable still, but I can't allow her to possess me; I must hold on to the dignity of my free will. For all that, I have not once been able to get the better of her. I waste my strength as though I were striking at water. In view of this, what purpose can such a portrait serve? I undertook it to prove that I still had power to betray her, when she had left me nothing else. But what's the use, even if I win? Not much of a victory, the torture of the thing one loves best; and that applies to her, too. It's as though we were both afraid of something; but why? Of what? Of happiness, as she said? Perhaps; the kind of happiness we can't understand because it's so different, a shadowy thing, and we're always taught to grasp at substance and let the shadows go. But I want her to be real; passionately, I want it. Real to me, as she has been all these years. I know that such a relationship would be in the ordinary human way too good to last, but I thought that I could keep her safely in my mind, I didn't understand that a living thing must change. I suppose that this will in some way give her freedom, and I'm made jealous and unhappy at the thought of what she may do when she's free. I can't think that I shall lose her altogether. We were so happy; she was so lovely. "Oh beauty, lone, and like a candle clear in this dark country of the world—"'

He looked up from his paper, feeling suddenly stiff and exhausted. Rain had ceased, but the room was almost dark, and when he looked at his watch he saw that it was after five. He stretched himself, and gathered the sheets in order to read them over.

The very first sentence, which he had forgotten, made him pause, and finally he ran his pen through it. He thought, 'Why should nobody read it? The shrew must be publicly tamed if the taming is to do any good. Someone must read it. Philip would do. I'll tidy up a little and send it straight to him.'

He found it hard, after this decision, to let the intimate passages stand. He tried to find an excuse for cutting them by saying that they concerned himself rather than her, and therefore were out of place; but honesty won. He left them as they were, with an angry jerk of his shoulders at the thought of another man knowing. When the reading was ended he put the sheets into an envelope addressed to his friend; there were stamps, for a wonder, in the little enamelled box, so that he had only to give the packet to his landlady when she came with tea, and ask her to post it. He delayed. He allowed her to go out of the room, then rang the bell, ashamed of his weakness. She went with it at once to the pillar-box at the corner, and he listened until he heard her steps again in the hall outside his door. Then he sighed, and began to consume his tea with appetite. As he ate he remembered patches and phrases of his story with discomfort, and thought, 'She's there; she's alive in that paper as she was in my mind. My treachery is artistically complete.'

Shame and anger at that treachery kept him from making any attempt to visit the scene of it. He was afraid of finding her and seeing pain in her eyes, afraid of not finding her lest she might have gone for always. He sat smoking all the evening, gulping down chapters of an indifferent novel, and finally went to bed, where he could not sleep. Everything in him that had gone to her making, idealism, shyness, protested against that brutal exposition. He thought that he could have no right to sleep until he had explained to her, and tried, now that the quarrel was out and over, to make friends. He shut his eyes, which had been fixed on the thin blade of light between the drawn curtains, but he could not immediately find himself at the manor. It needed an effort of will to draw it round him, and when he had the room to his liking the sunny coast that used to show so clearly through the windows was blurred as with rain. He did not call her. He waited, looking about the room with which he was so entirely familiar, and for an instant felt afraid. It seemed as though the solid walls just beyond his range of vision were flickering, wavering, like dark smoke. When he looked directly at them they stood still, but in another corner the unreal appearance mocked and angered him. He struck the walls with his hand, and they gave back the thick sound of old wood, while behind his back, as he knew, they were frail as charred paper. He made a tour of the room to satisfy himself; where he tapped it was solid, the rest was misty. He struck with a clenched fist and all his strength at last, and the ribbed carving of the doorway tore the skin from his knuckles. He stared at them, and at the window. The coastline was no longer visible, night had fallen outside, and he was able to persuade himself that the changed look of things had been due to the oncoming twilight. There was no sign of her as yet, and no welcome in the air of the house. He could bear it no longer and went back to his bedroom, still aloof from sleep. When he turned on the light beside his bed to see the time he looked at his knuckles; the skin was unbroken. He would have been glad, comforted, to find them bleeding.

He woke from a restless sleep at a quarter to nine; the packet must already have been delivered at Philip's house. There was nothing to be done, except one thing. He turned over in bed, pressing his face into the pillow, ashamed and unhappy, and lying there went again in search of her to explain, only to explain.

This time the effort of will would not serve him. His manor was not there. He commanded and conjured in vain, advancing his will against the different country; it was not there. The eye of his mind caught for a second or two, and hardly apprehended, the stormy edge of a moor and a curved headland. He cried out, 'At least I can remember!'

And memory painted for him two or three flat little scenes; but he struck down the canvas before they could be finished. There was no life in them, and he was afraid lest he might see her stiffly smiling, motionless among the rigid trees, dead as they.

An hour later Philip in his office was surprised to learn that Anthony was waiting to see him. The latter did not shake hands; he was trembling. He said abruptly, 'I sent you a manuscript.'

'Yes; I read it in the train, coming. An odd story. I didn't know you went in for that kind of thing.'

'Where is it? I must have it.'

'Here. What, are you off to an editor at once with it?'

Anthony was not listening. He snatched the papers out of Philip's hand and turned away. Philip went with him to the doorway, talking.

'You know, the woman in that thing is extraordinarily good. She's real.'

Anthony halted and looked at him.

'I mean to say, she's vivid, alive. It's unaccountable, because there isn't anything in the actual writing. That's not offensiveness on my part; I mean that she seems actually to be living.'

'Oh God, yes,' said Anthony, and bent his head as though to kiss the manuscript before he put it away in his breast pocket.

10 Teigne

The Clivedens went the way of all the rest. The country people who lived in the shadow of Teigne knew why, and watched the breaking without pity; it was too inevitable for that. Teigne was ravenous and strong. It could wait. Flesh and blood had no chance against the immutable and mysterious stone, built to endure; and so the Clivedens went, as others had gone, sadly.

The first owner, a Jacobean merchant with a purchased baronetcy, had built it on the site of an old low-lying farmhouse. He was a man with ambitions, and since he could find no purchasable dwelling adequate to his new dignity, he decided to build such a castle as should astound his little world and proclaim him not unworthy of the gratitude of his King; so he set them all to work, stone-masons and carpenters and woodcarvers, making a ludicrous castle whose appearance set the local squires rocking in their saddles as they rode by. It had a great square keep of red stone, with a court leading nowhere, enclosed by a wall with little round inaccessible turrets; beyond the court lay the house. When at last, after seven years, the great building was finished, it occurred to him that he must beget sons to inherit, and here was a problem, for his wife was barren and her blood as good as nameless. Teigne worked for Sir Abraham; she died, and he was free to choose.

On this matter country opinions, three hundred years later, were divided, some saying that this was the first crime of all upon which the rest followed, others that the roots of the evil lay deeper in time. However that may be, it was after this happening that the evil took shape, and the proverb was made which read:

Sins die by water,
Souls die by fire;
Teigne stone and mortar
Kills heart's desire.

Sir Abraham Greatbatch, being free, looked about him for a wife who should advance his consequence and continue his line. His wealth tempted Anne, the only daughter of Baron Morden of Bere. She married him, and went to live in the red castle whose anachronisms were a constant source of amusement to her brothers. At first she looked with aversion at the carved figure of Dame Elizabeth, her predecessor, kneeling stiffly, with round pink cheeks and an old-fashioned ruff, under the south window of the church; but later, when she knew that her baby was to come, she felt sad for the barren wife, and would sometimes go to kneel beside the effigy, until Sir Abraham rated her for Popish practices, and forbade the church on week-days. All his anxiety was for the child, his hope. He would not permit the fancies of a woman, that frail but most necessary vessel, to endanger the precious life as yet hardly begun. He was harsh with her for the sake of what she carried, and she began to fear him, not understanding that in her melancholy and brooding hours he saw a threat to the unborn.

As the months went by, this severity was modified, but the mischief was done. Anne's mind, exalted by her condition and denied relief, for she had no companionship, turned inwards, considering how best she might thwart her husband. She began to be careless in household matters; but he was indifferent, caring little for food, and as yet unaccustomed to the working of a great house. She found in a chest some linen that had belonged to Dame Elizabeth, and wore it; he laughed, and commended her for her thrift. Then as her time came nearer, she abandoned such follies, and became afraid.

Her fears, restlessly darting from one object to another, gave her no peace. Sir Abraham was patient with her, and kind, as a man will flatter a dog lest it should break some precious thing held in its teeth, and she saw in this forbearance some sinister meaning. Stories had reached her, which at the time she would not heed; she remembered them now, and shivered, imagining that if the child came to harm she might not live. In this she wronged Sir Abraham, who was not needlessly ruthless; and besides, she was protected by her great name.

One day towards the end of the seventh month, going into the little room where her husband often sat, drowsing amid his books, Anne found him seated in his chair looking out at her with his face drawn down, the mouth and cheek falling sideways. The mouth worked slowly, with a grotesque movement as of an animal chewing, but no sound came from it. She halted, staring at the twisted figure; then, holding her skirts, ran silently away, down the oak corridor, down the stairs, out into the woods behind the house. As she went, she felt that her mouth moved as his had done, aimlessly mimicking the silly grimace. She ran on; and late that night they found her lying among the heaped brown leaves of the beeches. She must have been there for hours; the leaves were thick upon her stiff green skirt. They brought her back, and in the morning the child was born dead. Sir Abraham did not seem to heed when they told him, but slobbered a little, and peered out from the prison of his paralysed body with dull eyes.

After his death it was discovered that he had left the great house to his wife, 'to be held for my son until he shall attain manhood'; the will was dated April the twenty-fourth, the day on which she had told him that she was pregnant. Through her it passed to her nephew, Paradine Hastings, who sold it to the Carnabys; but soon Walter Carnaby had to take refuge in Holland—Charles II had a long memory, and a long arm for traitors—and Teigne again stood empty. So for two hundred years the lords came and went; and it was curious to see how in the village the same names persisted through the centuries, on tombstones, in farms; Marshalls, Corbets, and Goodbodys lived and got issue and died, generation after generation, while the names of the masters of Teigne shifted about, in and out of the great families of the south of England. The village people were sorry for the gentry, but indifferent. Their interest was reserved for the manner of the master's undoing, and in the course of two centuries they were afforded examples of every variety of ruin. Teigne broke the masters, their fortunes, their spirits, their health, their hearts. The village looked on, changeless, and thanked God on Sundays for a lowly station in life.

Sir Roger Cliveden bought the property in nineteen hundred and four. He was, like the first builder, a very recent knight, but the name was an old one, though it had lately come to riches. He loved the place, and filled it with young people; his little son grew strong in the shadow of its woods. For ten years it was a happy house, until the outbreak of war. Young Roger was sixteen then, and fretted at the thought that since it must be over by Christmas he could never take his part in the pageant. His father, too, was of opinion that six months would see the end of it; and secure in that hope allowed the boy to join his school OTC so that he might learn to handle a rifle and drill a squad, and become familiar with the more ornamental duties of a soldier.

But the war went on, doggedly, stupidly; and the day came when Roger Cliveden was given a commission and sent out to Flanders with a battalion of the county regiment. A week later he was dead, shot through the throat as he ran towards the dark shattered trunks that once had borne green leaves, and were marked on the map of the section as Courlay Wood.

Sir Roger took it well, everyone said. The news arrived on Saturday, when Teigne was filled with young men and women, dancing, forgetting. Sir Roger told no one, not even his wife. The guests went on Monday, and those who saw it in the papers next morning were shocked, and secretly glad that they had not known. It was an ordinary tragedy. Teigne had known worse miseries, and witnessed more shameful deaths. It was strange, therefore, that the death in battle of a half-grown boy should prove to be the signal for the destruction of Teigne. Sir Roger was not superstitious, but he began to understand the attitude of the country people, and to look on his house with their eyes. It seemed to him unnatural that the living fact of his son should cease, should be dispersed, and the clean flesh rot that had been so loved. From the woods to which Anne had fled in her terror he spied upon the malignant house, watching it as though it were an enemy; it stood, triumphant, secure, and the great artificial keep mocked him with its strength. He would have no panel carved and set in the hall, nor any monument raised in the church as his wife wished, to commemorate their loss; but he ordered the stonemason to trim a little oblong slab of granite on which the words were cut—'In memory of Roger Cliveden, who died attacking a wood such as this, August 1916'—and set it up where the beeches grew tall. Then suddenly, despite the protests of his relatives, he decided that they must go from Teigne.

It was a difficult time, an absurd time to put a big house upon the market. It was a year after the boy's death, and the war went drifting on, and the profiteers did not care to display their money too openly, and no bids were made for Teigne, which was inconvenient and remote. Sir Roger lowered the price. His agent protested, and secretly discouraged several offers which approached the new figure.

One day in December, a slim and elegant gentleman called at Teigne. He was shown into the hall, and messengers were sent to search out of doors for Sir Roger, who came in at last, and stood rather doubtfully contemplating the visitor, as though wondering what in the world any person so well dressed could have to say to him. The visitor was at no such disadvantage. His swift eye appraised Sir Roger, and found him perfectly adapted to his panelled setting; the grey hair and thin nose were admirable. As he introduced himself, Mr La Vie, an artist at heart, winced at the thought that he had come prepared to divorce this stately gentleman from his appropriate surroundings. He observed that it was a fine day and that the house was of remarkable interest; then, realising that the preliminaries and fine shades of dealing would be wasted here, bluntly offered a price, backed by unexceptionable references, which Sir Roger as bluntly accepted. The bargain was accepted, though the business must go through the hands of solicitors and agents, and there must be months of delay before it was concluded. They were both men of their word. But Sir Roger, looking at the purchaser's exotic clothing, asked what he meant to do with the place when he got it.

'Not much shooting; no frivolities,' said Sir Roger.

'I shall find occupation,' the visitor answered.

'There's hardly any land; a few fields, and two or three acres of woodland. About that—but I can settle with your representatives. And of course the village—'

'The land does not interest me,' said Mr La Vie.

'Upon my word, Sir,' said Sir Roger, 'I don't know if I'm to take your offer seriously. You haven't seen the house; you don't want the land. You buy a property as if it were a pair of gloves.'

'In both cases I know what I want.'

'Well, if I may say so, it seems an extraordinary way of doing business.'

Mr La Vie smiled. He knew more of the ways of business than Sir Roger did.

Together they went over the house; and whereas previous intending buyers had considered the size of the rooms and their outlook, and had commented on the endless passages in connection with the kitchen, Mr La Vie paid no attention to these things, but looked attentively at the ceilings, fire-places, and the mouldings of the doors. Sir Roger was bewildered, and felt very much inclined to ask him point-blank what use he intended to make of the house; but he had given his word as regarded the sale, and he was weary of the place and its memories. It was not worth while; and the lawyers would settle that clause about the stone in the wood.

Mr La Vie stayed to luncheon. During that meal, made difficult by the hostile, enquiring presence of Lady Cliveden, he was told something of the history of the house, and the local proverb concerning it; but his calm was unruffled. He smiled, and Sir Roger, who had began to dislike him, hoped in his heart that the curse might have some virtue in it still.

By the end of May the Clivedens were gone. Their successor came in an opulent car a week after their departure, and put up for two days at the Five Bells in the village, an object of rather contemptuous interest to all the inhabitants. The landlord said, talking in the tap room, 'Ah, pay a grand price to come in, 'e did; 'e'll pay a bigger to come out.'

His audience agreed effusively; but then they always did when the landlord delivered a judgment. Everybody wondered when the great pantechnicons would come with the furniture, and which of the firms in the county town would get the job for decorating. They observed all the movements of Mr La Vie, and the caretaker who came one night to the Bells had a good deal to say of him.

'Tapping at the wood, and looking at it through one of them reading glasses. Writing in a little book all the time. I tried to get a sight of it, but it was writ too small.'

'How about Falkiner's cottage?'

'Will he keep James Goodbody on?'

'How'd I know? He didn't say a word. Not so much as asked after my leg, though I dragged it cruel. Them's not gentry ways.'

'Ah, but them's not gentry,' said the landlord, and this summed up the impression of the tap-room council.

Mr La Vie went away, speeding south in his opulent car, and for a month nothing happened. Then Teigne heard that the county town builders had been given a contract, but not to decorate. They were to pull down; to pull down Teigne. The country people were disturbed, like a swarm of bees when their hive is destroyed. For centuries the great house had provided them with themes for speculation and legend. They were used to it. They liked to feel it there, powerful still. They could not know why Mr La Vie had made his decision.

In his rather dark but splendid sitting-room he had told his mother of the interview with Sir Roger, and spoken of the ill-luck which went with his purchase. His mother, who retained the older form of the family name and took curses seriously, was upset by his story. She discouraged him, and refused flatly to live under such a roof.

'Well, if you won't, you won't,' said Mr La Vie at last. 'But I tell you what I'll do. I'll cut my losses. We'll gut the place and leave it. And by the time I've sold the woodwork and the ceilings and one or two other things there may not be much loss to cut. How's that? That doesn't give it much of a chance to do any mischief.'

Mrs Levy agreed.

'What about buyers?' she asked.

'I could sell the interior five times over,' he replied.

'Over the water,' she supplemented, and they both laughed.

In this way the destruction was planned, and according to plan was carried out by the firm in the county town. Every inch of woodwork was stripped from the walls; foot by foot the moulded ceilings were dissected, a difficult matter, for the old plaster held strongly; the doors were taken out; the staircases, hollowed with treading, were loaded on to vans. Windows, floors, lead roofing, gutters, pipes, everything moveable was taken, until only the red shell of the house stood, gaping. Mr La Vie was there as the last load was driven away, and he stood in the shelter of the wrecked doorway to watch it go; when he could no longer hear the sound of wheels, he spat on the threshold and walked briskly to the village by a side-path through the woods.

He had not overstated his case when he told his mother that he was sure of buyers. They came to him from the four winds, American gentlemen with money and English gentlemen with taste; even one gentleman from a Museum came. They bid openly and secretly for the spoils of Teigne, and Mr La Vie, smiling, told himself that he still had an eye for a good thing. Yet, as once he had regretted that all this beauty must pass from those to whom it should belong into the hands of those who could afford it, so now he hated to think that it had been broken apart from the shell that had held it safely so long. He was not proud of the deal. It had been profitable, but he was not tempted to repeat it. One could not reputably live by eviscerating old houses, and it went against the grain with Mr La Vie. So he returned to his lawful enterprises, and as senior partner in the firm of Chester, La Vie, of Bond Street, began once more to distribute pictures, fans and Renaissance jewellery at prices which were a sufficient indication of the reverence in which he held such things.

He loved his galleries. The frail beauty of his wares possessed him with ecstasy. He touched them gently, and tried not to part with them. Sometimes he would buy some exquisite fan, or beaker of coloured glass, and put it aside, hidden so that no strolling casual customer might find it; after a day or two the lure of the treasure would prove irresistible and he would go secretly to look at it, and smooth it with a forefinger. In his divided mind dealer would war with artist, and the victory went always to the latter, so that the lovely thing would be ravished from the galleries and Mr La Vie would sit late that night turning it fondly in his hands or seeking a place for it in the crowded cabinets of his study.

Mr Chester could never understand these lapses. He was a businesslike, stolid person, who dwelt among precious things as though they had been turnips, and the eccentricities of his partner were painful to him. But, as he would sometimes explain to a customer, punctuating his speech with significant nods, La Vie was an artist as much as any of these fellows that lay on paint or sing at the Queen's Hall; he was proud of this alien quality, and he had discovered that it appealed to a certain type of customer.

'I'm only a business man,' he would explain, 'I can't tell you about that. We'll ask La Vie. He knows the history of all these things as though he'd made them himself.'

Then, hastily, fearing lest his last sentence should create a false impression, he would add, 'Funny thing is, he doesn't do anything. Nothing to show for it. Can't use his hands at all.'

Theirs was a tactfully conducted and confidential business. They did not often bid at sales. But if some collector wished to dispose of duplicates, or if some lady, last of a family, found herself burdened with unproductive heirlooms, Chester, La Vie, could be trusted to come to some arrangement. They acquired privately, and sold to well-known persons within a limited social circle. They were honest, deliberate. They knew.

It was a comparatively small matter which revealed to them both that there was something wrong with Mr La Vie. A very junior dealer had come with a ring which he said was more in their line than his. Mr La Vie was called to inspect it which he did in his usual leisurely competent way with the aid of a glass; but the glass in this case was unnecessary. It was a plausible Renaissance jewel, one great baroque pearl forming the head and body of a sea-horse; the ordinary kind of monstrosity for which there was a market. This one, however, was not genuine. The colour of the gold was wrong, the method of securing the pearl was wrong. Mr La Vie, handing it back to the dealer, told him so.

'Fake?' said the dealer, vanquished, but good-humoured, 'Fake or not, it's a beautiful thing.'

'No,' Mr La Vie answered, as though repeating the words after some invisible dictator, 'Fake or not, it's an ugly thing.'

He sat back, horrified at his own revelation; and when the dealer had departed, the ring in his pocket, he rose and paced about the galleries, miserable because he had lost his conception of beauty, and could not find it among the things which hitherto had brought him comfort.

Later he confided his troubles to Mr Chester, who laughed robustly, and urged him to take a day off.

'You're run down, that's what's the matter with you,' Mr Chester declaimed, standing four square in the little office, 'You get away into the country. You can trust me with your pretties for an hour or two.'

Accordingly, next day Mr La Vie made no appearance in Bond Street, but summoned his chauffeur and drove into the country to appease his questioning mind. They went north into Hertfordshire, and secure in his glass box he surveyed the fleeting hedges with dreary eyes. There were some lazy fields, and a number of fields busy with standing crops. Bridges humped themselves to give the motorist a disagreeable switchback feeling as he rolled over them. Once he saw a mill-wheel slowly churning a quick brown stream to froth. He drove past country policemen, affable on bicycles; and there were the usual children caught back by the skirts, and the usual little towns disfigured by garages plastered with advertisements in primary colours.

Mr La Vie, pressing his shoulders against the yielding cushions, stared indifferently upon it all. He was arguing with himself, trying to make accepted things resume their previous unquestioned status.

'Beauty,' he thought, 'what we're all after. It must exist. It would be too cruel—have I been fooled all these years? What are we here for, anyhow? Is it that there are so many kinds? Why am I cut off, then? I've always kept to the sort I could understand. But now—'

As they left the country behind them, turning in to London again, he was not made wretched by the transition, nor was he conscious of the horrors that elbowed his car as it followed meekly behind a towering tram. It seemed hideous, yet he could not condemn it, for he was bereft of all his standards, and his problem was vivid and restless as ever. He defended himself against the attacks, telling himself that the matter of the ring was unimportant and that his subsequent lassitude and distress of mind were nothing more than a physical intolerance of routine. He tried to be amused at the exaggerated tumult of his ideas, and went up the steps of his mother's house smiling. He reflected that the country didn't suit all people; too stimulating, too big, too much repetition; field after field, and the same sky meeting them all. It was enough to upset any man who wasn't used to it. He was talkative at dinner, but now and then he caught his own eyes in the bevelled glass of the sideboard opposite his chair, and looked away quickly. He could not bear to give that sideboard the benefit of the doubt.

He tried no more experiments, and returned next morning to Bond Street.

Mr Chester, approaching in a hearty manner to question him, was foiled by an assumption of the absent-minded silence which his partner's reputation as an artist excused. All that morning, whether he spoke with customers or walked among the treasures displayed, or merely sat at his desk pushing back the skin from his fingernails the same question bothered him.

'It isn't in these things. Where, then? Can't you buy it and sell it? For centuries people have said these things were beautiful. They can't all have been wrong. I thought it was to be found in things that people had made with their hands, made carefully and with love; but it's not. Nature—no, not for me. Though even those things are made, carefully too, for all we know. I don't understand.'

He ranged among the cabinets and tables, stooping, minutely examining. He saw little pieces of yellow and grey metal, thin sticks of ivory inlaid with dull stones, thread worked painfully into meaningless patterns, aimlessly repeated, mirrors whose dark glasses reflected him and offered new problems to bewilder him. He turned his back on them all and went again to sit at his desk, frowning at his nails.

At about half past five a customer entered the gallery, a countess whose income was so deplorably irregular that it was never possible to forecast whether she came to sell or to buy. Mr Chester, who greeted her, was soon able to discover, by her admiration of everything she saw, that she did not come as a purchaser. She hovered before a dessert service of painted glass, wailing that it was too heavenly to exist; in a Venetian mirror she tilted her hat to another angle, exclaiming that it was abominably put on; finally she produced from her bag a jewelled watch, dusty with pink powder, the face of it painted with the judgment of Paris, and on its back the letters M. A. twined in a cypher with a crown above. Mr Chester took it, and inwardly assessed the value of the sapphires in the monogram, but he would not commit himself. He said, as was customary, 'A lovely thing. We'll have to show this to La Vie. He's the expert.'

'Oh, but of course,' the countess agreed.

Mr La Vie was summoned from his desk and came slowly forward, going carefully, from habit, among the crowded tables. The countess tittered, as Chester handed him the watch, 'You won't be too hard on me, will you? Really, you know, it's historical, my poor watch. I do so hate to part with it. But now-a-days, what is one to do? It's so impossible to make ends meet, isn't it? You'll be kind, won't you, Mr La Vie?'

'My partner hasn't been at all well,' said Mr Chester, 'but it will do him good to look at such a beautiful thing.'

His words were for the jewel, but his eyes for the countess, who bridled.

'You know, it used to belong to Marie Antoinette. It's tremendously old, and so attractive, don't you think? You must really be generous. I could easily have found an American for it, but I brought it to you.'

Mr La Vie studied the watch coldly, turning it over, and peering at it closely. He opened the case, and saw, engraved upon the gold rim which the case covered, the words, 'Boehme, Wien.' Austrian made; a gift perhaps from Maria Theresa to her daughter. The crown was not the royal crown of France, but a coronet such as the daughter of an empress might bear. A gift to the child princess before her mother had arranged the marriage with France. Exquisite work. The countess talked on.

'You must never let my husband know. He's so old-fashioned. He'd starve surrounded by heirlooms rather than sell. He gave me this, though. It's quite my own. I do not think that's such a foolish attitude to take up. The times have quite gone by, haven't they? Do tell me your verdict, Mr La Vie.'

She turned suddenly to him, and he, startled from his preoccupation, let the precious thing fall from his hands, face downwards on the floor. There was a little tingling crash. Mr La Vie, stooping, saw that the glass was broken and the enamel blotched with white; a dust of coloured particles lay at his feet. He did not know that he had laughed as it fell, not harshly, but delightedly, like a child pleased by the noise. Now his partner and customer saw his face alter. He made a little gesture towards them with his hands as though to implore their help. Tears came to his eyes, and he said wildly, forgetful of race, of dignity, of all save his immense trouble, 'Christ! What's got me? I don't care any more—'

And began to sob, standing helplessly in front of them.

It was almost a pity that the villagers of Teigne could not have witnessed the scene.

11 The Pledge

In the old town was a most unexpected street, which, neglecting the opportunity offered by the level land to the north, turned away southwards to go shouldering up the hill in whose lee the town had been built, and under whose sheltering trees it lay like a ship at anchor. The street was like a street of ships, and had been built by seafarers. The houses were ribbed with oak, their upper stories leant forward so that to a person standing in the street they seemed like wooden hulls curving to earth instead of water; their flanks showed round windows here and there, portholes against which on stormy nights the rain flung itself with a sound as of spray. The street was like that. People had heard of it, and came in cars and buses to ascend it on foot, for the incline baffled all mechanism; these outlanders could be seen any day, staring right and left with the wistful look of those who have been told what to admire, but are uncertain as to details. Their conversation as a rule was fragmentary, owing to the climb. They said, 'This'll soon get that fat off you, Annie.'

'Charming, of course, but almost too artificial.'

'I should think they must get a lot of painters coming here in the summer.'

'My! If my husband could see this street he'd want to buy it right up.'

'I wouldn't live in one of them, not if you was to pay me. I do like a nice bright room. Where we live we got a great big window where you can 'ave a nice pot of ferns—'

But the inhabitants of the crooked leaning houses were used to it; and the street, oddly enough, did not break out into little tea-shops with orange curtains, or little antique shops with brass candlesticks writhing in the window. A certain tenacity and unfriendliness came to the aid of the inhabitants. They refused to resign their houses, and the visitors had to retire to the far end of the town where in a charming but adroitly aged hotel they might consume the cakes and purchase the Staffordshire figures which the barbarians of the street denied them.

The barbarians, in spite of their houses, had ceased to think of the sea. They had forgotten it, since it no longer occupied their immediate horizon. It had gone, leaving the marsh behind it, rich land where sheep were pastured; and so gradually did the meadows slope to a shingle and the shingle to water, that although it was only two miles distant the sea was not visible save on bright days as a thin silvery line. They built no ships now, and no houses save in ignoble rows with disciplined roofs. They were no longer adventurers and free men of the sea; the land held them fast. Only the strangers remembered.

Miss Alquist lived in one of the narrow houses halfway up the street of the ships. She was a newcomer. She had arrived one day from the outer world, unheralded, and at once, by artifice or simply by strength of character, had contrived to secure a foothold among the ship-dwellers. She lodged with a family of them, renting one room at first, and gradually, as the elder children married, extending her domain till she possessed the whole ground floor with a lien upon the kitchen. As time went on she proceeded, to the dismay of her hosts, to oust their furniture and replace it with odds and ends of her own, which came sewn up in sacking from some place abroad whose name the Frants could never succeed in reading. They found themselves crowded in the remaining rooms, compelled to uncomfortable proximity and obsessed by the rejected furniture which advanced upon them like a tide with their lodger's every acquisition.

Miss Alquist never considered the inconvenience, and had never been heard to apologize. She was shabby and haughty and quite without consideration for the Frants, who, though appalled by her assurance, lacked the courage to send her packing. It is possible that had they tried to do so she might not have consented to go, and before that only too probable situation the stern overnight resolutions of the Frants would pale to morning civility. Her advantage was a moral one, and her strength lay in this, that for some reason unknown she loved the street of the ships. This passion, unsuspected by the rightful heirs, would have astounded them. They found sufficient matter for astonishment in the account of her possessions and the manner of the arrangement; for whereas they had iron beds with speckled knobs of brass, tables made of bamboo, and gilded vases, Miss Alquist kept her rooms bare, uncarpeted and vaguely redolent of salt and spices. She slept in a little narrow bed which had no wire mattress but was corded with rope; a bright coloured blanket covered it. Under the window of the back room stood a big dark chest with brass corners from which the smell of spices seemed to come; but in all the years of her residence the Frants had never once found it unlocked. That, with a small folding chair and hanging curtains in two corners, was all the furnishing of the bedroom.

The sitting-room, with bow windows looking on to the street, was almost equally bare. There was a wooden chair with a cushion tied to the seat, comfortable enough, though foreign looking; a table covered with a shiny cloth; a brass lamp; above the fireplace the photograph of a man. Near the window was a wooden stool, and the floor, like that of the bedroom, had no carpet or rug on the clean boards. There were five or six books huddled against each other on the window-sill, into which the Frants had never looked. They were not curious in such ways. But one most unaccountable fact they had observed, that three or four times in the year other belongings would make their appearance, from the depths of the chest as it was supposed. They would follow each other in order, obedient to the canons of some private and unguessable ritual which went forward within their owner's mind.

First, towards the end of May, a strip of silk, claret-coloured, and embroidered in gold, with flowers of yellow and faded blue, would one day be laid across the table; it was not wide enough to cover the whole surface, but, being rather long, hung down richly at either end with flowers and golden scrolls crowding together to fulfil their pattern. There for about twelve hours it would lie without explanation, and at the end of that time be engulfed, to reappear no more until another year summoned it.

Next, about five or six weeks later, on the dull black of Miss Alquist's everyday blouse would be displayed an ornament like a large round brooch, of a marvellous blue, with patterns and whorls of silver, and in the centre a bird with an orange breast. It looked soft, as though the bird and the circling pattern had been worked in silk; but Miss Alquist had once vouchsafed the information that it was made of feathers.

After this, no splendours would be set forth for nearly six months, when beneath the photograph, blurred with enlargement beyond its capacity, a little jar would be placed, coloured a clear brilliant green fading to white; in this jar flowers grew in what seemed to be red soil, but which was in fact composed of tiny grains of powdered coral, the flowers themselves were of coral, pink and white, with carved spiky leaves of greenish-brown tortoiseshell. They looked so real, though fantastic, that it was almost shocking to hear them faintly rattling when someone trod heavily in the room overhead.

These were the only treasures on which the public eye might rest. They were sufficiently provocative, and each year as the ritual proceeded there was speculation in the Frants' kitchen.

Miss Alquist disregarded hints and questions. She could be intimidating for all her shabbiness; her very sniff and the lean foreign look of her was enough to disquiet the ordinary questioner, and by degrees her hosts became accustomed to her apparition of the silk, the brooch, and the cold flowers, and accepted them as the years passed almost without comment. They had ceased to hope for any explanation.

All day long, save for a short foraging expedition in the morning, Miss Alquist sat in the wooden chair by the window making ugly little pictures in wool on a coarse stretched canvas. Nearly all these pictures represented ships, not sailing ships, but steamers, and one dirty little steamer in particular with two crooked funnels belching thick smoke, cutting stolidly forward through a grey woollen sea. No picturesque aspects for Miss Alquist. Even on canvas she permitted herself no illusions. The things had movement, though; the clumsy lurch of the broad-beamed tramp, the lift of the stem as she sank in the trough of a wave, the smoke streaming away in a cross wind, it was all recorded and set down in stitches. What became of these pictures when they were finished could never be discovered. Perhaps they descended into the oblivion of the brass-bound chest. Perhaps they were despatched as gifts to distant relatives whose existence was not otherwise recognised; if so, they were not acknowledged, so far as the Frants knew. In the thirteen years of her residence in the street only five letters had come to Miss Alquist, and these were type-written, and presumably to do with money; for she had an account, piteously small, at the local bank, on which she drew, every four weeks, an unvarying sum, and paid at once in cash for every need of her life—house-rent, food, and at rare intervals clothing.

That was her day. But in the evening, earlier or later according to season, she would fold up her work, or replace one of her uninteresting looking books, and go out. Slowly she would climb the street—the Frants' house was at the northern end, near the High Street—looking about her, seeing for the thousandth time the detail of a door, the colour of a roof in sunlight above another in shadow. And towards the top of the street where the porthole windows were more frequent, she would draw long breaths and sniff noisily. Passers by, or watchers in doorways who observed her, always thought that the steep ascent had distressed her; but they were wrong. Her thin body was healthy, though she took no exercise save this. She breathed deeply, expanding her narrow chest, because at this point, among the jutting house fronts, the round sea-windows, and with the flying buttresses of the church rigged against the sky, she felt at home. Treading freely, casting looks of disdain at the tranquilly smoking householders who watched her daily progress, she would climb to the summit of the hill, which below the churchyard became a cliff, falling sheer to the green flats which stretched away to their shadowy junction with sea and sky. There she came every evening, to the same angle of the churchyard fence; and every evening, watching the marsh darken, she would forget its lush earthy green, seeing instead the green of shoal water breaking to white against the cliff. That was how it had been; no grass nor sheep; no smoke, no crawling river with banks of yellow mud; no land to tame men's bodies, but the clean water shifting, flowing, offering and claiming life. Something in her, some legacy from unknown seafaring ancestors, hungered for this to be as it had been. Each day, coming to this place, she felt the passion in her, alive, incommunicable, that recognised and answered the passion of the sea. Motion, colour; fear and defiance; all craving and all fulfilment was there. She was stirred by the sight of that calm, distant water to a great longing for new perils and adventures of the soul, and these she might command, in imagination building the tumbling waters to storm, or subduing them at will. Standing there in the last light of the sun, a small, unconvincing figure, hands resting loosely on the wooden rail, she had experienced all the terrors and revulsions of one who has submitted himself to the powerful sea. She thought how danger might rise in the tropics. Out of a dark breathless sky would come a single gust of hot wind; it died down, and she could hear again the thud of the engines and the water whispering as it slid along the side. A feeling in the air of expectation, vigilance. Another gust, suddenly pushing against the ship like a hot hand; and now the reflected lights began to dance and to heave themselves into twinkling ominous patterns, and the severed water no longer whispered evenly, but came slapping sharply against the plates.

She knew how a steamer might lie waiting for the dawn outside the harbour of an Eastern port; the pale green of the water, reflecting untroubled the lines of the masts and ropes; the fishing boats with their top-heavy triangular sails veering by on the wind that blows before sunrise. She knew the grey-blue of the early sky. She saw the coolies running and yelling, with little baskets of coal no bigger than so many flower-pots, running, sweating, getting the bunkers filled somehow amid singing and sudden unreasoning quarrels. She watched the sky go green and the coast darken as night came; the stars were tremendous and their colours distinct, yet a swift wind might extinguish them in half an hour and set the water leaping and playing, pale with phosphorus, against the hull. She knew the unfathomable blue of mid-ocean, opaque, the colour of lapis-lazuli. She heard the hours go clanging by and the hurry of feet and voices in the night when the watch was changed. She knew monotony; the endless horizons of the sea, the eternal similarity of distant coasts, the throb of the screw. She learned to long for the shore life, and to hate it. She watched the streets of the world; Australian streets with sporting placards at every corner, and sellers of lottery tickets offering their wares to hurrying men with wrinkled eyes; streets of Japan, with vertical shop-signs, and paper fish floating above the houses; South African streets where huge negroes wearing buffalo horns and kirtles of feathers stood in the shafts of the rickshaws.

This was Miss Alquist's life. These were the voyages on which she set out every evening during thirteen years, or longer, who knows? They were the voyages of which he had spoken, from which he had brought back the gifts which looked so exotic in her bare rooms, and which she followed in her heart; but the best of all was that which should have been the last. In it she stood on the bridge of a vessel steaming up Channel, and saw the sequence of lights winking out the course. A heavy sea came clouding over the bows, and sank in little whiffs and rattles of spray against the decks, against her cheeks. Lights of France to starboard; La Vache booming out her warning, fog off the coast. Voices below on the fore-deck, and a laugh, one of the hands playing the fool, all the rest thinking of home, and the drawn red blinds of stuffy little parlours, or bars with the strong lights glittering in gilt-framed mirrors. Quiet lights those, not the restless warning lights of the sea; a firm road to tread; stillness, welcome, safety; and their ship driving back to it all through the spray.

Strange that she should so love the sea, which had robbed her of her lover. At first she could not look at it. She remembered how once, just before the news came, she had gone down to bathe in a little sandy cove; suddenly she had become afraid, angry, and standing waist-deep in the water had struck down at it with her clenched hands, hating it because it yielded and slipped away, not resisting her strength. She had not known then, and the little scene remained in her mind unexplained. Since, she had come to think of the sea as a loved thing that had blundered cruelly. She could not forgive the townspeople their apathy with regard to it. They had been glad when the sea, that had made them, departed. They lived within sight of it, oblivious, tilling the reluctant land, ignoring the treasure withdrawn from them. Their town was dead; better if it had gone down in flames, never to rise, when the French raiders sacked it long ago, in the first years of the fifteenth century. Going home down the tall street early darkened by its own shadows, seeing as she passed candles burning without fear of wind, seeing the people eating, secure and warm, Miss Alquist felt a kind of despair.

It was on an autumn night, an October night still and misty, that it happened. Mrs Frant remembered very well how the mist began to roll in from the sea, like the ghost of a tide, at about half past five in the afternoon, when the sun was dropping and Miss Alquist had set out on her pilgrimage. They heard her return, and could follow the sound of her footsteps from room to room, and could distinguish the tinkle of china as she prepared her supper. They did not consciously reckon up these sounds, to which they were so accustomed that they must rather have noticed their cessation than their sequence. The Frants finished eating, and Mrs Frant piled up the greasy plates on a tray to take them down to the scullery. It will be remembered that Miss Alquist rented the ground floor. Mrs Frant came downstairs carefully, the tray held out before her so that she might see where she was treading, and had reached the kitchen before she raised her eyes. Then she saw that Miss Alquist was standing quite motionless by the door which led to her bedroom, apparently listening. The attitude was not strained or unnatural; that is to say, it would not have seemed so had the tense figure relaxed after a moment. Mrs Frant said afterwards that they seemed to stand there for half an hour, the one stiffly with closed eyes, all senses save one forced to quiescence, the other with her tray held before her, staring, and wondering what sound could ever come up Ship Street that was worth listening for like that. Just as the immobility had lasted long enough to frighten the watcher, Miss Alquist turned away abruptly and went into her bedroom. Mrs Frant advanced towards the sink with her crockery, mentally calculating whether they could afford to give up their lodger if she should turn queer. Her back towards the bedroom, she filled the sink with boiling water, shook in some soda from a tin, and began to scrape the fragments of cheese and bacon fat from the plates. Then she heard a step, and looked quickly round, apprehensively. Through the door she could see Miss Alquist standing with her hat on, and her hands fumbling at her bosom; then the figure moved and there came the sound of steps on the boards, the opening of the street door, its gentle closing. Miss Alquist had gone out. Mrs Frant was so much astonished that she tumbled the plates into the hot water and left them to soak while she went upstairs to consult with her husband. He, too, was astonished, and went at once to the window; the mist was impenetrable, but they could hear plainly the short quick steps going up the hill towards the church.

'Looks like she don't know what time 'tis,' said Frant, 'did she go out for her usual?'

Mrs Frant did not answer. They had both watched her go out, just after five.

'Thick night, too,' said Frant, closing the window. "Well. None o' our look-out.'

'Not our look-out,' Mrs Frant echoed angrily, "T'll be our look-out if she comes over funny and tries to kill us all in our beds one night.'

She had been frightened down there in the kitchen. Frant, who had not seen the still figure, grunted, and took up his paper again, comfortably saying, 'You don't want to go thinking of such things.'

Mrs Frant looked up and was about to speak; but realising how foolish the thing must sound told in her words, sighed, and went, not without qualms, back to the sink and the crockery. From time to time she stopped her washing-up to listen, holding her hands still in the water. Ship Street was silent. The old walls cut off the sounds from neighbouring houses; no one passed on the cobbles. She dried the plates, and hung up the cloth on the line that was stretched across the kitchen from window to fireplace; then slowly climbed again to the upper room where her husband sat. His pipe filled it with rich smoke; the new wick of the lamp gave a good light. Mrs Frant took her chair by the fire and gradually forgot, in that atmosphere of familiar warmth, that half an hour ago she had been frightened by the sight of a woman listening.

Listening, astounded, to the thud and rustle of surf, breaking, so Miss Alquist thought, not a hundred yards away. At first she did not heed it; a trick of the blood, perhaps, rushing in her ears. But it would not be denied. It was real. When she understood that, she was filled with a mad hope that the sea had come back to claim the town, advancing without cause, as it had retreated. The sound persisted, and she made her decision, to go up at once to the cliff by the church. From there she could watch it come crawling over the fields, lapping towards the town. In some haste she put on her shoes and hat, but delayed, strangely enough, over another matter which puzzled the Frants afterwards; then she set out, walking quickly through the mist to the churchyard. She was happy, until as she went it occurred to her that perhaps owing to the mist the sea might not be visible; but when she came to that part of the cliff from which she was accustomed to look across the marsh, she clasped her hands, pressing them in a kind of ecstasy against her breast. For the night was clear, with a half-moon rising, and not a quarter of a mile away she could see a line of white that sometimes drew back hissing, and then launched itself forward, at every such attack gaining a little ground. It seemed to her a battle of two surfaces; one dead, motionless, blindly resisting, the other vivid, alive, wrinkled into a million tiny strengths which at last must overwhelm the single strength of the land. It had reached the outlying dwellings. She saw it close round a cottage, coming creeping and fawning to the threshold, mounting in little waves and surges towards the windows, higher, higher. The glass burst inwards under the impact of a larger mass of water, which poured through, foaming over the jagged edges noiselessly. She observed this silence, and accepted it, though it had been the sound which had summoned her; now she watched while the drama played itself out, and found it natural that it should be presented without sound. Every moment the liquid glittering surface increased, and the dull squares of grass yielded to it, dwindling one by one. The track of the moon grew longer, and was broken into shifting ripples of light, multiplied as the sea advanced stealthily, but more swiftly than before. At this rate, she thought, another five minutes must bring it to the foot of the cliff, and she strained towards it, gripping the wooden railing, thinking rather confusedly of those cities in the Old Testament, overwhelmed that the power of God might be made manifest. She thought of the limitless strength of the sea; of its hills and shadowy valleys, hidden too deep for light to discover them; of the strange jewels of the sea, living creatures, and pearls crusted together in obscurity. There were mysteries there of which the land could know nothing, wonders consummated in the utter darkness, shapes moving above in their own radiance, broken ships like leaves drifting down. She would not open her eyes, she resolved, until she heard the first beat of the waves against the foot of the cliff, for when the water had attained its goal there would be sound again. She began to count the seconds, blindly waiting; sixty rather slowly, and sixty again; and again. Now surely the victory must have been achieved, the walls of water must be piling up in withdrawal to fling themselves in a last assault upon the rocks that withstood them. Another minute went slowly by. She opened her eyes, looked, and felt the blood run to her heart.

There, across the brilliant pathway of the moon, a shadow was passing on the water. She could see and recognise the sturdy hull, the twin funnels streaming smoke, coming as she had seen it so often in thought, northwards, up-channel, home. In an agony of joy she sprang forward, stretching out her arms; heard a cry, the sound of rending wood; and fell.

They did not find her till morning. The Frants, after a little vague speculation, retired to bed and slept heavily as was their custom. Miss Alquist had her key, and there was no need to worry. But Mrs Frant, as she came last into their bedroom, secretly locked the door. She said nothing to her husband; she was taking no risks. At six o'clock next morning they heard a frantic knocking, which at first they ignored, thinking Miss Alquist must answer it; but it was repeated past bearing, and finally Frant, grumbling, went down to the door. Tom Eldridge, a young farm labourer, cousin to Mrs Frant, stood there. He was very white, and would say nothing but, 'You got to come with me, Ted.'

'What you want? Coming making a row like the end of the world. Can't you say what it is?'

'She's dead.'

'Who's dead?'

Tom Eldridge would not answer, except to repeat, 'You got to come.'

The two men went together into Harbour Street and woke the constable. While they waited for him to come down Frant asked again for details. The boy shook his head. He did not want to talk about it. When the constable was ready he led them down the steps, cut in the rock, which led to the foot of the cliff. She was there, on the grass. The constable knelt by her, felt her heart, then looked attentively at her face, and up at the height from which she had fallen. From below they could see the gap in the railing, and beside her, but a little away, lay a fragment of rotten wood.

'Not marked,' said the constable.

He laid her back on the grass, and suddenly put a hand to his sleeve, twisting the cloth as though to wring water from it. The other men saw his fingers come away glistening with moisture.

'Dew,' said Frant, 'or the mist.'

'Ground's dry,' Eldridge answered, breaking silence.

The constable felt the grass. It was dewy, but not soaking. Her skirt and jacket were heavy and stiff with water. He looked again at the dead face, and rose to his feet, wiping his right hand across the front of his coat. He said, without relevance as it seemed, 'I seen two men that died o' drowning—'

He stopped, and screwing up his eyes peered towards the quiet sea as though measuring the distance; then with a quick movement he put the wet palm of his left hand to his mouth, and held it so for an instant, tasting, the big red hand spread out over his face. They watched, with a growing discomfort. Abruptly the hand was dropped; young Eldridge knew that the palm had tasted salt.

Fearfully, with hunched shoulders, they stared down at the little dark figure, lying so easily; it was only then that Frant saw pinned on her breast the brooch, the blue brooch made of feathers.

12 The Pythoness

Interest in Spiritualism need not imply that an inquirer has the religious temperament. He may attend meetings of a circle for half a dozen reasons; curiosity as to the next life, its habits and values; scientific inquiry; a mere taste for the marvellous; and occasionally, rather pitifully, a genuine and overwhelming desire to get in touch with some loved person lost.

All this is mere preliminary, to explain how I came to be sitting in circle with three men so entirely different from me and from each other as Tarrant, Pybus, Mortimer; and one woman so inexplicable as the medium, Mrs Bain. Tarrant was one of those people that all the more showy religions cater for; he liked marvels. The blood of St Januarius liquefies for such as these, and bull-roarers whirl in African caves. Pybus was the earnest inquirer. He found spiritualism logical; it satisfied his intellect; having swallowed the camel of survival after death he ceased to strain at the gnat-like tactics of the spirits, who in their endeavours to resume contact with the world moved birdcages, rang bells, and brought from other climes such mementos as safety pins and faded flowers. (Apports was the technical term for these. They were diverse, their one common characteristic was portability. The spirits never, in my experience, astonished us by materialising a grand piano in my dining-room where we sat behind locked doors.)

Then there was the medium. Mrs Bain had good looks of a large sort, but it would have been difficult to imagine falling in love with her—for me, at least; her natural voice, that most revealing attribute of man or woman, was tinny and self-assured, though it could put on a deeper note in the cabinet. Whether or no she was honest, she gave value for money. I believe the truth to be that she did possess certain powers which she eked out, poor creature, with safety pins and the like; destroying credibility by the very means she adopted to bolster it up.

I repeat that, diverse as were all our needs, she gave us good value, Lance Mortimer in particular. He had been going to her for some time, even before his wife's death; indeed, I believe it was Aileen, the wife, who induced him to attend this circle in the first place, and naturally after she died he gave it more of his time and interest than ever. Personally I was always a little sceptical about the messages Mrs Bain obtained for him. She had known Aileen well, and the confection of detailed messages having the ring of truth seemed to me in the circumstances to be a little too easy. Possibly I wrong Mrs Bain. At any rate Mortimer seemed happy and reassured by the messages, which was the chief thing. He never missed a meeting, and three months after his wife's death had lost almost completely the dragged and haunted look which came on him during her illness.

I have said that to me it was impossible to imagine falling in love with Mrs Bain; impossible that any man of education and intelligence should do so. She appeared to read nothing, to be interested in nothing; she was big and badly dressed. I admit that at moments she was impressive, while the trance was on; there was one occasion when she stripped off every rag of clothing in the cabinet and marched into the room stark, reciting something in a language none of us could follow, and making curious gestures—of libation, I imagine; her empty hands curved themselves to the handles of an imponderable beaker. There was some discussion among the five of us afterwards—this was in Aileen's lifetime—as to whether we should tell her the details of her performance when she came to, but eventually we decided not to embarrass her. On this occasion she was quite unconscious of her actions; the display was altogether too crude to have been the result of conscious deliberation; nakedness, after first youth has passed, and in a heavy muscular woman, lacks allure. We repeated to her so much as we could remember of what she had spoken—there was a refrain, like the 'Pray for us' of a litany, which we were able to write down—and left it at that. I believe, personally, that for once some very old wine was poured into a new bottle.

But this was the performer; the woman was one who would terrify the average man, if he ever looked at her twice. And so I am quite unable to put into words my surprise when, strolling through Hyde Park one evening, in that unfrequented patch near the police station, I saw her sitting on the grass, with Mortimer beside her. She was unmistakable. It was summer, and she had taken the hat from her heavy black hair, which had never been cut, and was never tidy; a coil of it had come down, and lay askew on her shoulder, while her dress, though it was of some light-coloured stuff, somehow looked frowsy. She had her back to me, but I could see Mortimer's face. It was the face you may see often enough in the Park of an evening, eyes intent, mouth restless, desire written plain on it for any passer-by to read. The sight sickened me, somehow. I had known gentle Aileen, his wife, rather well.

Mortimer was talking, urging something, looking steadily, as lovers do, at her mouth. She listened, not interrupting, but her right hand plucked at the grass, and when he seemed to have done she shook her head vigorously, so that the coil of hair slipped down further. When she answered, the timbre of her voice carried, though not the syllables; she seemed to be denying or refusing something. Mortimer became more urgent. On that her restless hand seized the discarded hat, and crammed it on anyhow; then, with an ugly, plunging movement like a cow, she got to her feet and, looking down on him, rapped out something final. Unexpectedly she turned my way, and met my eyes. A cloud of red came over her sallow face, but she walked towards me.

'Quite a surprise,' said she, in those tinny accents of hers, shaking her head; the coil of black hair tumbled forward over her shoulder. 'I never!' said she, hastily stuffing it under the hat with her thick fingers. 'What you must think of me—'

'Hello, Mortimer,' I said, looking past her.

He had risen, and was coming towards the pair of us, seeming none too pleased at the interruption.

'We've been getting a breath of air,' Mrs Bain explained.

'Very wise,' I said; 'it's hot.'

Then there was nothing more to say. I raised my hat to her, and started to move on; it was so very evident that Mortimer didn't want me. But as I took my first step Mrs Bain fell in beside me, saying: 'I'm going your way, if you don't mind being seen with me.'

I said something about my delight. She added, with what seemed deliberate intent: 'Mr Mortimer's had as much fresh air as he can stand. He ought to be getting home.'

Mortimer said nothing whatever to either of us. He took off his hat and we walked on, leaving him standing on the path.

I had nothing in particular to say to Mrs Bain, but I made some sort of conversation about the dresses and the grass. She answered absently and kept looking at me sideways. At last, just as we were halting to cross the Row, she suddenly spoke.

'I suppose you think there's something a bit funny going on.'

I could not pretend to misunderstand, though I did not want confidences.

'There's no reason, you know, why you shouldn't sit in the park with Mortimer.'

She answered, in tones that sounded just a little shocked: 'Well, but he's only been a widower three months.'

'Widowers don't have to shut themselves away from the world nowadays.'

'No,' said she dubiously; 'only a person ought to show respect.'

'Aileen Mortimer was a very generous and sane woman,' I went on, 'as you know. You might have sat in the Park with her husband in her lifetime with her full consent. Why should it be different now?'

'I don't know, I'm sure,' said she; 'only it isn't like the same—'

'Shall we get across?' I asked her, for really I found it intolerable to discuss Aileen with her, and I did not want to be drawn into any comment on Mortimer.

She made no answer, and I hurried her across, through a gap in the traffic. She came meekly enough, head well down as is the way of women; on the opposite, the Knightsbridge side, I stopped, meaning to leave her and walk down alone to Chelsea. To my horror and dismay she was crying. Her great eyes were welling, tears had overflowed, making channels through the brownish powder she used; in another minute she would have broken into noisy sobbing there on the public path. I could hardly leave her boo-hooing after me like a punished dog and so took action at once; gripped her elbow, and piloted her into a providential tea-shop that I had suddenly remembered—quiet, and no more than a hundred yards away. The place was nearly empty; it was getting on for six; shoppers were on their way home. Mrs Bain gulped a 'thank you' and disappeared without shame into the Ladies' Room. I was curious, and sorry for her in a detached sort of fashion. It is so difficult to realise that ugly women must have their emotions too.

She came out, powder renewed in a muddy mass on her nose, and sat down by me at the table. Without studying the menu she asked for chocolate—chocolate at a quarter to six: and while the waitress went for it, talked.

'I ought to be ashamed of myself, Mr Findlay; I know that. Making a fool of myself in public'—('and of me, too,' I thought)—'like a kid of ten. D'you know how old I am? I'm forty-three.'

She looked it, certainly; she had never taken care, and nature had not been kind at the start. I said nothing. She was in the mood when a woman sees through the usual masculine futilities in the way of placation. She went on: 'Forty-three. Makes you think, doesn't it? I've been earning my living for twenty-five years, and you can believe me when I say I'm sick of it.'

The chocolate came, hot enough to waft steam even on that summer afternoon. I poured out my tea and added lemon, while she sipped the boiling thick stuff with a spoon.

'You're interested in your work, though, surely?'

'Look,' said she, pointing her spoon at me; 'I'm interested, and it's as honest a way to make a living as most others. Only just—I'm sick of it.'

She sipped more chocolate, and I could feel her waiting for me to make the first move. No purpose was to be served by waiting, and I obliged her.

'Mortimer, I suppose, was suggesting an alternative.'

'You're right, he was. And I refused. Refused dead, like that—' she made a slashing movement of her powerful hand—'and here I am, going on like a kid with a smashed toy.'

The eyes had indeed started to well again. I said hastily: 'Mortimer didn't mean to offend you, I'm certain.'

'Offend? Offend me? Oh, I suppose you think it was the other thing he wanted. It wasn't; it was marriage, flat out.'

That did surprise me, and perhaps my face showed it.

'Oh, I know. Mrs Mortimer's only been in her grave three months. You think it's not respectful. Nor do I, and so I told him. But it was hard work saying it. I suppose I'm what they call in love.'

She said that as though it were some remote condition familiar perhaps to doctors, but her face contradicted her, or, rather, it underlined the words, gave them force and beauty, for all the clotted powder and the reddened eyes. I said, smothering my convictions, for I had no wish that she should marry Mortimer: 'Well, you know, there's really nothing against it. He's free.'

She answered, staring into the cup, talking as if to herself: 'If only I could be sure—'

'Sure?'

'It's this way,' she said, and paused to gulp down the rest of the chocolate. 'I want to have a home of my own. And I'm fond of him, I don't deny. Fond—' she considered the word, and altered it. 'I'm mad about him. But there's things to be considered. For one thing, I'm not his class.'

There was no answer to that. It was pretty evident that they could have nothing in common, that there was not one chance in fifty of the marriage being a success.

'For another, I'm older than him. He's thirty-eight—five years—that makes a lot of difference. And I couldn't think of marrying him for a year; it wouldn't be right. That brings me up to forty-four. So, you see, looked at all round, it's silly. I see that as clear as you do. Only—'

I was sorry for her. This outburst was genuine, and in refusing Mortimer she had done the only possible thing; but the cost of the decision I could fairly estimate. After all, Mortimer made a fair amount of money, lived comfortably, had a position in the world. She was a vagabond, without a home or a future or any background save that which some psychic laboratory afforded. It was much to give up voluntarily, for the sake of common sense; I respected her, and told her so. She said, with a big, tremulous smile: 'Keep your bouquets a bit longer. I mayn't stick to it.'

'I shan't blame you,' I said, 'if you don't. What about the circle? You'd better not be seeing him.'

'No, that's right,' she agreed with a sigh. 'We'd better wash out the sittings for a while.'

'How long will it take to—'

Get over it, I meant, and though I left the actual words unsaid she answered them.

'I don't feel as if I ever should, come to that. Better say I'm going away.'

'I'll tell Mortimer.'

'Well, I'd be obliged. I don't want to get in touch with him, you see.'

'How about money?' I said on an impulse; 'can you carry on?'

She looked vague, and said she could manage. We went together out of the shop, which was closing, and I saw her on to a bus before I walked thoughtfully home.

There was to have been a meeting next evening, but I sent out cards, with some invention about Mrs Bain's having been called away suddenly, to put off the others. These cards should all have been delivered next morning, in plenty of time to warn; nevertheless, at nine-thirty that night, our usual hour, Mortimer was shown in.

'No sitting to-night, I'm afraid,' I said. 'Didn't you get my notice?'

'I got it, thanks,' he answered; 'that's why I'm here.'

He looked sick and dangerous, and I could easily trace the cause even before he spoke again.

'What did you say to her yesterday? I want to know.'

There was no sense in refusing to discuss the matter, since he already knew all that she had told me. I let him have the whole of our interview in the tea-shop, ending with: 'And she's right, you know. What she says is unanswerable. She's thinking for both of you. I respect her, and her decision, and so will you if you're wise.'

'What do you know about it?' he broke out in fury; not rowdy fury, but a deadly white quiet. 'What do you know of what's behind it all? You with your respect, you're half dead!' He used a curious phrase then. 'I've earned that woman, and I'm going to have her.'

'That's your affair. I won't help.'

'I don't want your help. Where's she gone?'

'I don't know.'

This was true; I was surprised that she should so soon have cut herself adrift. He considered me, whistling softly through his teeth.

'You're a liar, but it doesn't matter. I'll find out.'

'If you love her, you'll let her alone.'

'I can't let her alone,' said Mortimer, snarling, and turning to the door.

He might never have found her but for one thing; she had to live, and she knew only one way of earning money. If I had pressed a loan on her there in the tea-shop it might have prevented the whole tragedy—and yet, I don't know; I couldn't have kept on subsidising her, and she must, sooner or later, have gone back to her trade. She went far enough off, but mediums are easy to keep track of, especially such a woman as she was, well known and nearly honest. Mortimer ran her to earth in Edinburgh within three months of her departure from London, and began without delay or haste to make his siege.

Poor woman! She did resist as she had promised; fled the town, tried to get passage to America, and was brought up short, like a dog on a chain, by the imperious eternal need of money. He followed again and found her in some sort of dingy lodgings, where he fairly bullied her into consenting.

All this I had from her long afterwards, and I remember the words she used: 'They say if a man gets thirsty enough he'll drink seawater though he knows it'll send him off his head. I'd got to that state. I knew it was mad, but I was thirsty for him.'

It would have been superhuman to expect her to put up yet another fight. She had done her best for the decencies, and for the ultimate happiness of both of them; he, and the world, and the circumstances of her life would have none of her best. She gave in.

Having yielded, she kept nothing back—no rashness, no absurdity of affection. She let herself go with his desire like a flower dropped on a quick stream; or, rather, since that comparison suggests something frail, like a whole tree swept towards Niagara. She would not marry him, so far she held out, until the year was past from the date of his wife's death, but she planned, doted, spent fifteen hours a day in his company, and with a snap of her big fingers gave her whole spiritualist connection the go-by.

She it was who wrote to me, for I believe that after those half-dozen sentences exchanged between us on the evening of her flight Mortimer would have seen me dead and damned before he put his foot over my door. She, on the other hand, remembered that I had understood both sides of the question. I wrote back congratulating, and suggesting that they should come one evening to dine. She accepted enthusiastically by telephone.

'Oh, please, Mr Findlay,' I heard her unlovely voice; 'if it isn't a rude question, will anybody else be coming?'

'That's as you choose,' I answered. 'Plain party, or coloured; you shall decide.'

'Oh, then, just us, if you don't mind, Mr Findlay.' She had that infuriating trick of using one's name at every sentence.

'Unless—' the voice trailed off.

'Unless?' Then I suppose I must have caught her unspoken thought. 'What about Pybus and Tarrant, if they're in London? A final meeting of the circle?'

'Oh, yes,' said she, noisily glad; 'that's what I was hoping you'd say. After all, it was with you all, and sitting for you, I met Lance. It would be nice to say sort of good-bye.'

'You're giving up your work, I suppose?'

'Lance says I've got to,' she answered, and the clumsy words, as she spoke them in her unbearable voice, gave an impression of joyous surrender difficult to describe.

So this was the party, four men, one woman, just as we had met often before. Pybus and Tarrant turned up first together, so that I was able to let them know the state of affairs. They were incredulous, as I had been when I came upon the ill-assorted couple in the Park.

'They say,' said Tarrant, 'a man always goes for the same type of woman. Here's proof he doesn't. You couldn't have two women less alike than the Bain and Aileen.'

'Few husbands have energy enough to experiment in domesticity,' I said, busy with the sherry. 'If a man's happy with one type he'll stick to that.'

Pybus, always literal, took up my words as he accepted his glass.

'Wasn't Mortimer happy, then, with Aileen?'

Tarrant jumped on him, of course. Aileen, so fine, such a darling, who wouldn't be happy with her? Pybus, making appreciative faces over his sherry, agreed that he had said something idiotic, and the topic dropped—dropped, and took root in my mind uncomfortably, like the barbed seed of some desert flower. They went back to the marvellous alliance.

'She's older than he is. And—how about Bain? Who and what was Bain?'

'He's dead, she told me once.'

'Well, it's Mortimer's funeral. I wouldn't care for a wife myself that had been long on this job.' Spiritualism, Pybus implied.

'She's giving it up.'

Tarrant laughed.

'How can she give it up?' Which was just what Mortimer had said to me, concerning his pursuit of her. 'She's—a sort of spirit right-of-way. After there's been going and coming for years you can't suddenly padlock a gate that people have got used to using.'

'You can,' said Pybus, the literal. 'It's entirely a question of how long the trespassing has been permitted.'

'She's been working as a medium for twenty-five years,' I said, and Pybus' face fell.

'What I mean is,' Tarrant went on, 'she won't be able to help stuff coming through. It's a queer situation. Suppose Aileen wanted to get in touch with Lance?'

'Talk of something else,' I said; 'they're on the stairs.'

A moment later they were in the room. She came first, untidy as ever, but grander. Her hair was wound up in a large bun, lop-sided already, and secured with a flashing slide of some kind at the back. Her dress was a savage orange colour which must have killed any clothing set near it save masculine blacks and whites—a terrific dress, but her face dominated it. Big and untended and uncouth as she was, there was about her a happiness so shining that it lent her almost beauty; as the two men congratulated, and she smiled with her eyes on Mortimer, I could read astonishment behind their civil masks. They were used to her as the medium, a powerful blank body, strong enough physically to stand the strain of the trances, having no very definite personality to oppose the entrance of the other-world forces, whatever they were. The instrument had become a woman, and though I was prepared for it, knowing the circumstances and having had that conversation in the tea-room, it was something of a revelation, even to me.

Mortimer, too, looked different, settled, as if at last he had come home. There had been hunger in that face when I last saw it snarling over his shoulder, and now that the hunger was appeased he was again the pleasant-mannered fellow that his club knew; the snarling face became something seen in nightmare, and which for her sake I hoped he might never show again.

Yet, despite the perfect contentment of the chief guests, or possibly because of it, our meal was not successful. The talk was spasmodic, gusty; it rose and died, and even the wine could not keep it to an even flow. The truth was, of course, that we were about the most ill-assorted party conceivable, having only one interest in common—a topic barred by the idiotic prejudice against talking shop. Somehow or other we laboured along, in friendly but difficult converse, to the moment of coffee, which at my suggestion we took at the table, all sitting together round the candles. It is a good moment, that after-dinner quarter hour's dawdle, wine circling, smoke ascending, and whether or no there is talk seems to matter little enough. I saw Mrs Bain, as she stirred her coffee, gaze about her with kindliness. We had always held our circle in the dining-room, which lies at the back of the house, insulated from noise, and she was evidently remembering. I put it to her.

'A penny, Mrs Bain?'

She came back to reality, looking a little puzzled.

'Penny? Oh, I see what you mean—for my thoughts. I was thinking about all that had happened in this room. We got grand results, didn't we?'

Everybody nodded, and there was a murmur of 'That we did. Thanks to you. Wonderful phenomena.'

She went on, looking steadily and lovingly at Mortimer:

'I'm giving it up, you know, for good.'

'You won't be able to,' said Tarrant, who, it must be remembered, was a believer born. 'It will come over you sometimes, a rush of communication.'

Mortimer laughed rather shortly.

'I'll keep her to earth,' he said, and glanced over at her for response. But for once she was not looking at him. She was staring down into her coffee cup, where the round of shining black liquid seemed to hold her eyes. Tarrant was going on with his argument, using over again his simile of the right-of-way.

'There aren't so many short cuts,' he persisted, 'and those there are get known; both sides of the fence they get known. How many mediums are there—proved, honest ones, I mean—in London? And how many wanting to use them on the other side? Do you suppose they're going to sit back and let—'

'Look out,' I said sharply.

Mrs Bain's head had fallen forward, though her eyes still were open, staring into the dark pool of the cup. Mortimer swore, and thrust back his chair. He was sitting on my left, opposite her, and I shoved him back and down. It is not healthy for sleepwalkers to wake them in mid-progress, and the same holds good for people entranced. I had, I may say, from the first moment, no doubt whatever that this was a genuine performance. Her colour was deathly, the breathing had slackened, the pupils of her eyes were contracted as if she had taken a stiff shot of morphia. She had looked like that once before, on the occasion when she stripped, and I remembered these preliminary signs most clearly.

Mortimer subsided under my hand, but spoke to her.

'Ruby, come back. You're having dinner with Findlay, not giving a sitting. Ruby!'

She took no notice at all, she who all the evening had been

quiveringly alive to every glance and gesture of his. She stared into the cup, opening her mouth now and then. It was Tarrant who said, triumph in his whisper: 'Better let her get it over. What about the lights?'

'No!' said Mortimer loudly. 'Ruby, listen to me.'

'She doesn't hear you,' Pybus told him unnecessarily; 'something's coming through.'

Tarrant got up quietly and, leaning over the table, blew out the candles, our only illuminants, one by one. We sat in the silence and dark, I with my hand still on Mortimer's arm, listening to strong sighs that came from her, seeming to shake her; great sighs, deep and endless, as though her whole trunk were hollow, a mere cavern for air. Then a voice sounded, broken and often half-lost, like some person speaking against the wind.

'Cruel,' it said. 'Oh, cruel! You hurt me so.'

Nothing more for a minute. I took upon myself to be leader, since the others were silent.

'Who are you?' I asked. 'Will you tell us who you are?'

'He knows,' answered the voice; 'Lance knows.'

'Have you a message for Lance?'

A laugh; a pause; then a little husky sound of singing, an old song, familiar words, the folk-tune of 'Lord Rendel'.

'Oh, that was strong poison, Rendel my son;
Oh, that was strong poison, my pretty one—'

I felt the muscles contract in Mortimer's arm as involuntarily my fingers gripped tighter; we were both hearing the same thing, Aileen's light voice with a touch of County Kerry in it, singing an accustomed tune through the mouth of her supplanter. I remembered, troubled, that on this day a year ago she had died.

'Aileen,' I said, 'we know you now. What have you come to say?'

The voice fluttered on with its song.

'Oh, make my bed soon;
I'm sick to my heart, and fain would lie down.'

Still Mortimer did not speak, and I supposed that the shock of the thing was keeping him quiet. We all of us knew that voice and recognised it with the conviction that this was no trickery. Aileen spoke quite inimitably. This was herself.

'Lance, Lance,' it went on. 'What are you doing, my dear one? I'm sick, take that dope away. Must I have it, Lance? Ah, you've killed me, my poor creature, my dear lover; wasn't I dying fast enough—was that it? It's kind stuff you're using, gentle stuff, sleepy; but oh, the cruel pain at my heart! You wanted that big woman, did you? Poor Lance, and I was in the way, my sweet pretty one.' Then the voice went wavering off into its tune again.

'I'm sick to my heart, and fain—and fain—'

It went away in ghostly heavings and sighs, cavernous breaths on which now and then a note of the song could still be heard riding. There was a pause, a deadly five seconds. Then the arm under my hand flexed, Mortimer's fist drove at me in the dark and caught me over the heart; there was the screech of a chair on the parquet, and a shaft of light struck in upon us through a door torn open. In an instant a wave of noise seemed to rise; feet scuffling, the voices, angrily loud, of Tarrant and Pybus in the hall, a struggle in which a mirror went down, and through which I could hear the scrape of steel. Mortimer's blow had been fierce enough to sicken me. I sat limp, hearing the struggle, which at the height of its din suddenly died away to silence, following the sound of a man's fall.

'He's done it. My God,' from Tarrant; 'how do you stop blood?'

'You'll never stop that,' Pybus speaking. 'Better than the hangman's trap, anyway.'

I got to my feet with a groan, and pitched forward to the door, to whose handle I clung, looking out. Mortimer had made a job of it with one of the Chinese swords hung for ornament on the wall, my yellow wall that was streaked where blood had spurted towards it from the side of his neck. He died while I watched, with a writhing of the face, a rictus above clenched teeth that I do not now care to recall. We stood away from him, and stared down on him dying, without compassion of any sort for the man who had murdered Aileen. Not one of us doubted that; and if it may sound absurd wholly and instantly to believe a woman whom we knew to be not above using the tricks of her trade—well, we had seen the glow of her happiness before that voice came out of nowhere, singing and murmuring damnation to her hope. We looked down on him, and then round at each other, silently with a question. What to do?

Before there could be any consultation, a sound from the dining-room made me start and turn; that most ordinary of sounds, a long, untrammelled yawn. I went in at once, shutting the door behind me, and switched on the lights. Mrs Bain was lying back in her chair, very white but conscious, and rubbing at her eyes with the heel of her hand like a child.

'Where's Lance?' she asked first, smiling. 'And the others? You look washed out, Mr Findlay. Whatever have I been up to?'

'Something came through,' I began, stammering, for there were sounds outside as if they might be lifting him; 'something rather shocking—'

She glanced down at once at her ornate and hideous dress, but it was not disarranged, she was clad as fully as its cut permitted.

'Fancy!' she said archly, 'It must have been bad for you to look like that. I'm tired too; dead tired. But what's the odds, so long as you're happy? We always did get good results, didn't we, in this circle?'

13 An Experiment of the Dead

It was a most shocking surprise to that highly respectable firm of solicitors, Messrs Walker, Paradise, and Walker, when Lady Paula Lidyard went off the rails, causing almost as much confusion and loss of life as might an express train similarly fated. She had been in the habit of drinking too much, spending too much, and risking her neck in swift vehicles far too lightly; but she had somehow kept clear of scandal, which to the legal mind (and indeed to most other minds) meant lovers. Then, at forty-six, what must she do but fall in love with a boy of twenty-three, a young soldier, and announce that she intended to marry him.

Alaric Lidyard, who had been married to her for twenty years, and was a little sorry for the young man, refused flatly to give her her freedom. Mr Percival Walker listened, nodding comprehension, to his reasons.

'She'll get sick of him, y'know. And it's not fair to young Ninian. He'd have to send in his papers—they don't care for this sort of thing in the Brigade. He won't take her on, if it means blowing all his prospects sky-high. We'd better sit tight till she quiets down.'

Mr Walker agreed heartily with this solution, which was well within the traditions of his firm.

'Quite,' said Mr Walker, 'quite. We may safely leave the whole matter to Time.'

With which words, followed by a smile as of parchment cracking, he sent Alaric Lidyard to his death.

For Lady Paula, caught in their trap of inaction, sought escape as an animal might. There was an accident; the car in which she was driving her husband to a dinner-party on the other side of the county turned over into a granite quarry. Lady Paula, bleeding and exhausted, was picked up by a passing motorist as she stumbled, in her evening shoes, towards the nearest village for help. Alaric Lidyard lay at the bottom of the quarry with the car on top of him. When they recovered his body, the head was found to be smashed in.

All very natural, given the weight of the car, and the thirty-foot drop. But an alert young doctor noticed one or two things. He observed that the head wounds, under their mask of blood, were numerous, smallish and deep. A blood-stained spanner was found, hidden under a pile of stones. There were inexplicable stains on the grey upholstery of the car. In short, the conclusion was inescapable. Lady Paula had halted the car, struck her husband repeatedly with the spanner, killing him; then, getting out and putting the car in gear, had sent it with its freight straight at the fence that railed the quarry.

The Coroner's inquest, the trial at the Assizes, took their course. Messrs Walker managed with despairing skill the only defence on a criminal charge that had ever come the firm's way. In vain. Paula Lidyard, daughter of one of those earls whose names in white paint adorned Messrs Walker's deed-boxes, was to die, hanged by the neck, on a given date in November.

The day after the announcement that her appeal had failed, an odd-looking figure called upon Mr Percival Walker. He had the look of a not very exemplary clergyman, grossly fat, and of an appearance disturbing to confidence. He spoke well, however, and made an extraordinary request in very seemly language. Briefly, he wished for an interview with Lady Paula in prison; an interview with her alone.

'Impossible,' said Mr Percival Walker with finality. 'Apart from the technical impossibility of introducing a stranger at this time, I may say it is not likely that a gentleman of your cloth would meet with a good reception.'

'Is she bitter?' asked the clergyman, eagerly. 'Terrified? Reluctant to die?' Mr Walker regarded him stiffly, and the visitor resumed, more calmly: 'The fact is, I am a relative of Lady Paula, and I have a communication of some importance to make to her.'

Mr Percival Walker looked at the visitor's card, which read: 'The Reverend Dionysius Luan,' and turned his eyes towards the red volume of *Burke's Landed Gentry*. Mr Luan followed the glance, smiling.

'By all means,' said he; 'you will find me there. Her first cousin. No cure of souls—at present.'

Mr Walker did not consult the volume. Recollection stirred in him; this was the son of Lady Paula's only uncle; a recluse, the author of books on certain occult subjects, a practitioner of certain odd and mystical experiments. Certainly, he was the nearest relative of the firm's unfortunate client. All the same—

'May I know your purpose in wishing to see her?' enquired Mr Walker.

'I can only inform you that it is a private matter of the first importance—to me, at any rate,' the clergyman answered; and there was a kind of urgency, almost a glitter, in his small, sunken eyes.

Mr Walker turned the matter over. Taking into consideration his visitor's cloth, with his relationship to the condemned woman, he thought it might be done. The clergyman beamed and swallowed, clasping his fat hands together in gratitude. Would Mr Walker be so good as to approach the proper authorities? And communicate their decision? Mr Luan could not really express his obligations. And the date of the execution—so soon? Unhappy woman, poor Paula!

With this lamentation the clergyman heaved up from his chair, shook hands with a clinging pressure, and went rolling and labouring out through the old-fashioned high doorway.

Mr Walker, moved by a need for air, opened the window a little wider after his departure.

Ten days later he sat opposite Mr Dionysius Luan in a railway carriage. Both men were reading; but while Mr Walker deplored the Gadarene course of British politics as revealed in the pages of *The Times*, Mr Luan was deeply intent upon a red leather book which had the appearance of a manual of devotion. He seemed to read always the same few pages, turning back again and again, as though committing some passage to memory. Once, when moving lips and half-shut eyes showed him engrossed, the book slipped to the floor. Mr Walker, active and polite, bent quickly to recover it, glancing as he did so at the open pages; he observed that one was devoted to a diagram in black and red, which might have been an astrological design, except for certain symbols which had no obvious connection with astrology. He had time only to notice this, and to read a few words in large type which headed the opposite page, when Mr Luan took the book from him, eyeing the solicitor shrewdly as he offered civil thanks. Mr Walker had not sat thirty years in his swivel office-chair for nothing; he met the look as blandly as he accepted the thanks, with some comment upon the difficulty of combining high railway speeds with ordinary comfort. He had half a mind to enquire of Mr Luan the meaning of the words which had caught his eye: 'If you would have a dead man's spirit to attend you, and do your bidding in all things, there is a way, how it may be done.' But the clergyman, having stowed the red-covered book in his pocket, seemed inclined to doze, and Mr Walker, who regarded his client's occult studies with the disfavour natural to a priest of the obvious, permitted him to sleep.

Arrived in the northern town, they went direct to the prison. It was arranged that Mr Luan should wait with what patience he could upon an unyielding Office of Works chair, while Mr Walker interviewed his client, and prepared her for the visit to follow. He returned in a short time, shaking his head, with the news (to him not unexpected) that the condemned woman had no wish to see her cousin, and that the matter could not be further pressed.

'One cannot insist,' the solicitor told Mr Luan. 'A condemned person retains certain rights.'

Mr Luan deliberated; then, slowly drawing a note-book from his pocket, wrote a few words, tore and folded the sheet, and courteously requested Mr Walker to deliver the note.

'Pray take it. I believe she will see reason. It is,' said Mr Luan, with an odd smile, the smile of a man thinking of treasure, 'a necessity that she should see me.'

The note was delivered and read. Five minutes later Mr Walker, secretly marvelling, was informing the clergyman that his cousin had changed her mind. Mr Luan showed no surprise, but got to his feet with a kind of clumsy sprightliness and went billowing down corridors at the heels of a wardress to that apartment known to prison officials as the solicitor's room. Lady Paula stood there, a wardress by her, at the other side of a wide table. Her eyes had lost none of their defiance, her hair was black as he remembered it; she still had beauty, but it was contradicted and marred by the line of her mouth, cruel, wholly relentless. She spoke loudly and at once, without greeting.

'Is Ninian coming? What's the message? Why the hell doesn't Ninian come?'

Mr Luan glanced at the wardress and spoke with the authority his cloth permitted.

'I presume I may speak with the prisoner alone?'

The wardress hesitated, and compromised by retiring to just outside the door, which she left half-open. Lady Paula gave a contemptuous short laugh. Then, seeing the gold chain stretched across her cousin's ample black waistcoat, said suddenly: 'What's the time?'

Mr Luan told her. She began to tap with her fingers on the table, almost as though she were counting, then broke off.

'Well, what's the message from Ninian? You said you had a message.'

'I have none,' answered Mr Luan placidly. 'It was a ruse, to speak with you.' She did not move; but gave him, without turning her head, a hooded look. He continued: 'I have something to say more important than any message from that young man.'

'In two days I shan't be alive,' said Lady Paula harshly. 'Two days and a few hours. I shall know more about it than you, in two days. I don't want to talk about religion, thanks.'

'Nor do I wish to talk about religion,' replied Mr Luan.

Lady Paula stared, gave a half-laugh.

'What sort of a clergyman do you call yourself?'

'Wait,' said Mr Luan, one fat hand raised. 'Listen, if you please.'

The wardress, standing by the door, could see Mr Luan's face. His lips moved without pause. The condemned woman sat, flung sideways on her chair; her expression showed scorn, and later a kind of angry curiosity. The wardress looked away, after a glance at her watch; six minutes yet remained of the quarter-hour permitted. She was a religious woman. The attitude of her charge to the prison chaplain had distressed her, and it was with satisfaction that she perceived the attention with which Lady Paula now heard this stranger clergyman. She began to walk a few steps this way and that, outside the door, to give them an illusion of greater privacy.

Her next glimpse of the pair showed Mr Luan pushing a red-bound book towards the prisoner, and she was about to interfere, for, according to regulations, no interchange of books or papers was permitted; but the prisoner did not open the book, merely laid her hands on it, from which the wardress supposed that it must be a Bible, and let matters alone. The prisoner, hands crossed one above the other, seemed once more to be repeating some formula after the clergyman, and when this was over kissed the red book, though with no very devout expression, and thrust it back along the table. By the wardress's watch it was almost time to interrupt them, but apparently the ceremony was not ended, and it was possible to stretch a point in the interests of salvation. She ceased her march, however, and stood in the doorway as a hint to the two engrossed persons; from this vantage point she heard, with some amazement, Mr Luan recite as follows:

'By which kiss thou, Paula, dost covenant and agree after death to be my servant in the spirit, to go wheresoever I shall bid thee, whether in earth or hell, and to obey me in all things, because by my knowledge I have power to constrain thee. Fiat, fiat. Say, now, after me, Amen.'

'Amen,' said Lady Paula's voice. It was mocking, the voice her husband and lover had both of them known. 'But it looks to me as if you'd made a rotten bargain. I never could do as I was told. And I don't suppose people change much—afterwards.' Mr Luan smiled indulgently. She persisted: 'No, seriously—of course, I mean, it's all quite mad, but just by way of curiosity, what would happen if I turned out to be stronger than you?'

Mr Luan looked at her: at the dominant mouth, the eyes expressionless as those of a snake; and, despite his confidence, felt a little disquieted. She went on: 'After all, I've committed a murder. What have you done? Where does this power of yours come from? You've read a lot of books. I—' She looked at her hands, which had beaten out Alaric Lidyard's life—'I've done things.'

'I must take my chance,' said Mr Luan, and made a curious gesture with his left hand in the air. Paula Lidyard leant back, surveying him with amusement and contempt, as she might have watched an unwieldy animal doing tricks. So thought the wardress, coming forward at this moment. Her prisoner disregarded her entirely, as she had been accustomed for forty years to disregard persons in attendance on her.

'Can't we go on?' said she. 'You take my mind off things. Can't we seal it in blood, do something dramatic?'

'Unnecessary,' said Mr Luan, not smiling at this little joke, and pocketing the red book as he rose.

'You may shake hands,' the wardress told her charge, who laughed and blew Mr Luan a kiss.

'Good-bye,' said she, 'and here's to our experiment. Lucky for you, wasn't it? It's not every day you get hold of a collaborator who's going to be hanged'—The word, thus defiantly and loudly spoken, caught her back into nightmare. She went out with the wardress; and Mr Luan heard her outside the door: 'What's the time? There aren't enough clocks in this damn place. Tell me the time, can't you?'

In their hotel that night Mr Walker inquired more particularly if the interview had been a success.

'I think so,' answered Mr Luan slowly. 'Yes, I believe so. Time will show.'

This, Mr Walker's own favourite maxim, had a reassuring sound. He had not been easy in his mind concerning the clergyman. Certain further memories had come back to him, one unsavoury business in particular, with an odour of black magic about it, from the far-off days when Mr Luan had been an undergraduate at Cambridge. He rebuked himself now, and took up the conversation.

'Lady Paula has been something of a problem to the chaplain, I understand. It is shocking,' said Mr Walker, pausing to clip a cigar, 'to consider what she has done with her opportunities, her determination, and her great beauty.'

'Has she then such force of character?' enquired Mr Luan, earnestly.

'That,' answered Mr Walker, pausing deliberately, 'would be an understatement.' His bright small eyes concerned themselves with the tip of his cigar, but he was well enough aware of his companion's interest to continue: 'She is a woman of one idea at a time, impeded by no scruple that I have been able to discover. She wanted entire control of her husband. That implied the death of her mother-in-law—oh, believe me, I have no doubt of the fact. She has twice done murder, each time for the same reason; that she might have what she wanted.'

'And what do you suppose she may want now?'

'Life,' answered Mr Walker, without hesitation. 'She wants to go on living. The life of the body, I mean, for that has been her sole concern. I should say that what she now deeply wants is a body to dwell in. But there is no way out for her this time, unless'—he regarded his companion with a half-smile—'unless your studies can find her one.'

'My studies?' repeated Mr Luan, quickly for him. 'I am no wiser than my neighbours. What studies do you imply?'

Mr Walker reminded him that one of his published works had to do with thaumaturgy. He did not remind him of that unsavoury affair at Cambridge, whose details still dwelt vaguely at the back of his mind. Mr Luan laughed; disclaimed any practical belief in such matters, and feared that Lady Paula must place no reliance on him.

'A dangerous soul,' then said Mr Walker to his cigar. 'This will sound to you superstitious, Mr Luan, but I cannot imagine so much violence, so great determination, ended by so simple and obvious a process as strangling.'

'It may be diverted, however,' answered Mr Luan, turning up his eyes, 'to other purposes. Yes, to other purposes.'

Mr Walker made no direct answer, for he found his companion repulsive in these occasional sanctimonious moods.

It had been decided that the solicitor and the clergyman should remain at hand in the northern town until Lady Paula could have no further need of their services. During the brief period of waiting Mr Luan betrayed a certain very natural restlessness and discomfort of mind. Occasionally he questioned Mr Walker with notable intensity concerning Lady Paula's character, laying stress in particular upon its ruthlessness and strength. Could it be true that she had committed two murders? Two? Was she indeed so accustomed to have her own way in all things? Mr Walker, having answered, with some impatience, that it was so, Mr Luan would return to the study of his red book. It never left him. Its bulk showed in his pocket, or else he was handling it, not reading, but holding it as though he found it comfortable to his fingers. Once he inquired of his companion if he intended to be present at the execution. Mr Walker replied with distaste that such attendance was no part of his duty.

'It would be interesting,' began Mr Luan; and checked. 'I should be glad to know how my cousin conducts herself.'

'I may tell you this much,' said the solicitor on an impulse, looking at him sideways, 'the interview with you appears to have done Lady Paula some service. She is no longer frenzied at the thought of death.'

'I am happy to hear it,' said Mr Luan, the tone contradicting the words.

'She has swung to the other extreme,' Mr Walker went on, 'as is her wont. She seems to anticipate the hour, almost—I was going to say, almost with zest.'

He observed Mr Luan's cheesy face take on a more absolute pallor at this; and indeed, he personally found the new attitude of the condemned woman disturbing and unnatural. He changed the subject by ringing the bell, and giving precise orders about being called in the morning.

Mr Walker that night slept but ill. So did Mr Luan, if the evidence of his neighbour's ears might be believed. Each time the solicitor woke, and he woke at all hours, he noted a heavy shuffling tread next door, which told him that Mr Luan was awake and troubled. Mr Walker too was by no means indifferent; and he heard the bells of a church strike the hour of execution, almost with relief.

A minute later, just as the clanging of the bells died down, he heard a different and more sinister sound from the room next door; it was, unmistakably, the sound of a fall. Mr Walker snatched his dressing-gown and ran out into the corridor. Mr Luan's door was shut, but it opened to a turning of the knob. He ran in, pausing to press a bell for help, and looked about him.

Mr Luan lay by the window, grossly sprawled on his back, the red-bound book beside him, open as it had fallen. Mr Walker, in his concern for the man, could not but recognise that same page, that diagram, which he had seen for a moment in the railway carriage two days before. Even as he clasped his fingers upon Mr Luan's pulse his eyes were taken by the clear ancient print, headed with words in larger type: An Experiment of the Dead. He read again, and on, while his fingers noted the pulse's leapings: 'If you would have a dead man's spirit to attend you, and do your bidding in all things, there is a way how it may be done. Get a promise of one that is to be hanged—'

A movement distracted his attention. Mr Luan's large head was moving from side to side, as though to free the neck from some constriction, and as Mr Walker watched, the clergyman's eyes opened and surveyed him; bewildered, yet with a kind of triumph. They rolled once or twice, as the head had rolled, then blinked at Mr Walker; who gently shaking the wrist he still held, asked: 'Are you better, Mr Luan?'

The answer came slowly, in a voice whose words and quality Lady Paula's solicitor heard with the sick certainty of recognition: 'Hullo!' said the voice which was not Mr Luan's, though it came from his throat. 'What—what's the time?'

Notes on the stories

BY KATE MACDONALD, WITH CONTRIBUTIONS BY EMER O'HANLON

1 Grey Sand and White Sand

up to town: to London, presumably to drop back into a more sociable life, in touch with artists and their friends.

put salt on beauty's tail: an old-fashioned method of capturing a bird is to put salt on its tail.

2 The Rite

hatless: before the 1950s in Britain a woman not wearing a hat out of doors was not dressed correctly, or was indicating a personal freedom that could be read as childish or intimate.

the dust clouded: country roads were rarely 'made' in this period. Asphalt and tarmac only became the norm after the 1940s, and so roads were routinely dusty or muddy.

solitary measure: a solitary dance.

3 The Outcast

hollow square: the four-sided shape on the parade-ground made by soldiers about to watch the execution of one of their own number, for breaking military law.

the parlour: the parlour or front room was traditionally the 'best' room in a private house, used only by favoured visitors or those from a higher social class. Old-fashioned inns kept the parlour as a private room for guests of the higher classes, and for women travellers who would not have been allowed in the main bar in any case (women drinking in bars risked being treated as prostitutes). This spatial segregation by class and sex persisted in pubs and hotels in some areas of the UK until the 1980s.

I'll lay: I predict.

it'll be to do again: he's planted a yew tree, but has no expectation that it will live beyond the spring.

our memorial: a war memorial for the soldiers from the village who had died in the First World War.

Gippo: derogatory rural term for a gypsy.

grenade: a military insignia of the Royal Regiment of Fusiliers, consisting of a metal disc depicting a flame erupting from the top.

4 As Much More Land

laedunt omnes, ultima necat: Latin, 'Every (hour) wounds, the last one kills'. A traditional motto for sundials.

monthly: a monthly periodical.

been confined: have given birth to their children.

the service was finished: when the servants had taken away the last dishes from the meal.

Think'st thou that Faustus: from *Dr Faustus* by Christopher Marlowe (first performed in the early 1590s), from the scene in which Faustus has signed his pact with Mephistophilis.

Bluebeard: in the folk tale Bluebeard's new wife is told that she may not enter the one room in the castle from which he has banned her, in which he keeps the bodies of his disobedient wives.

In my school-days: Bassanio's remark about shooting arrows is a metaphor, from Shakespeare's *The Merchant of Venice*.

th' Antartique pole: from *Tamburlaine the Great Part II*, by Christopher Marlowe (1588).

schools: Hugh's final examinations at the University of Oxford.

sash: each part of a sash window slides upward and downward, and they can be locked at the centre where the frames meet when fully closed.

bandbox: a box made of a continuous band of light wood or cardboard bound in an oval with a lid and base, used for storing small items or hats. They are often used as similes for neatness and tidiness.

egg-and-spoon: this may be an alternative name for the classic egg and dart plasterwork that decorated edges of ceilings.

Let no deluding dreames: from *Epithalamion* by Edmund Spenser (1594), a marriage hymn anticipating the bridal night.

If snow be night: the third and fourth lines from Shakespeare's Sonnet 130, which begins 'My mistress's eyes are nothing like the sun'.

I disbelieve: a pastiche of the Nicene Creed, a central statement of faith for Anglicans, which negates some of its principal ideas, and paganises others. Saying a prayer backwards was held to be a practice in black magic, but here Hugh is merely being a clever undergraduate.

My soul, like to a ship: the dying words of Vittoria, a murderess, in the Jacobean playwright John Webster's *The White Devil* (1612).

Hell is murky, light thickens: phrases spoken respectively by Lady Macbeth and Macbeth in Shakespeare's play (1606), which is technically Jacobean since it was first performed three years after Elizabeth's death.

A thing armed with a rake: from the Cardinal's speech in the scene where he is murdered, in John Webster's *The Duchess of Malfi* (1612)

He that died a Wednesday: from Shakespeare's *Henry IV Part 1* (1597), Falstaff speaking of honour.

Lord, what fools—!: The spirit Puck speaking of humans, from Shakespeare's *A Midsummer Night's Dream* (1595).

5 Young Magic

white daisy: a Michaelmas daisy, which can grow to four feet high.

cats' cradle: a game played with string or elastic held and twisted around the fingers of both hands.

the stuff: old-fashioned term for dress-making fabric.

chilblains: an inflammation of the skin and underlying tissues on finger and toes, usually caused by too much exposure to cold temperatures. Warming up too quickly beside a fire can also produce a similar reddening of the skin.

monthly nurses: a nurse who would care for a newborn baby and the mother.

temporised: played for time, said things of little importance.

Spartan, little fox: Plutarch's *The Life of Lycurgus* tells the story of a Spartan boy who stole a fox, and then, on seeing his trainer approaching, he hid the illicit prize under his cloak. The fox began to scratch and tear at the boy's flesh, to get free, but the boy refused to give away the fact that he had been stealing, or to acknowledge his own suffering, and he died from his wounds.

coaxed a pipe: sucking on a lit pipe to make the tobacco draw properly, which requires concentration.

Edgware Road: they are joking about lifestyles below their class.

Punch: *Punch* was a humorous weekly magazine from the Victorian period, still going strong in the early twentieth century, famous for its cartoons and comic sketches, which were, as is referred to here, often repeated over the years.

Ebury Street: a pleasant street in Belgravia, west London, within easy reach of the richer area of Mayfair but with lower rents.

sentimental education: this lady has been flirting with James in a semi-maternal way.

marble halls: a quotation from the popular song 'I Dreamt I Dwelt in Marble Halls' from the 1843 opera *The Bohemian Girl*.

6 Disturbing Experience of an Elderly Lady

a little rankly: a discreet way of suggesting prostitutes.

Brookwood: Brookwood Hospital was a hospital for the mentally afflicted in Surrey, south of London.

pink paper: cheques used to be bi-coloured in cream and pink, to prevent forgery.

Gardez: French, the imperative 'keep'.

his faithfully: the convention for signing letters used to be 'yours faithfully' for people you did not know, and 'yours sincerely' for people you already had a connection with. Intimate friends and relations would be given a less formal signature.

7 Good Company

Vengono: Italian, 'They come'.

Terraemotum, pestum, bellum Procul pelle et flagellum Appropinquet civitatis Quae tuae fidit pietatis: Latin, 'When the earthquake, pestilence, and war have passed, let a scourge approach the city in which you place your trust and piety'.

O virgo gloriosa, laudens, audi vota: Latin, 'O renowned Virgin … praising (you) … Hear (our) prayers.

Ora pro nobis: Latin, 'Pray for us'.

nunc te lilis, nunc te rosis Sponsus ornat odorosis: Latin, 'The groom presents you now with sweet-smelling lilies, now with roses'.

Golden Legend: a thirteenth-century compilation of the Lives of the Saints.

8 A Curious Story

Tristan: in the many variations of the legend of Tristan and Iseult, the central consistent image is the pair of lovers drinking a love potion from a cup.

Siddons: Sarah Siddons, née Kemble, was a great British tragic actress of the Regency period and early nineteenth century.

Venice Preserv'd: a Restoration play by Thomas Otway, first performed in 1682.

hare's-foot: the foot of a hare is long and delicately furred; they were routinely used for applying stage make-up before artificial versions were manufactured, although the artificial versions retained the name of the real thing.

facetious guide: Simpson used William Clarke's *Every Night Book, Or, Life After Dark* as a source for these quotations (1827), particularly pp77-78, which contains most of the phrases she quotes here, in a different order.

"flowers to strew her corse": from Charles Lamb's *Tales from Shakespeare* (1807), retelling the story of Romeo and Juliet.

10 Teigne

OTC: Officer Training Corps, an army cadet force for public schoolboys.

unexceptionable: references to which one could not take exception, acceptable.

Queen's Hall: a concert hall in central London.

11 The Pledge

lee: the side sheltered by a hill or a tall structure.

lien: a form of ownership by virtue of physical proximity rather than legal possession.

tramp: a tramp steamer has no fixed itinerary, and is available for hire at any port where it is offered.

clanging by: on board ship the passing of time is sounded by bells to indicate the changing of the watch.

La Vache: presumably a foghorn off the coast of France.

12 The Pythoness

pythoness: the name given to the Oracle at Delphi, who would see visions and foretell the future on request.

portability: the inference is that fraudulent mediums hide such objects on their persons and produce them during a trance, claiming they are gifts or tokens from the dead.

cabinet: a room or closed cupboard in which the medium would sit alone to make contact with the spirits before emerging to allow the other participants to join her in that communion.

took off his hat: a gentleman would raise or take off his hat on greeting and saying goodbye to a woman.

a quarter to six: drinking chocolate or hot chocolate was then a drink for breakfast, or afternoon tea, but not during what Findlay would categorise as the cocktail hour. This suggests that Mrs Bain's social codes are entirely different from his and Mortimer's.

plain party or coloured: referring to the Victorian practice of issuing prints of well-known stage actors as 'penny plain or twopence coloured', in which the plain ones were cheaper than the hand-tinted versions. It was a common metaphor for choosing between something simple or slightly livelier.

twenty-five years: in English law a path for which there is documented proof that it has been used regularly for at least twenty-one years then becomes a statutory right of way, and cannot be closed.

talking shop: if colleagues dined together out of office hours it was not considered good manners to discuss business affairs during dinner.

wine circling: the decanter of port being passed around the table.

'Lord Rendal': more commonly known as 'Lord Randall', a early British ballad about the poisoning of Lord Randall by his lover.

13 An Experiment of the Dead

send in his papers: resign as an officer in his regiment, because being involved in a divorce case at this date was scandalous.

hanged by the neck: the death penalty would not be abolished in Britain until 1965.

Burke's Landed Gentry: a standard reference work listing the names and estates of families in Britain and Ireland who owned land. Inclusion in this, or in *Debrett's* for the nobility, was a guarantee of class position.

Gadarene: the Gadarene swine were unfortunate enough to be possessed by demons, which were exorcised from a man's body at Jesus's command.

Office of Works: the former British government department that was responsible for buildings, fittings and repairs.

thaumaturgy: the study of the practice of magic, or of miracle-working.

Elinor Mordaunt
The Villa
and The Vortex
Supernatural Stories, 1916–1924
Edited by Melissa Edmundson

The Villa and The Vortex
Supernatural Stories, 1916–1924
by Elinor Mordaunt

Elinor Mordaunt was the pen name
of Evelyn May Clowes (1872–1942),
a prolific and popular novelist and short
story writer, working in Australia and
Britain in the first thirty-five years of
the twentieth century.

Melissa Edmundson has curated this selection of the best of
Mordaunt's supernatural short fiction, which blend the technologies
and social attitudes of modernity with the classic supernatural
tropes of the ghost, the haunted house, possession, conjuration
from the dead and witchcraft. Each story is an original and compelling
contribution to the genre, making this selection a marvellous new
showcase for women's writing in classic supernatural fiction.

Stories include:

- The Villa', in which a Croatian mansion does things to its
  unlucky owners.

- 'The Country-side', in which a very ordinary infidelity demands
  the ultimate sacrifice.

- 'Hodge' (previously published in *Women's Weird*) in which
  a teenage brother and sister resurrect a prehistoric man
  and bring him into their home.

- 'Four wallpapers', in which stripping off the wall coverings
  of a Spanish chateau re-enacts a family tragedy.

Women's Weird
Strange Stories by Women,
1890–1940
Edited by Melissa Edmundson

Women's Weird

Strange Stories by Women, 1890–1940

edited by Melissa Edmundson

Early Weird fiction embraces the supernatural, horror, science fiction, fantasy and the Gothic, and was explored with enthusiasm by many women writers in the United Kingdom and in the USA. Melissa Edmundson has brought together a compelling collection of the best Weird short stories by women from the late nineteenth and early twentieth centuries, to thrill new readers and delight these authors' fans.

The thirteen authors include:

- Charlotte Perkins Gilman, author of 'The Yellow Wallpaper', with her story of a haunted New England house, 'The Giant Wistaria' (1891).

- Edith Nesbit, best known for her children's fiction by E Nesbit, her horror story 'The Shadow' (1910) is about the dangers of telling a ghost story after the excitement of a ball.

- Edith Wharton, the chronicler of New World societal fracture and change by new money tells an alarming story of Breton dogs and a jealous husband, 'Kerfol' (1916).

- Mary Butts, modernist poet and novelist, wrote 'With and Without Buttons' (1938), a story of some very haunted gloves.

Women's Weird 2

More Strange Stories
by Women, 1891–1937

Edited by Melissa Edmundson

Women's Weird 2

More Strange Stories by Women, 1891–1937

edited by Melissa Edmundson

'Terrifically enjoyable, surreal'
— *The Washington Post*

'Thirteen stories mixing unknowns
with household names' — *The Guardian*

A second anthology of classic Weird short fiction by women authors, containing thirteen remarkably chilling stories originally published from 1891 to 1937, by women authors from the USA, Canada, the UK, India and Australia. Featured stories include:

- Barbara Baynton's 'A Dreamer' (1902), a rare sighting of early Australian Weird.

- Katherine Mansfield's 'The House' (1912), in which a dream of a happy life has to end.

- Bithia Mary Croker's 'The Red Bungalow' (1919), colonial Weird takes its revenge.

- L M Montgomery's 'The House Party at Smoky Island' (1934), nothing like *Anne of Green Gables*.

- Stella Gibbons' 'Roaring Tower' (1937) is as unexpected as *Cold Comfort Farm*.